continued . . .

"Shirley Jump packs lots of sweet and plenty of heat in this heartwarming first book of her promising new series."
— Virginia Kantra, *New York Times* bestselling
author of *Carolina Man*

"Fans will enjoy following the sisters' paths to love and the quaint and quirky setting."
— *Booklist*

"An exceptional, humorous romantic writer."
— New York Journal of Books

When Somebody Loves You

SHIRLEY JUMP

BERKLEY SENSATION, NEW YORK

BERKLEY
SENSATION

An imprint of Penguin Random House LLC
375 Hudson Street, New York, New York 10014

WHEN SOMEBODY LOVES YOU

A Berkley Sensation Book / published by arrangement with the author.

ISBN: 978-0-425-27937-3

PUBLISHING HISTORY
Berkley Sensation mass-market edition / October 2015

PRINTED IN THE UNITED STATES OF AMERICA

10 9 8 7 6 5 4 3 2 1

Cover art by George Long.
Cover design by Jim Griffin.
Interior text design by Kelly Lipovich.

Penguin
Random
House

Dedication

*For the dozens of starlit nights on the pier, the magical
moments spent kayaking among dolphins and manatees,
and all the sweet memories yet to come.*

Acknowledgments

I was one of those little girls who loved horses, and always wanted one of my own. I remember trying to convince my dad that we had room for a horse corral behind the garage, forgetting that we lived in the middle of a busy intersection and there were no horses allowed within the town limits. Or the fact that the poor horse would have had a corral the size of a postage stamp. My aunt had two horses and every time we went to her house, I would get to ride on the back of Old Bay, the sweeter and gentler of the two, and dream that he was my very own for a little while.

But I didn't know anything at all about quarter horses when I started this book, so I had to rely on help from lots of wonderful, knowledgeable, and helpful sources. Thank you to Carl Allison and Pepir Jernigan for pointing me in the right direction of people who knew lots about horses, to Heather Atton Cook for her wealth of information on reining, to Bev Petterson and Jessica Anderson for helping me shape this from an idea into something that could work, and a special thank you to Katie Carris, whose years and years of quarter horse experience gave me a nice foundation to work with. Any mistakes are entirely my own, and I apologize to all the horses, breeders, and riders out there in advance if I goofed, which I've been known to do, a time or a hundred.

This book also wouldn't have been possible without the great support of so many close friends who listened to me on long runs and bike rides while I worked out my plot and stressed about deadlines and life. Thank you to all of you (and you know who you are!) but a big thanks especially to Pauline, Tina, Joanna, Shayne, Michael, Leo, and Doug. Without you guys, this last year's journey would have been a lot longer and tougher.

Chapter 1

When Elizabeth Palmer's mother died in 2004, she left her only child three things: a fake ruby ring she'd bought at a garage sale, a tattered apron with a plastic name tag hanging askew from the corner, and one piece of advice: *never bet on a losing horse.*

The trouble with that advice was figuring out ahead of time which horse was going to lose, and which one was going to have a final kick at the end. Something Winnie Palmer had never quite gotten the knack of doing. She had, however, wasted nearly every dime of her diner paychecks at the track, betting on everything from dogs to ponies, searching for that elusive ticket that would drag her out of a life of poverty and set her down smack-dab in one of the mansions she cut out of the Sunday real estate section and tacked onto the fridge with little horseshoe-shaped magnets.

Elizabeth's mother had been like Delta Dawn, that hopeless romantic in the song immortalized by Bette Midler.

Standing in her Sunday best every spare minute of the day, hoping for some miracle to bring her to the castle in the sky. In the end, all it had taken was a few thousand Marlboros to give Winnie the gift of emphysema and a one-way ticket to a castle-less plot in Whitelawn Cemetery.

Whenever Elizabeth hit a crossroads, she would think *what would Mom do?* And then she did the exact opposite.

Until yesterday, when she'd quit her job, giving up medical insurance and a biweekly paycheck for a chance at pursuing the only dream she'd ever allowed herself to have. Now she was stuck in the middle of Nowhere, USA, and trying not to hyperventilate.

She needed something to eat. And a bathroom. Maybe then she could take a few deep breaths and convince herself that throwing away job security was a smart move for a thirty-year-old with bills to pay.

What had she been thinking?

That she needed a way out of a dead-end administrative job that was heading down a hellish road of bad fluorescent lighting and endless reams of computer entries and a fiancé who told her via text that, whoops, sorry we wasted two years together, but he was in love with the fifty-year-old cougar on the second floor.

And most of all, that Elizabeth wasn't happy. She wanted more from her life, more from her days, and the only way to do that was to . . .

Do what her mom had done. Believe in the impossible, and take a leap into the unknown. Even if doing so scared the heck out of Elizabeth.

Elizabeth glanced again at the official assignment sheet from the horse-breeding magazine that had given her a chance with her first-ever freelance job. In a moment of insanity, Elizabeth had proposed an article on a topic she knew nothing about—breeding and training quarter horses. But after three hundred and seven query letters and two years of trying to break into a national magazine, Elizabeth wasn't about to admit that to the editor at the quarter horse magazine who said yes to Elizabeth's query letter. She'd wanted to be a writer most of her life, penning her own stories when she was a little girl, then taking on the company newsletter at Miller's Property Management, and churning out a monthly quartet of articles. That newsletter writing, as boring and dry as it was to write yet another article on "managing weeds on your property," was the one thing that made the rest of her days—spent doing bookkeeping—tolerable.

Then her boss decided to axe the newsletter program, which put Elizabeth square in the cold world of numbers and columns every single day, eight hours a day, with no creative break to look forward to. She'd started churning out query letters left and right, hoping for a break, any break. The original plan had been to add freelancing on in her spare time, but when Roger fell in love with the cougar, that had been enough. Either she was going to make a go of this writing thing or forever dream about the job she really wanted.

Every time she wanted to hyperventilate, she reminded herself that she had a solid six months of savings in her bank account, a strong résumé that would land her another dead-end administrative job in a heartbeat, and no ties to force her to stay in one place. And that her path of planning and schedules and responsibility had, in the end, left her lonely and unhappy, two adjectives she no longer wanted in her life. Okay, so maybe she wasn't as impulsive and crazy as she could be. She'd done this whole thing with a safety net, after all.

So early that morning, she'd stowed an overnight bag in the trunk of her Honda, then headed out of New Jersey and down to Georgia. She had called the Silver Spur Ranch yesterday afternoon, talked to some woman named Barbara Jean, and made an appointment to meet Hunter McCoy at seven that night. An initial meeting, she thought, gather a little background information, do the formal interview the next day, and be back on the road by lunchtime.

Then she'd hit Atlanta at rush hour and spent an ungodly amount of time trying to get through the city center. By the time she got to Chatham Ridge, she was ravenous. She hadn't spied anything resembling a drive-through in at least half an hour. Damn. She should have stopped when she was on an actual highway instead of these rural roads that rippled through Georgia like veins in a bodybuilder.

Even though it was close to seven, the temperature outside had gone from hot to holy hell in a matter of hours, and the sunny day she had welcomed when she'd stepped outside this morning had spiraled into the depths of Dante's inferno.

Otherwise known as Chatham Ridge, Georgia. Population: Not Nearly Big Enough.

The sun was just starting to wane when there was a low, menacing rumble from above and the skies opened up. Rain began to fall in thick, heavy sheets that pummeled her windshield and taunted her wipers. Elizabeth drove slowly down Main Street, peering through the veil of water, looking for something—anything—that would sell food. The lights were off at the little white building with a hand-painted sign that read BOB AND MARY'S SUNDRIES. There'd been a single gas pump out front, a pile of cordwood stacked and bundled with a makeshift sign that read THREE BUCK BUNDLE. But it was closed, as was the hardware store, the art studio, and the bank.

Finally, she spied lights and a tiny neon OPEN sign outside a brick-front building on the corner of Main and Pecan. She pulled in, then parked and made a break for it. She'd left her umbrella at home and the storm lashed at her pale pink dress shirt and dark blue pants with fat, soaking slaps. Too late she realized she hadn't run into a restaurant but rather a bookshop/coffee shop. She stood in the entryway, dripping a puddle onto the hardwood floors and trying to catch her breath.

A buxom woman with a pile of gray hair swirled onto her head in a loose bun came bustling forward, her arms outstretched, her face bright with greeting. Before Elizabeth could react, the woman had wrapped one arm around Elizabeth's shoulders and was tugging her into the store and over to a small café in the corner.

"Sweetie, you look about half drowned. Come on in. Let's get something in you and dry you off before you catch your death." She swung a bar stool away from the counter and pressed Elizabeth into it. "You sit tight and I'll be right back with a towel."

Then she hurried away, disappearing behind a swinging door. Elizabeth swiped the damp hair out of her eyes and looked around the bookstore, really a converted Colonial Revival home. It was warm and welcoming, she thought, feeling like a home more than a store. The hardwood floors gleamed, their darkened planks worn and dented from years of tread. A dozen bowl-shaped chandeliers hung over the space, casting a warm bright light into the nooks and crannies. The walls were a pale straw color, with thick wood molding that had the occasional hiccup flaw marking it as hand hewn. A sign above the café counter read HAPPY ENDING BOOKSTORE, in a bright pink curlicue script. The shop was large but cozy, with rows and rows of bookcases stuffed with books that formed a rainbow of straight lines. At the back of the store, a six-pack of wingback chairs ringed a small circular table set before a fireplace with a tiny flickering flame teasing at a pile of logs, and Elizabeth wondered if that was what you got with a Three Buck Bundle.

"Here you are, sweetie." The woman draped a fluffy white towel over Elizabeth's shoulders, gave her a firm squeeze to cement it in place, then went back to the other side of the counter. "I'm Noralee Butler, no relation to Rhett."

Elizabeth couldn't help but smile. "Nice to meet you. I'm Elizabeth Palmer."

Noralee cocked her head and studied her. "Let me guess . . . New York?"

"New Jersey. Born and raised in the lovely city of Trenton."

"Can't say I've ever been there. I hardly ever leave my little corner of paradise. I figure the Lord planted me here so I could bloom, and that's what I been trying to do for near on sixty-two years now."

Elizabeth had exhausted her repertoire of small talk. "Do you serve food? I stopped in just to grab something to eat. I'm supposed to be out at the Silver Spur Ranch by seven and it's already past that."

"Hunter McCoy's place?" Noralee waved a hand. "Oh, I know Hunter. I'll give him a call. He'll understand."

Before Elizabeth could stop her, the woman was dialing, talking to Hunter, saying something about giving this poor creature a sandwich and a sweet tea, then she covered the phone and looked at Elizabeth. "You got a place to stay, honey?"

"I was planning on staying at the Motel 6 in the next town over." She had another thirty miles to go to get there, and maybe she'd feel up to it after she had a little something to eat.

Noralee's brows wrinkled. "Oh, I know that motel. And believe me when I tell you their idea of a *sleeping establish-*

ment is pretty light on the sleeping and the establishment. Besides all that, in this storm, you'd be lucky not to get washed off the road, straight into a ditch. Don't you worry, honey. We'll get you something to eat and then you can head over to Hunter's. He's got a house big enough to hold a Boy Scout Jamboree, so I'm sure he can put you up for a day or two."

"I can't stay—"

"Hunter?" Noralee said into the phone. "This girl needs a place to spend the night, too. Oh, she's no trouble at all. You got that big old house. . . ." A pause. "Okay, good. I'll let her know."

This had already gotten out of hand. A journalist didn't spend the night at the house of the person she was supposed to be interviewing. "Mrs. Butler—"

"Oh, I'm not a Mrs., and nobody 'round here calls me anything other than Noralee. 'Cept for Cooter Whitman. That man's full-time job is giving people nicknames. Now, don't you worry about Hunter. He's as fine a gentleman as they come. I'm not even sure they make gentlemen like him anymore. So, sweetie, if you want to catch Hunter—"

"Oh, no, not at all. I'm here to interview him, for a magazine. Nothing more."

"Well, won't that put a feather in the town cap? I'm just sayin', Hunter is the most eligible bachelor in this town right now and I haven't met a woman yet who hasn't fallen half in love with him from the minute he said *ma'am*." She waved toward the corner of the room. "Now you go get yourself freshened up and by the time you come back, I'll have something warm waiting for you."

Elizabeth ducked into the tiny one-stall ladies' room at the back of the store. She washed up and tried to do her best to clean up the raccoon eyes of her mascara and the wet tangle of her blond hair, loosening it from its usual clip and letting it hang around her shoulders to dry. She blotted the worst of the water with the towel, as she peered into a reflection that screamed *needs a good night of sleep*. That hadn't happened in a long time, and she doubted it would happen today. Elizabeth sighed, then headed back to the counter.

Noralee stood there, as proud as a peacock, beaming at Elizabeth. "Glad you had a chance to get the drowned rat off you. Now you sit right down and enjoy yourself." She patted the chair.

Elizabeth wanted to say she'd get the food to go, but then she looked down at the plate and saw a muffin as big as a grapefruit sitting there, warm and welcoming. The scent of blueberries wafted up to tempt her. Butter pooled in the crannies of the halved baked treat, and before she could think twice, she'd eaten the whole muffin and washed it down with a full glass of sweet tea. "That was delicious."

"Why, thank you. It's my grandmama's recipe. Lordy, that woman could bake a porcupine and make it taste like something from a fancy French restaurant. You come by here on a Tuesday and I'll have her praline cookies. They're usually gone within an hour. My most popular treat, next to the books, of course."

"It's a very nice bookstore."

"It was my mama's. Course, it was a dress shop when she owned it. She was always saying to me, Noralee, you get your head out of that book and live your life. Now I'm living my life, with my head always in a book. Funny how things work out like that." Noralee leaned in, her soft green eyes bright with interest. "Tell me what you're reading now."

"Oh, I don't read much."

"Well, that is just a crime. I will make it my mission to find the right book for you. In fact, I'm going to talk to the

Southern Belle Book Club tonight and see what they think. That's why you caught me here after hours. It's about time for those ladies to come on in and fill this place with chatter. Their meeting isn't for a couple days, but sometimes they come in just because they want something to eat and a place to talk. And, of course, that's what I'm here for."

As if on cue, the door to the shop jingled and a quartet of women dashed inside, laughing and talking as they doffed their umbrellas and shook the water off. For a second, Elizabeth felt a stab of envy at the easy roll of conversation between them, the kind that marked lifelong friendships. They seemed happy, at ease in their place in the world, and at that moment, Elizabeth wanted to stay.

She shook her head and cleared her throat. "I, uh, should get going." Elizabeth slipped off the bar stool and reached for her purse. "How much was the muffin and tea?"

"Oh, sweetie, you don't owe me a dime," Noralee said. "You just promise to come on back sometime soon. I guarantee I can find you something to read that'll change your life." She drew out the middle syllable of *guarantee*, as if the word was running away.

Elizabeth had no intention of returning. She was here long enough to get the story, then get back to Trenton. With one last thank-you to Noralee and a glance at the book club, already settling into those wingback chairs by the disappearing Three Buck Bundle, Elizabeth headed out into the rain again and down the road toward the Silver Spur Ranch.

She found it twenty minutes later, tucked at the end of a long, dark road. The storm had strengthened and now Mother Nature was attacking her car with fat droplets that hammered a one-two punch at her windshield. The wind had kicked up and was buffeting her little car. Elizabeth flicked on the high beams, and concentrated on the road between quick swipes of the wipers. The ranch itself was dark, but the main house at the end of the drive was ablaze with lights flanking the front door and either end of the wraparound porch. Twin rockers sat on the porch, seeming to beg someone to sit and stay awhile.

No matter what Noralee had said, Elizabeth wasn't staying here tonight. It wasn't professional for one, and for another, one woman's word that Hunter McCoy was a gentleman didn't make it a fact. She'd get the initial meeting out of the way, then find someplace else to stay the night.

Elizabeth took a deep breath, then got out of the car, using her notepad as a shield against the rain. She charged up the stairs and raised her hand toward the doorbell. The door opened before she touched it.

A tall man filled the doorframe, literally. He was at least six-two, with broad shoulders and a commanding presence that charged the air, making Elizabeth draw in a breath. His brown hair curled a little at the ends, as if he'd gone too long between haircuts, softening the look of command his body wore. One lock of hair fell over his brow, emphasizing eyes so blue they could have been oceans all on their own. He had on worn, comfortable jeans, a thick cotton white button-down, and a glare she could spot from Alaska.

So this was Hunter McCoy.

"Sorry you've come all this way," he said, "but I want to make one thing clear before we go any further. I don't know what Barbara Jean and Noralee told you, but I'm not interested in being in a magazine."

That was a curveball Elizabeth hadn't expected. "I'm sorry, Mr. McCoy, but I thought my editor spoke to you—"

"She did. I told her the same thing I'm telling you. I don't want to be in the magazine. You can stay here tonight, especially since this storm isn't gonna lighten for at least another couple hours, then get your things and be gone in the morning."

"But Barbara Jean said—"

"Barbara Jean means well, but she thinks our DNA allows her to make my decisions for me. I don't want to be in a magazine. I'm a private man, and that means I like my privacy."

"But it's a wonderful opportunity for people to find out about your breeding operation and—"

"If people want to find me, they know how. It's a small town, and I'm the only decent quarter horse breeder in the county. And people talk at reining competitions. Word gets around when you have quality horses." He gestured toward the open door behind her. "Are you done letting the storm into my house?"

She debated telling him good-bye and just hitting the road again. But that would mean she had failed at her very first freelancing job on her very first day. Did she have it in her to send another three hundred and seven query letters, just to get a second chance? "I appreciate your honesty, Mr. McCoy," she said with a smile, as if she had no problem with him refusing the interview. "And you know, you're right. It *is* a long drive back to New Jersey. So if it's okay with you, I'm going to take that offer of hospitality and stay here. I just need to grab my bag out of the trunk." She started toward the car before he could change his mind.

"Wait."

She turned back.

He put out his palm. "Give me your keys. You get inside, dry off, and I'll grab your bags."

Elizabeth stared at him. Was this perfect stranger offering to do the chivalrous thing and get her things out of the car? In this Noah's Ark storm? She thought of all the men she had known in her life and couldn't list a single one who would do the same thing.

"Keys?" Hunter said again.

"Oh, oh, yes. Sorry." She fished her keys out of her pocket and dropped them into his palm. "It's just . . . I didn't expect you to do that."

"My mama raised me to be a gentleman, and not just when it's convenient or I'm trying to impress a pretty lady." A grin flitted across his face and filled her gut like honey drizzled on toast. Did he mean she was the pretty lady, or was he just saying that? "Wait here, ma'am."

Holy cow. Noralee had been right. The way that man said *ma'am* set off a riot of fireworks in Elizabeth's body. She fanned at her face, suddenly feeling ten degrees hotter.

He ran outside and, a minute later, was back with her small overnight bag and her briefcase, shiny new leather, bought for this very occasion. He set them by the door, then turned back to her. His gaze dropped and lingered for a moment. "I . . . uh . . . should get you a towel or something. You're . . . soaked."

She glanced down and realized that her shirt, which had been merely damp at the bookstore, had gotten so wet by her second run in the rain that it plastered the thin pink satin to her chest, outlined the lacy scoops of her bra and soft peaks of her nipples. Like a real-life wet T-shirt contest. Oh Lord. She yanked the briefcase up and pressed it to her chest and tried not to look disconcerted. "That would be great. Thank you."

Hunter disappeared down the hall. Elizabeth leaned against the wall and let out a sigh. Great. So much for making a professional impression.

Her gaze landed on a small table to the left of the door. An empty crystal vase sat to one corner behind a small framed photograph of Hunter and a pretty blond woman. She was leaning into him, one hand possessive and protective on his chest, and looking up at him with a smile so wide, it seemed to last forever. Hunter had a cowboy hat tugged down on his forehead, masking his expression, but Elizabeth could see that his attention was locked on the woman in his arms. A wife? Fiancée? Girlfriend?

Regardless, it was a picture of love. Pure, unadulterated love. The kind Elizabeth had only seen in movies, and didn't believe really existed. Heck, maybe it didn't for Hunter and this mystery woman, either. For all Elizabeth knew, they could have had a big fight five minutes later over taking out the garbage or what to eat for dinner.

Hunter returned and Elizabeth jerked her gaze away from the photo. "Here's a towel. Guest bedroom is at the top of the stairs on the right. I don't get many guests, so it's clean, but probably a little dusty. Breakfast is at eight, on the dot. You miss it, you're on your own. Good night."

Then he turned on his heel and disappeared down the hall. Apparently, that was the extent of his hospitality to unwanted reporters camping in his guest room. For an easy, quick assignment, Elizabeth had a feeling she was in for a Herculean effort.

∽

Hunter McCoy stood on the front porch of the small white farmhouse that sat at the edge of the Silver Spur, sipping a cup of coffee and watching the sun rise. He'd watched near every sunrise behind his property, for as long as he could remember. Course, when he was a boy, he'd watched the sunrise with a mug of chocolate milk, standing tall and straight next to his dad and his granddad, pretending he was holding a cup of coffee like the men he'd so admired. Now it was just him running the Silver Spur. But that hadn't stopped the morning tradition. In Hunter's mind, it was a way to commune with his father and grandfather, maybe soak in a little of their wisdom as the sun crested over the trees at the far side of the land that had been in the McCoy family for as many generations as the state of Georgia had been in the union.

The sun started like a shy child, peeking between the trees, washing a slight gold over the long squat stables, the smooth oval training corral, the old red barn, the blooming flowers in the far pasture, then finally reaching tentative fingers across the lawn, up to the steps of the porch. The birds chattered in the trees, rising in volume as the land went from dim to bright. The horses nickered in their stalls, and from far down the road, Joey Barrett's rooster crowed. At his feet, Foster, a furry lump of a dog that was part golden retriever, part moocher, snoozed in the early morning light.

For years, this land, this place, had filled Hunter with peace. But as he stood on the porch for the ten thousandth time, sipping another coffee he barely tasted, peace eluded him. He dumped out the coffee, then laid the cup on the railing and headed out to the stables. Work, that was his salvation. The only thing that kept him from drowning in a pit of his own misery.

He noticed the reporter's car still sitting in the driveway, caked with mud now that the rain had stopped. She was a tiny little spit of a thing, that Elizabeth Palmer, one of those take-charge women from up north who didn't take no for an answer. Hunter made a note to talk to Barbara Jean. He'd made it clear, hadn't he, that he wasn't interested in the magazine article? He wanted his peace, and by God, if he couldn't have that, he'd at least have his days uninterrupted, one following after another until they became a blur and his mind stopped whirring.

He greeted each of the horses in turn, running a hand along their velvety muzzles. Foster followed along, nosing at the horses and moseying through the barn. Hunter stopped at the last stall and waited at the gate, but the bay roan mare inside didn't move from where she stood at the back of the stall. He clucked his tongue. "Hey, Dakota. Wanna come see me today?"

Diamond Heel Dakota's dark brown tail flicked left, right, and she shifted her hooves, but didn't move. The pale-colored mare with the dark legs and dark mane and tail had been here for a week now, and had yet to warm up to anyone. Hunter never should have bought her—she was scarred and skittish and had turned mean in the years since Hunter had last seen her, and according to Billy Ray, Dakota was long past her reining days, too, especially since that accident two years ago. A practical man would have let the horse go, because seeing her made a part of Hunter hurt in ways he couldn't begin to explain. Maybe it was guilt, maybe it was a desire to fix things long past fixing. But when Billy Ray said he was just going to send her off to the slaughterhouse, Hunter had pulled out his wallet and taken her home.

Hunter reached in his pocket and withdrew a small red apple. "Got a treat for you, Dakota." Foster perked up, wagged his tail.

The horse didn't move. Hunter stood there a while longer, then set the apple on the gate. "I'll be back tomorrow, Dakota. And the day after that."

The stable door opened, casting a shaft of light down the long wooden corridor. A single shadow followed, the long, thin figure of Carlos, who had been the right-hand man at the Silver Spur for forty years. "Hey, boss. Our girl talking to us today?"

"Nope. Maybe tomorrow."

Carlos cast a doubtful look toward the last stall on the right. "She's stubborn, that one. There's a reason Billy Ray unloaded her on you."

"She's difficult. Not impossible." *She's been hurt. I understand that.*

Carlos chuckled. "You're always the optimist."

"I don't know about that. I just see . . .," *a second chance,* ". . . hope in her, for the future, for the ranch. And I want to get my money's worth."

Carlos shook his head and clapped a hand on Hunter's shoulder. "You can pretend all you like that this is about dollars and cents, but I've known you a long time, boss, and not only are you an old softie when it comes to these horses, but you've also always run this business like it's a family."

Maybe because it was pretty much all the family he had left now. The horses, the workers, the hay in the stalls, the beams above his head. It was what got him out of bed in the morning, what kept him putting one foot in front of the other. Without the Silver Spur, Hunter would have curled up into a corner a long damned time ago. Dakota gave him a reason to try, as if healing that horse could help mend the mistakes of the past. So far, Hunter was batting a thousand.

"We got work to do," he said to Carlos.

"We always do." Carlos grinned, then headed off to feed the horses.

Hunter started toward the water troughs, then stopped when the front door opened and the reporter from yesterday came out onto the porch. She stood there, her face upturned to greet the sun, wearing a pair of black dress pants, low heels, and another of those silky shirts—this one dry and dark blue, which sent a ribbon of disappointment through Hunter.

He shook it off. He wasn't interested in her. Hell, he hadn't been interested in anyone for so long, he wondered if maybe he should add *monk* to his job title. He had his work, and that was all he wanted, all he needed. This little spit of a thing standing on his porch was another complication—and Hunter was going to handle her like he handled all other complications.

By shaking her off like a burr on his leg.

Chapter 2

After Elizabeth woke up at the butt crack of way-too-early, she eyed the window in the second floor room and wondered if it was possible to sneak out without breaking a leg. Maybe if she tied the bedsheets together, or fashioned a rope out of the drapes?

She'd lain there, a hand on her chest, concentrating on long, deep breaths. She was in over her head. What had she been thinking? Why had she thought this would be a good idea? She wasn't the kind of person to up and quit a perfectly good job just to follow some silly dream she'd had when she was an overly emotional teenager, filling lines of a composition book. She wasn't a professional journalist—she was just some bored bookkeeper with a few newsletters under her belt and a crazy fantasy of being a writer.

Not to mention, the hunk of a man she was supposed to interview made any kind of coherent thought impossible, even if he was a little . . . prickly. In his teeny-tiny Facebook photo, most of his looks had been obscured by a cowboy hat. She hadn't been prepared for how . . . overpowering he was up close. The kind of overpowering that made her common sense flit away.

Yes, she'd leave. Drop Hunter McCoy a note and tell him she'd forgotten a meeting with the prime minister of England or developed a sudden case of malaria. Something believable like that. She had gotten up, gotten dressed, and had her bag in her hands, ready to leave, when she heard the screen door below her open with a squeak and shut with a slap.

She glanced out the second story window, and past the edge of the porch roof, and saw a sliver of Hunter standing on the back porch with a cup of coffee in his hands. He stared at a giant field of bright yellow and orange flowers or maybe at the trees just beyond them, for a long time, a man who seemed to have no trouble staying quiet, still, at center with himself. She felt almost like a voyeur watching him. Of course, if she were a true voyeur, she'd be watching him do something else, but that was not what she was here for. Not at all. Nope, not going to happen, not today, not tomorrow.

Okay, so the man was good-looking. She'd met good-looking men before. Plenty of them.

Except none of the men she had met said *ma'am* quite like he did, like the word was a caress, sliding down his tongue—

Not constructive.

Hunter shook his head, muttered something under his breath, then he tossed out the rest of the brew and headed to the barn. She watched him stride across the lawn, the dog at his heels, and lowered her bag to the floor.

Hunter McCoy walked like a man with a mission. He had purpose, confidence, in his steps, a man who knew his place in the world. She envied that.

So what was she going to do about it? Go crawling back

to her dead-end job and those flickering fluorescent lights? Or was she going to suck it up, get out there, and get this interview done? One article didn't make a career as a writer, but one article did take her a step further into the writing career she'd dreamed of since the first time she'd picked up a pencil.

She headed downstairs and out to the porch. The warm Georgia sun greeted her like a hug, and she paused midstep to take it in, let it settle into the pores of her skin. In a few hours, it would probably be hot and sticky and miserable, but right now, the air felt like heaven.

"Mornin'," Hunter said as he returned from the barn. The word was half grunt, borderline unfriendly. In the distance, pairs of horses moved through the corrals, mommas with their foals, tails high and proud and streaming in the slight breeze.

"How early do you get up around here?" She stretched and tried to rub the sleep out of her eyes. Good Lord, the sun had barely risen and here she was, having a conversation. Before coffee. Surely, a sign of the apocalypse.

"As early as I can. It's a ranch. Work's never done. And in my world, the animals eat before the people." He started to move past her.

"Wait a second, please. I know last night you said you didn't want to do the interview—"

"I'll say it again this morning, if need be."

"But . . ." She refused to take no for an answer. There had to be a way to convince him that this would be worth his time. "But I can do this quick as a bunny and be out of your hair before you know it. That way you'll make me, my editor, and Barbara Jean happy."

He chuckled and shook his head. "You're like a dog with a bone, you know that?"

She raised her chin, shot him a grin. "I'm from Jersey, Mr. McCoy. *No* isn't in my vocabulary."

He gave her an assessing look, his gaze sweeping over her dress pants, low heels, and a new shirt just like the one from yesterday. "Looks to me like you're dressed to take me to dinner, not ask me a bunch of questions I don't want to answer."

She glanced down at her clothes. "I didn't realize there was a dress code for an interview."

"There is if you're gonna be around horses. And men who work around horses."

She could see him relenting. It was in the teasing light in his eyes, the way he had yet to leave. "I'm sure I'll be perfectly fine in this. I wasn't planning on talking to the horses. Just you. Surely we can sit here and—"

"Darlin', I don't sit for anything other than meals, and half the time, I don't even do that. This is a working ranch, which means if you wanna to talk to me, you gotta trot along behind me all day. And if you want to be more than just a gnat on my ass all day, you'll lend a helping hand."

Darlin'. Oh my God. If she'd thought the way he said *ma'am* was sexy, that was nothing compared to the way *darlin'* rolled off his tongue. She had to take in a breath before she could get her brain back into the realm of common sense. Like the part where he said he wanted her to help him, and that he would do the interview. "Wait. Did you just say that you want me to . . . help?"

"Everybody 'round here pulls their own weight. Part of the deal. You get a roof over your head and three squares, and in exchange, you pitch in."

Pitch in? Surely he didn't mean she'd do anything with the horses, or the barn. Maybe she could sweep the kitchen or something, uh, not ranch-y. Or domestic-y. Maybe this was a good time to tell him that her best and only homemaking skill was ordering moo shu pork. Martha Stewart would surely be horrified, but Martha Stewart wasn't standing in Elizabeth's Anne Klein pumps, trying to land a career-starting interview. She sensed that Hunter was the kind of man who respected hard work, and if she wanted to get him to open up, she was going to have to, as he said, pull her own weight. Or fake it.

"I'd be glad to help," she said. "Do whatever you need." Besides, she hadn't planned on being here for more than a day at most. She could feign skill at whatever task he gave her for twenty-four hours. Couldn't she?

He smirked. "Whatever I need?"

"Well . . . I mean . . . not *whatever*, but . . ." Damn. The man kept turning her into a stammering fool. She was a Jersey girl, for God's sake. She could handle New York City traffic, rowdy construction workers, and uppity doormen. She could surely handle one cowboy with a Southern drawl. "I meant work. Nothing untoward, of course."

"Of course. Nothing *untoward*." The smirk lingered on his face. "If you're going to pitch in, then I suggest you change or those pretty little shoes are gonna be ruined."

"This . . . this is all I brought. Maybe I could run to the mall or—"

Hunter rolled his eyes. "You told me yourself, you're a Jersey girl. Surely I'm not supposed to tell you how to dress yourself? Come find me when you have some boots and some common sense."

He turned on his heel and started off across the lawn. Elizabeth hurried down the steps and after him. Just as Hunter had warned, her heels caught in the damp grass, thickened into mud by last night's rain. She jerked off the shoes and ran barefoot to catch up with his long strides. The mud kicked up around her as she ran, peppering her skin and clothes.

"I'm not leaving," she said. "I'm here to do this interview, and if that means I have to follow you around barefoot, I will."

A grin played at the corners of his mouth. "Are you normally this much of a pain in the ass?"

She parked her fists on her hips. "Depends. Are you normally this impossible to deal with?"

The grin widened. Lit his cheeks, raised his brows. "I'm not impossible. I'm practical. I have a business to run here. I don't need to be mollycoddling some reporter who didn't have enough sense to bring a pair of boots to a ranch."

"I assure you, I don't need any mollycoddling. I am quite capable of taking care of myself."

"You"—he took a step forward, then, before she could react or catch her breath, he swiped away a hunk of mud that had plastered itself to her face and dropped an amused glance to her mud-splattered silk shirt and dress pants—"are the very definition of a woman who needs mollycoddling."

"You have read me wrong, Mr. McCoy." She drew herself up, trying her best to look strong and resilient in an outfit better suited for a dinner party than an interview. And trying to pretend that the momentary touch of his finger on her forehead hadn't ignited a flame deep in her nether regions. She must be hypoglycemic or something, because all this man had to do was breathe and she wanted to faint in his arms like some nineteenth-century virgin. "And if you allow me to follow you around today, I will do my job without interfering with yours."

He considered her. "One time," he said after a while, raising a finger. "You get in my way one time, and the interview is over."

"One strike and I'm out?" She grinned. "You're a tough ump."

"I have to be, Miz Palmer. This"—he waved at the acreage that encompassed the Silver Spur—"land is more than just a place to raise some horses. It's life, pure and simple, and I don't take that lightly, not at all."

"Neither do I," she said.

His gaze swept over her again, discerning, disapproving, but still slightly amused and maybe just a bit curious to see where this would lead. "We'll see about that."

Chapter 3

❧

In the end, Hunter had heard his mama's voice in his head admonishing him about being rude to visitors, and he'd led a still-barefoot Elizabeth Palmer back into the house. The fancy heels she'd had on earlier had clumps of wet grass stuck to the heel, and her pant legs were wet and clinging to her ankles. She wouldn't last five minutes on the Silver Spur dressed like that, and that silky shirt she had on would be glued to her skin as soon as the heat and humidity started rising. The thought of that shirt plastered to her skin—just like the one last night—sent his mind spinning down some treacherous paths. Best to get her what she needed and get her the hell out of here.

He had no idea if there was a store nearby that would have what she needed, and he didn't want to waste time giving her directions or shuttling her to town himself. Before he could think twice about what he was offering, his mouth was moving. "I have some extra women's clothes that are about your size," he said.

"That would be great. Thanks." She followed him up the stairs and down the hall to a bedroom that hadn't been opened in two years.

As soon as he stopped outside the door, he regretted doing this. What was he thinking? Offering this infernal woman, a woman he didn't even want in his house in the first place, some clothes? These clothes in particular?

His hand rested on the knob. It was cold to the touch, a hard, inanimate sphere of brass. He rested his opposite palm on the pale oak door, as if he could feel the past through the cracked surface. His eyes closed, and his heart clenched, and bile rose in his throat.

I'll be right back.

He'd left this door closed for two years because a part of his heart had heard *I'll be right back*, and thought if he just left the room as it was, just let time stand still in that space, she would return. Roaring into his life with that throaty laugh of hers and those legs that stretched a mile.

I'll be right back.

But Jenna hadn't been right back. The wife he was supposed to have and the life he had planned were gone in an instant, on a rainy, moonless night. All he had left was this closed bedroom door and a granite headstone in the Chatham Ridge cemetery.

"Uh, is the door locked?"

Elizabeth's voice drew him back to why he was here. The reporter. Damn it. This was why he didn't want people around. Why he had told Barbara Jean to cancel the interview. Because reporters asked questions and the last thing Hunter wanted to do for anyone was provide answers.

"I just remembered I have to give Dakota some medicine.

You'll find boots and jeans in there. But don't touch anything else. And shut the door when you're done." Then he let go of the handle and stepped back, spinning on his heel and heading down the stairs again as fast as he could. He heard the door open above him, and he hurried back outside before he threw Elizabeth Palmer and her questions out of his house.

Carlos was out in the paddock, working with one of the colts, giving it a beginner lesson in running the barrels. The eager colt looped in and out of the barrels, his tail high, his pace good, strong. He'd make a fine racing horse someday, and that gave Hunter hope for the future. It had been a while since the Silver Spur had had a winner on their roster. And an even longer while since they'd had a balance in the black in their books.

Barbara Jean would tell him that this interview was exactly the kind of publicity Hunter—and the ranch— needed. That even a small mention in a magazine like that would get the ranch's name in front of the people who made the decisions, who were looking for strong, trained foals ready to drop into their racing programs.

But Hunter knew that he had to be careful. If he let this reporter start asking questions, she'd open the one door he kept locked all the time. The one in his head that still blamed himself for Jenna's accident, the one that told him half the reason the Silver Spur was doing so poorly was because Hunter wasn't up to the job. Hadn't been up to the job in a long damned time.

Yet, like a glutton for punishment, he kept on trying to make the impossible work. His father would say that either made him a dreamer or a fool. Or both.

Hunter headed into the barn, ignoring the mile-long to-do list in his head, and heading for Dakota's stable. Foster kept pace at his master's heel, tail wagging, eager to start the day.

The dog loved being around the horses, almost as if they were part of his canine family.

The apple was gone. Hunter took that as a good sign. Dakota had ignored yesterday's apple, knocked the one from the day before onto the floor of the stable. But third time was the charm, and she'd eaten this one. He lifted the latch on the door to her stable and let the door swing open a couple inches.

Dakota watched him with wary, wide eyes. Hunter didn't take a step, just let the door do all the moving. Foster snuck around Hunter's legs and poked his head into the stall.

"Hey there, girl," Hunter said softly. "I'm not going to come in there. Not going to make a move you don't want me to make. Just standing here, talking gibberish you probably don't understand. You have a history here, girl, even if you don't remember it. Your momma and your daddy were amazing horses. And I bet they made you into something amazing, too."

Dakota raised her head, rolled back her upper lip, and bared her front teeth.

"Is that horse going to bite you?"

Hunter didn't turn toward Elizabeth's voice. Didn't move at all. He kept his eye on Dakota, his tone as easy and gentle as before. "Nope. That's just her way of processing the new world around her. It's called flehmening. Horses do it to get a better smell of new things." Like unwanted reporters walking into the stable.

Foster edged forward a little more, his tail beating against Hunter's leg. Dakota snorted and shifted her weight. Foster stilled, waiting until the horse calmed, then he moved another couple steps into the stable.

"Is the horse going to crush the dog?" Elizabeth asked. "She keeps moving her feet."

"They're saying hello. Testing the waters," Hunter said,

then went back to talking to the horse. "He's a good dog, wouldn't hurt a fly. You can trust him."

Dakota shifted some more, lifting her hooves, putting them down again. Another snort, then she lowered her head, eyeing the dog. Foster just kept on wagging his tail, as friendly as an overeager neighbor.

Something trilled, and the sudden noise scared Dakota, who reared up and backed into the stall, hitting the wooden wall with a thud. Foster scooted out of the space, and Hunter backed up, still talking soothing quiet words as he moved. "It's okay. Just a stupid noise. Won't—"

The noise happened again. Hunter whipped his head around and glared at Elizabeth. "Shut that goddamned thing off. Are you trying to get me killed?"

"I'm . . . I'm sorry." She fumbled in her pocket and muted the sound, but the damage was already done. Dakota was snorting and pawing at the ground, her tail flicking fast, ears pinned flat on her head.

Hunter let out a curse, then closed the gate. He whirled on Elizabeth, grabbing her arm and hauling her out of the barn. Once they hit the bright sunshine, he realized he was being an ass and let her go, then waved at the building behind them. "What were you thinking? You don't scare a horse. Especially one that's been through all this horse has been through, and a horse as important as her. It took me a week to get that horse to let me get that close. And you undid all that with one stupid cell phone."

"I'm . . . I'm sorry," she said again. "I didn't realize I had the sound on."

Her voice filled with contrition. He should have taken her apology and let it go, but then he saw the boots. Those damned boots, fitting another woman like they were made for her. An insane part of Hunter wanted to tell Elizabeth to take off the jeans she'd donned, rip off those boots, and return them both to the dusty room on the second floor. A room waiting for a miracle that wasn't going to come.

Instead, he pointed at the road, letting his better nature take a backseat again. "Do me a favor and get the hell off my land."

∞

Elizabeth stood on the grass, watching the retreating figure of Hunter McCoy. This time, he climbed on a tractor and headed for a field on the east end of the ranch, effectively preventing her from following. Even the dog gave up and headed for a nap on the porch. Elizabeth didn't blame her. That man was about as friendly as an IRS auditor walking into a mobster's office. Best to give him some time and distance to cool down.

Except, he did have those moments when he'd begin to smile, or when he'd tease her. Those were the moments that told her as harsh as he'd been so far, there was a good guy somewhere underneath the bark.

She started walking back toward the house. As she did, she pulled out her phone and hit redial. The few seconds it took for the call to connect to a friendly voice seemed interminable. Chances were good that Sophie Green, a travel writer by trade, was probably trying out a luxury spa in a small European town or zip-lining through some remote forest. Sophie, Elizabeth's best friend since first grade, and her polar opposite, was the one who lived for adventures, who took off here, there, and everywhere, because a whim hit her. When they were little, Sophie was the one talking Elizabeth into cutting school or playing a prank on the science teacher. But the minute they graduated, Sophie had been gone, darting away like a bird in search of better lands. These days, the best friends kept in touch with text, phone, and social media, but it wasn't quite the same. "Sorry I didn't answer when you called," Elizabeth said when Sophie answered. "What's up?"

"I was about to ask you the same thing. Since when do you, the one who is so dependable I could set my watch by you, just up and leave town without a word? And without taking me along for the escape?"

Elizabeth grinned. Just hearing Sophie's voice lifted Elizabeth's mood. She'd been there through Sophie's marriage, her divorce, and the many ups and downs in between. "I made an impulsive decision," she said.

"You? Made an impulsive decision?" Sophie laughed. "What kind of drugs were you taking?"

"None, though I could use some Valium right about now." So far, her new career was sinking faster than the *Titanic*. She had an uncooperative interview subject, about one sentence of material, and no fallback. This was the kind of insane thing Sophie would do, not Elizabeth, and she wished desperately that her best friend could be here to talk Elizabeth off the ledge. "I would have taken you along with me, but there's no mall for at least fifty miles."

"No mall? My God, you must have totally left civilization." Sophie was the one who most loved to shop, indulging her love of shoes every time they passed within a hundred yards of a store. She might jet off to remote destinations, but she rarely stayed longer than a few days, hurrying back to the world of towel warmers and room service. "Where did you go? The Amazon rainforest? One of those tiny islands where the people run around naked and eat tree bark?"

"Chatham Ridge, Georgia. And as far as I know, no one here is naked or eats tree bark." That wasn't to say that Elizabeth hadn't pictured Hunter McCoy naked a couple times. Maybe a couple dozen. Elizabeth blamed it entirely on the remote quiet of the ranch. Gave a woman altogether too much time to fantasize.

"Chatham Ridge?" Sophie said, like the word was a lemon wedge. "What the hell is a Jersey girl doing in Georgia?"

"Working." She clutched the phone tighter and ducked under the shade of a tree. "Remember that query letter? The editor I e-mailed it to bought my story idea, Soph. She wants me to write it. Assuming, that is, that I can get the man to sit down long enough for an interview."

"Wait. Is that the same query letter you banged out that night we had too much wine and saw that guy's picture on Facebook?"

Too many bottles of pinot grigio and a little idea strolling through social media had resulted in her coming across Hunter McCoy's picture and proclaiming that she needed to meet that guy. Sophie had joked that it would be a great query letter and helped Elizabeth compose it. They'd hit send, then sat back and had another bottle, sure that the whole thing was just a lark. Now it was an honest-to-God chance, and Elizabeth wasn't going to let it go. "Guess it's true what they say. Writers do their best work drunk."

Sophie laughed. "Is he as gorgeous in person as he was online?"

"Yes." Elizabeth let out a breath. "Definitely."

"You said that with a sigh. Is he a hundred times sexier or a thousand?"

Had she really sighed? Must be the lack of coffee. Not the way he said *ma'am* or *darlin'* or any other of the gazillion words in the English language. "He's a pain in the butt is what he is. He's . . . uncooperative."

"So? Charm him. Use your feminine wiles."

Elizabeth laughed. "You have known me for twenty years. I don't think I have any feminine wiles."

"Sure you do. They're just hidden under all those buttoned blouses and grandma hairstyles. Bat your eyelashes, unbutton the first few buttons of your shirt and add a little whistle to your walk."

"Whistle?"

"Shake your booty just enough to get the guy to whistle. He'll be so distracted by what's happening in the trunk, he'll forget everything else."

Elizabeth laughed and headed up the walkway to the porch. Her stomach rumbled, and she figured it might be a good idea to get something to eat and give Hunter a few minutes to cool off before she went back to the barn and tried again to get him to sit down for the interview. Then she could write the article and be on her way. She had her savings, but it wasn't going to last forever, which meant she needed to hurry up and make a job out of this writing thing, or be faced with the dreaded cubicle world again. "I'm not here to distract him. Just get my job done, get the article published and maybe"—she let out a long breath—"launch that career I've been talking about for the past gazillion years."

"You've got this," Sophie said, her voice warm. "Easy as pie."

"And as delicious as cake." Elizabeth smiled. The familiar refrain, something they'd said to each other years ago when they were both in elementary school and scared about the first day with the big kids, never failed to make Elizabeth feel settled and secure again. "Thanks, Soph."

"Anytime. And if that hunky cowboy has any hunky friends, call me. I'll run right down there, even if there isn't a mall. I could use a man who knows how to ride." Sophie let out a throaty laugh.

"I won't be here long enough to meet his friends. In and out, fast as possible." Before she started to think about how well Hunter McCoy rode something other than horses. Good Lord, her hormones were in an uproar lately. All the more reason to get this all done quickly.

Elizabeth said good-bye to Sophie, then hung up the phone and went inside the farmhouse. The scent of coffee and bacon drew her into the kitchen where she found a short, wiry brunette woman in her early sixties moving around the kitchen like a tornado.

She spun when she heard Elizabeth's footsteps, a cookie sheet filled with freshly baked biscuits in her hand. "Well, hello. I didn't know we had company for breakfast. I'm Barbara Jean. I'm supposed to be the office manager, but I'm pretty much the manager of everything for the Silver Spur." She laid the tray on the stovetop, then put out her hand.

"I'm Elizabeth Palmer. We spoke on the phone. I'm the reporter doing the story on the ranch." She went to shake with Barbara Jean, then hesitated at the sight of a giant horse head.

Barbara Jean laughed. "Oh goodness me. I'm walking around like a calf that doesn't know it's got its head stuck in a bucket." She tugged off the oven mitt and thrust out her hand again. "Let's try this again. Nice to finally put a face to the voice, Elizabeth."

Elizabeth liked Barbara Jean right off. She had a firm grip, an easy smile, and eyes that crinkled at the corners, like someone who had laughed a lot in her life. "Nice to meet you, too."

"Have a seat, let me pour you some coffee. And if you want a biscuit, better grab one quick before the he-men out there come in. There's nothing they like better for breakfast than my grandma's biscuits, and they'll be gone quicker than a monkey can shake his tail." Barbara Jean dumped the hot biscuits into a waiting ceramic bowl, then grabbed a fresh cup of coffee and brought them over to the kitchen table. "Sit, sit."

"Thank you." Elizabeth accepted the cup and warmed her hands around the mug. "This is such a beautiful ranch. And so quiet. I'm used to the Jersey traffic at night, but here, I slept like a log."

Barbara Jean perched on the opposite chair, her pale eyes sweeping over Elizabeth's frame. "You spent the night here? At Hunter's invitation?"

"I wouldn't call it an invitation. More of a no-choice deal. It was all my fault, really." She took a sip of the coffee, a rich, dark brew. "I was running very late, and it was raining, and I was tired. When I got to Chatham Ridge finally, I stopped in this bookstore and met the most lovely lady—"

"Noralee. Probably the smartest bookseller you'll ever meet. That woman can pair a book with a person in five seconds flat. And she has the most wonderful book club. My niece goes every once in a while and just praises that group to the heavens. If you're in town long enough, you should check it out."

Elizabeth sipped her coffee. Strong, rich, perfect. Even the hearty stoneware mug seemed tailor-made for sitting at this kitchen table, in this warm and cozy kitchen. "I'm not planning on staying long. Probably a good thing, because I underpacked for a stay on a ranch. Hunter had me borrow these jeans and boots."

Barbara Jean's gaze lowered to Elizabeth's feet then rose back up to her face. Barbara Jean's jaw dropped a little. "He told you to wear those? Actually gave them to you to wear?"

"Yeah." That sinking feeling filled Elizabeth's stomach again. "They were in one of the bedrooms upstairs, and uh, he didn't say anything other than I should wear them so I won't get all muddy."

Barbara Jean sat back in her chair and rested an elbow on the edge of the table. "Well, I'll be. Did he say anything about who they belonged to?"

"No." Elizabeth let out a nervous, staccato laugh. She had a feeling she had walked into a minefield she didn't even knew existed, and had no idea how to navigate. "Uh, is there a ghost I should know about?"

"Not a ghost. More of a . . . painful memory." Barbara Jean got to her feet, then placed a hand on Elizabeth's. "Hunter can be difficult, I'll be the first one to say that, but he's a man who loves the people in his life fiercely, so try not to judge him too harshly. And be sure to take care of those boots. They were once worn by someone mighty special."

Elizabeth wanted to ask who, and why that bedroom had been so dusty and unused. Hunter's mother's room, maybe? His wife's? Then she remembered the picture in the hall, the one with the laughing woman who looked like she belonged to Hunter. Were they her boots? And if so, why wasn't she wearing them anymore? Elizabeth had done research on the Silver Spur, but very little on Hunter's personal life. She hadn't thought it mattered—until now.

If these boots were associated with a painful memory, would it be better to get rid of them? But if she did that, he'd complain about her shoe choices again, and she couldn't exactly manifest some non-bad-memory boots out of thin air.

Maybe she should have gotten some kind of *Journalist Rules to Live By* book before she took on this assignment. Like, Rule #1: Don't stay at the interviewee's house. Especially if he's hot and distracting. Rule #2: Don't wear his dead wife/sister/fiancée/girlfriend's boots and bring up past hurts every time you walk past him. And Rule #3: Don't let any of the above make you fall for him in any way, shape, or fashion. Objectivity above all.

Hah. Given how her body reacted every time Hunter McCoy was within a hundred yards, there was a good chance her brain wasn't defining *objectivity* correctly.

Barbara Jean was back in the kitchen, buzzing around the space, turning out freshly scrambled eggs into a serving bowl, loading squat homemade jars of jam onto the counter, piling fresh grapes into a glass dish.

"Do you need help?" Elizabeth waved at the long line of platters and food lining the center island of the kitchen. "Seems like you're running a small restaurant here."

Barbara Jean laughed. "Somedays, I think I am. These men eat more than a herd of buffalo. But I have it all under control. Even Hunter knows better than to mess with my kitchen."

"Your kitchen? But I thought this was Hunter's house."

"Oh, it is, but he's about as useful in this room as a gorilla at a baby shower. His world is out there, with those horses he loves so much. And I . . . I take care of him best I can, so he can take care of them." Clear, powerful love filled Barbara Jean's face, and something deep in Elizabeth's gut hurt.

Hunter McCoy probably had no idea how lucky he was to have someone love him that much. Someone who made sure his belly was full and his house was clean and his life was in order.

"You sound like his mother," Elizabeth said. Like a mother everyone wished they could have.

"Oh, his mama died years ago, God rest her soul. The Lord didn't make a woman more wonderful than my sister Mary Sue. Patient as a saint and as loving as can be. I was the one who flitted through life like a butterfly, until the day came that Hunter and Amberlee—that's his little sister, who's almost a carbon copy of her mama—those two needed someone to take care of them. That's the day I came to live at the

Silver Spur and I've been here every day since. Even though both of them are way past needing me to fix their lunches and shoo them off to school, I'm still here. I love this place now. Love those two kids as if they were my own." The scent of burning bacon filled the kitchen and a small tendril of smoke curled out of the cast-iron pan on the stove. Barbara Jean spun around and flipped the bacon onto a waiting paper towel, then turned off the pan and waved away the smoke. "My goodness, about burned down the house. Just in time, too, because here they come. Be prepared, Elizabeth, for the invading hordes of marauders. They're about as messy as pigs in a bed, but I love them all anyway. We've got extra hands around this week getting in the last hay harvest and baling it up for the winter."

At that moment, the back door opened and a trio of men came into the kitchen, followed by Hunter. It could have been a hundred men, and Elizabeth's attention would still have riveted on Hunter. He had a way of filling a room, of dominating it, without doing much more than breathing.

The men doffed their hats, nodded a hello to Barbara Jean, then descended on the coffeepot and buffet she'd set on the island like people who hadn't eaten in a month. Elizabeth sat at the kitchen table, her coffee mug between her palms. Barbara Jean was right. In thirty seconds flat, nearly every bite was either consumed or heaped onto a stoneware plate. A few of the men stood as they ate, but a couple of them settled in at the table with her. They all cast curious glances in Elizabeth's way, but no one said anything until Hunter slid into the seat beside her.

"I see you don't listen," he said to her, but there was no malice in his voice, only a mixture of surprise and maybe a little respect. "Didn't I tell you to get off my land?"

Barbara Jean swatted Hunter with the horse head oven mitt. "You be nice, Hunter McCoy. This woman is doing you a favor, and you're treating her like she's a trespasser. Boys, meet Elizabeth Palmer. She's a reporter, doing a story on the Silver Spur, so be nice to her and mind your manners."

Hunter shot a glare at Barbara Jean. "You're the one who set this whole crazy thing up."

"Because it'll do the ranch some good to get some publicity. Might even make enough money to give me a raise." Her chin jutted up.

"Hey, if you're handin' out raises, I want one, too." A wiry sixtyish man with a deep tan nodded in Elizabeth's direction. "Pleased to meet you, ma'am. I'm Max. That heathen over there, eating over the sink like his mama didn't raise him with any manners is Baker. He might have a first name, but we never bothered to learn it."

Baker grinned. "That's because y'all can't remember two words at a time." He stepped forward, putting out a strong palm. Baker was a nice-looking man, dark hair, blue eyes, with a friendly face. "Pleased to meet you, ma'am."

"Hell's bells, Baker," Max said. "Seems your mama raised you right after all."

A thin, caramel-skinned man to Elizabeth's right laughed. "I hear Baker was raised by wolves. Keep him far away from Miss Elizabeth here or she'll get the wrong idea about the ranch." He nodded in her direction as he forked up a big helping of scrambled eggs. "I'm Carlos. You need to know anything about the horses, you can ask me. I've been here almost as long as Hunter."

"That's because Hunter's mama found you in a basket on her doorstep," Max said. "Look where a little pity got her."

Carlos laughed, then tossed a biscuit crumb at Max's

head. Barbara Jean wagged a finger at them. "Y'all start a food fight in my kitchen, and you'll be scrubbing this floor on your hands and knees."

The men continued to joke among themselves and tease Barbara Jean. The meal passed in a flurry of laughter and smiles, and before Elizabeth knew it, the men were scraping their plates and loading them in the sink, then heading back out the door. Hunter started for the door himself, but Barbara Jean stepped in front of him. "Don't you be running away, Hunter. You have an interview to do."

"I told you—"

"And I didn't listen. Plus, she's here now. So deal with what's on your plate before you go chasing dessert."

Hunter's stony face broke into a smile. "What the hell is that supposed to mean, Barbara Jean?"

"I don't know. But it's wise advice my grandma gave me, so I'm giving it to you." She pressed a sponge into his hands. "Stay here, clean my kitchen, and talk to Miss Elizabeth. I'm gonna go do some paperwork."

Before he could protest, she was gone. Hunter shook his head and smiled again. Clearly, for all his bluster and bluff, he had genuine affection for his aunt. He started the water and added some soap to the sink, then started loading in the plates. "There are days when I wonder who is the boss of who."

Elizabeth got to her feet and gathered the empty serving dishes. She loaded them onto the counter beside Hunter, then picked up a dish towel.

"What do you think you're doing?"

"Helping. I did say I'd pitch in. A little quid pro quo."

"Helping? Or just trying to suck up to me to do this interview that I don't want to do?" He circled the sponge around a plate and rinsed it, then laid it in the dish rack.

She shot him a grin as she dried the dish and tucked it into the cabinet. "Is it working?"

He washed another plate, then cast her a quick glance. "Maybe. Depends on how fast we get through these dishes."

"You've got the right girl here, then. I'm a master at this."

He cast her another sidelong glance. "The right girl, huh?"

"Well, for dishes. And . . . drying and . . ." Damn it, why did the man make her stumble and babble like an idiot? She could feel her face heat, and she hated that.

"And?" He laid a clean plate in the rack, then turned toward her, amusement all over him. He was teasing her, and he enjoyed it, and a little part of her was flattered. "Do you have other skills that I can put to use on this ranch?"

Oh, there were skills she wanted to put to use right now. But they all involved a bed and a long, hot night. Hunter's deep blue eyes held a tease in them, and a slight smile played on his lips. She wanted to unbutton his blue chambray shirt, tug it out of the waistband of his jeans, and bare what she was sure was a hell of a nice chest. His jeans hugged his hips, held in place by a dark leather hand-tooled belt and a silver buckle in the shape of a horse. Scuffed cowboy boots peeked out from beneath the jeans, speaking of a man who worked hard. She imagined him hot and sweaty, draping that shirt over a fence, then turning on the hose and asking her to rinse—

She cleared her throat. "Uh, I think we should get the dishes done before Barbara Jean comes back."

"Yeah. Good idea." Hunter went back to the sink, attacking the next plate as if it had insulted him. Or maybe she had when she'd changed the subject. The sexual tension that had been simmering between them a moment ago cooled.

Elizabeth didn't know whether to be relieved or disappointed. Or a little of both.

She dried the next plate, circling the rose-patterned off-white stoneware with the soft cotton towel. The plate, like the kitchen, had an air of history about it. From the scarred maple table to the deep white farm sink and the butcher-block countertops, every part of the kitchen—and of the house itself—spoke of generations of memories. She could imagine kids running through the kitchen on their way to the yard, or a dozen family members circling the island, waiting for the turkey to be cut. The white lace-edged curtains dancing in the slight breeze and the braided rug beneath the table made everything feel like . . .

Home.

She could have stepped into the pages of *Better Homes and Gardens*, standing here in the kitchen of this house that was filled with maple and lace and cotton. The world Elizabeth came from was all concrete and gray, as harsh and cold as the winter air that whistled through New Jersey in January.

And the men in Jersey—well, they sure as heck didn't look like the men in Georgia. Hunter had muscles riding on muscles, big strong hands that seemed like they could break the delicate dishes in two with a flick of the wrist. But he handled the washing with efficiency and care, his hands working through that soapy water in record time.

She watched his hands, one moving over the other, soap bubbles skating along his fingers and palms. How could such an ordinary act be so sexy? She wanted to be that plate, to be the one beneath his touch.

"I think that one's about as dry as a desert." Hunter nodded at the dish in her hands.

"Oh, oh, yes, it is." She turned away, quick, before he could see the heat in her cheeks. What was she doing, staring at the man like he was some kind of sex god? Which he most certainly was not. At all.

Okay, maybe he was. A little. A lot.

They went on washing and drying, working their way down the mountain of dishes created in a few minutes' time. Hunter McCoy wasn't a man who said much, and silence stretched between them, filled with the sound of running water and the musical notes of dishes stacked one upon the other. She expected the quiet to be nerve-wracking, that kind of awkward space between people who didn't know each other well, but with Hunter, the silence seemed . . . companionable. If she didn't think about how her body seemed to lean toward his, as if pulled by some electrical current on steroids.

"How long has your family lived here?" she asked.

"Are we starting the interview here, over the breakfast dishes?"

"Just making small talk." She slipped a bowl into the cabinet. "And yes, maybe doing a tiny bit of the interview."

"I'm not a small talk kind of guy," Hunter said. "Too much to do to stand around talking about things that aren't going to get my work done."

"That's not going to win you too many girls."

He arched a brow in her direction. "Is this part of the interview? Or part of your small talk?"

"Neither. Just a . . . comment." Damn it. What was she doing? Flirting? Asking if he was single? "This house just seems to have a lot of history."

"Four generations." Hunter scrubbed a cast-iron pan, then put it on the stove and flicked on the gas to dry the metal surface. "My grandfather's parents built most of it when they first arrived in Georgia. They were farmers, not horse breeders. My grandpa's the one who loved horses. When his parents died, he inherited the farm but the crops withered and died because he spent so much time in the stables and the training circle. He struggled most his life to make this ranch into something special."

"It's something special now."

Hunter shrugged and went back to the last few dishes. "It used to be. There was a time when the Silver Spur was known for having the best quarter horses in the South. We had a stud here that was just made for making champions. The ranch did well for a number of years. My dad was running it then, and him and my mama added on to the house, bought up more land, expanded the operation."

"Then what happened?"

"A few bad financial . . . decisions, one bad year when the horses got sick and wiped out half our stock. And a lot of our best horses were sold years ago, though I'm working on building up our breeding program. You name it, it happened to the Silver Spur." He pulled the plug and let the water drain, then wrung out the sponge. "Anyway, I've got to get back to work."

"Why don't I come with you?" She handed him the towel to dry his hands, then leaned against the counter. "You can talk and I can listen."

A grin flickered on his lips. "You don't give up, do you?"

"My mother always said I was stubborn."

"Stubborn, Miz Palmer," he said, taking a step closer to her, and causing her breath to hitch, "is a mule who won't take two steps. You're not stubborn. You're . . . difficult." Another step closer, until she could see the flecks in his eyes, feel the warmth of his skin, almost hear the beat of his heart. "Like a wild bronco that refuses to be tamed. And that's exactly what I don't need in my life right now."

Damn the man. He got her hormones all worked up, then said something like that.

"*You're* the one being stubborn and difficult," she countered. "I'm trying to help your ranch, not make your life difficult. Embrace change, Mr. McCoy. Sometimes it's good

WHEN SOMEBODY LOVES YOU

for you." At least, that was what she was trying to tell herself, after making several huge changes in the span of twenty-four hours.

Barbara Jean poked her head into the kitchen. "Hunter, the feed order's ready. Do you want me to send Carlos into town for it?"

Hunter paused a long moment, thinking. "Maybe it's time I picked it up myself. Embracing change, as Miz Palmer just reminded me to do."

Surprise filled Barbara Jean's face. "Are you sure?"

Hunter pulled his keys out of his pocket and jingled them in his palm, as if he didn't want to leave quite yet. "I haven't been sure about anything in a long damned time. But I'm tired of letting things go on the way they have. It's time the winds shifted."

There was an undercurrent here, a discussion beneath the simple one about picking up feed. Elizabeth stayed to the side, intrigued but quiet. The tension in Hunter's shoulders, the regret in his tone, all spoke of some past hurts she hadn't found in her preliminary Internet search. A part of her wanted to run up to her computer right now and google until she had the answers. But another part sensed the hurt in the air and wanted to leave it all be.

"Yes, it is time." Barbara Jean's features softened. "Why don't you take Elizabeth with you? Give her a behind-the-scenes look at the ranch and you two can talk on the way. And then when you get back, Elizabeth, you must stay for dinner. I'm making chili."

Hunter scowled. "I don't need anyone to go with—"

"You don't need to be arguing with me is what you mean to say," Barbara Jean said, shooing at him. "Now go on, you, and be nice."

"Aunt Barbara Jean, don't you know? I'm always nice."

Hunter shot her a grin that disappeared almost as fast as it appeared.

"Then prove it," Barbara Jean said, draping an arm over Elizabeth's shoulders and drawing her in, almost like she were part of the family, "and cooperate with Miss Elizabeth here."

"I said I was shifting the winds, not upending the world," Hunter said. His aunt stood there, giving him the Eye, her hands on her hips. Hunter let out a dramatic sigh, then gestured to Elizabeth, but she could see the sparkle in his eyes that tempered his words. "All right, let's go, before I change my mind and leave you on the side of the road."

"Hunter!"

"I'm kidding," he said to his aunt, then leaned in close to Elizabeth, his voice low, his breath warm. "Mostly."

Elizabeth laughed, then followed Hunter out of the house and down the steps toward his truck. "I thought Southern men were supposed to be hospitable and chivalrous."

"We are." Hunter circled around to the passenger's side and pulled open the door. "Life here is just like a Margaret Mitchell novel. At least, that's what it says in the travel brochure." Then he gave her a smirk, and climbed in the other side.

Chapter 4

Barbara Jean watched Hunter and Elizabeth leave, and felt hope for the first time in a long time. She'd seen Hunter smile, caught snippets of him teasing Elizabeth, the words floating in through the open window. This reporter was good for him, good for the ranch. And if there was one thing she wanted to see more than anything in the whole world, it was Hunter smiling.

The back door opened and Carlos strode into the kitchen. "Sorry to interrupt, Miss Barbara, but I wanted a refill before I get to work."

Her heart tripped a little whenever he spoke to her, and even more so when he smiled. She'd known Carlos for more years than she could count, almost as long as he'd worked at the Silver Spur, becoming so ingrained in the ranch, it was as if he lived there. He was a good-looking man, wiry but muscular, with grained arms and hands that came from working hard and loving your work. He always had a ready smile, eyes that seemed lit from within, and if he complained at all about the heat or the workload, she never heard it.

Barbara Jean pressed a hand to her hair, hoping she didn't look like she'd just rolled out of bed. "Sure, sure. It's no bother at all. Would you like me to pour some into a thermos so you can take it with you?"

"That'd be nice, ma'am. One of these days, I'll put a coffeepot out in the barn, so I don't have to come in here all the time."

"You've been saying that for fifteen years, Carlos, and I still see you in my kitchen every morning." She poured the coffee, then handed him the insulated travel mug.

His hand brushed hers as he took the mug, a moment that Barbara Jean had been waiting for. Every single morning, Carlos came back in after the other men had gone to work, always looking for one more cup of coffee. And every time she handed him the mug, his fingertips brushed along hers. A little charge of electricity flickered in her arm, and she was sure she was blushing. Her, a woman old enough to have grandkids, blushing like a schoolgirl at the touch of a man's fingers.

"I sure appreciate it," Carlos said. "And I'll give that coffeepot another thought. Though if I do get one, then I won't have any reason to come in here every day and see your smile." Then he doffed his hat and headed back out the door.

See her smile? Good gracious, in all the times Carlos had come in this kitchen, he'd never said anything like that. She watched him walk away, and wondered if he'd been flirting with her, or if it was just the silly imagination of a woman old enough to know better.

But as Barbara Jean turned back to the dishes, she started

to hum an old love song, and wondered if maybe Hunter wasn't the only one on the Silver Spur who was smiling.

∞

Wild bronco.

That was how Elizabeth would describe Hunter's ancient Chevy truck, for sure. The pickup jostled and tossed her from side to side as he barreled down the dirt road that ran behind the Silver Spur. The old Chevy creaked and groaned, complaining every inch of the way. Elizabeth gripped the handle above her door, sure the truck would bounce her right out if she let go. "You sure this thing won't fall apart?" she shouted over the roar of the engine.

"It hasn't yet." He grinned, then fishtailed a little as he took a turn off the dirt road and onto a stone road. Little rocks kicked up a spray behind the tires. A farmer waved as Hunter passed, and Hunter lifted a hand in response.

The red leather dashboard was faded and cracked, the seats held together with duct tape, and the paint job on the Chevy might have been green at one time, but was now more of a dirty gray. Given the smattering of hay on the floor and the sheaf of receipts tucked into the visor, it was clear Hunter used the truck for work and not impressing women.

Not that she wanted him to impress her, of course. That wasn't why she was here.

They turned right again, this time onto a paved road, thank God. The truck settled into the asphalt, running smoother—not smooth, exactly, but not shaking-like-you're-riding-an-eggbeater rough. "You might want to consider some shock absorbers or something for this thing," she said.

"What, and make it all cushy?" Hunter grinned again. "That takes all the fun out of the ride."

"You and I have very different ideas of fun."

"Let me guess. You like long walks on the beach and drinking wine under the stars."

Elizabeth scoffed. "I'm from Jersey. You really think I'm the long-walks-on-the-beach type?"

He slowed at a stop sign and glanced over at her, his eyes hidden behind dark sunglasses. "Then what type are you, Miss I'm-From-Jersey?"

"The practical type."

He laughed. "Right. Women say that and they mean the exact opposite."

"I'm serious. I like practical things. I'm not one of those hearts-and-flowers kind of girls."

"So if a guy gave you a blender for your birthday—"

"I'd thank him," Elizabeth said, then laughed. "Okay, maybe I would prefer a gift that wasn't an appliance. But that's only because I'm not exactly handy in the kitchen. In a pinch, though, I can whip up a mean margarita."

"Now we're talking." He slowed to circle wide past a tractor chugging along the shoulder. "I'll have you know you are riding with the two-time winner of the 'Ritas and Ribs Contest."

She shifted in the seat to face him. "You cook?"

"I grill and smoke." He wagged a finger at her. "There's a difference."

"Because grilling and smoking is the manly version of cooking." What was it with men and their grills? Most every man she'd ever known considered food you heat with an open gas-fed flame to be more masculine. Like they were cavemen taming fire or something.

Then again, Hunter McCoy had manly down to a T, with jeans that skimmed along muscular legs, that soft-as-butter chambray shirt open at the neck, the sleeves rolled up just enough to expose strong forearms and hands that made her want to melt. He'd tucked the cowboy hat into the space behind his seat, but every time he had it on, he made her feel safe in a weird way that had to go back to some childhood fantasy about men on horseback. Yes, he was . . . manly. Very manly.

"And what about the margaritas?" she teased. "Those are girly drinks."

"Not the way I make them." He winked.

Holy hotness. When Hunter winked, it sent a little thrill through her. "And how exactly do you make those winning margaritas?"

"Trade secret. If I tell you, I'd have to kill you."

"You realize I'm a reporter, right? It's my job to uncover the truth."

"My winning 'ritas and ribs recipes are locked up tight. Even Barbara Jean doesn't know where they are." He pulled into a parking space alongside a red metal building and turned off the engine, tucking his sunglasses in the visor. "And there's nothing you can use to tempt it out of me."

She cocked a grin at him. "Nothing?"

Who was this woman flirting with Hunter McCoy? Since when did Elizabeth flirt, period? But here she was, sitting in the passenger's side of a beat-up Chevy, tilting her head and giving Hunter what she hoped was a coquettish smile, as opposed to the serial killer smile she usually sported in pictures.

His gaze dropped to her lips, then up to her eyes, and the heat in the cab rose ten degrees. "Well, nothing is a pretty broad category."

As in him wearing nothing. Nothing between them. Or—

She shifted on the leather seat, and as she did, she felt a horrible tugging. She twisted around, but her butt stayed where it was. Oh, crap. "Uh, Hunter? I think I'm stuck."

Hunter arched a brow. "Stuck? Or just avoiding the feed store?"

"Stuck. Like really." She twisted again, got nowhere. "Stuck." She moved again and heard a horrible ripping sound. Elizabeth's face heated. "Either that's my seat or . . . my seat."

"Let me help you."

This was what she got for being flirty. All distracted, then tangled up in an embarrassing position. "No, you just go . . . buy feed. I'll get myself out of this mess."

"It's probably just a caught button. Let me try to—" He reached past her, his chest almost brushing hers, but she shifted at the same time, which put his palm smack on her butt. "Uh . . ."

"Sorry. There's not a lot of room here to work in." She shifted again, and his hand slid under her. That brought him even closer to her, so close she could see the pulse in his neck, catch the tempting fragrance of his aftershave. Something spicy and dark, like chocolate dusted with chili powder.

Yum. She almost wished she could be stuck here forever with him pressed against her.

"Hold still," he said, his voice low and gruff. "I've almost got it."

"Okay, but—" And she shifted again, trying not to be so close, because Good Lord, everything about him was making her melt in funny places, and wham, she ended up shifting right into his chest.

He lifted his gaze to hers. "You're making it harder."

God, she hoped so. Her heart raced, and it was all she could do to breathe and not close the last couple of inches between them with her mouth. The urge to kiss him was so strong, Elizabeth was sure Hunter could see it all over her face. She wanted distance, and wanted closeness, and wanted . . . out of this truck. "Uh, sorry."

"Stay still, darlin'." His breath was warm on her neck. He had a slight dusting of stubble on one edge of his cheek, and a crazy part of her was tempted to run a finger along that missed patch.

Instead, she froze where she was, and cursed the designer who had put buttons on the pockets of these jeans. There was a horrible tearing sound and then a second later, she was free. She shifted toward the dash, and Hunter pulled back.

"You're free."

"Thanks." The word came out with a slight hint of disappointment. Crazy. She didn't want to have Hunter climbing all over her, nor did she want to be a permanent part of his truck's upholstery. She looked over her shoulder. "Sorry about the seat."

"Nothing some more duct tape won't fix." He grinned. "This truck is near as old as me, so there's not much you can do to hurt it." He pulled on the handle and opened his door. "If you're done getting caught in my seat, I've got feed to buy."

She slid across the vinyl, careful to keep her button butt from catching, then got out of the truck and followed Hunter into a giant red metal building shaped like a barn. A curved white sign hung over the entrance, reading BROWN FEED & GRAIN, ESTABLISHED 1882.

"They've been here a long time," Elizabeth said, if only to talk about anything other than what had just happened in the truck.

"Yup. Four generations."

"Sort of like the ranch. Is that par for the course for business down here? Decades of relationships, your father dealing with his father, et cetera? Two families, friends for generations, like *Big Valley* or something?"

He stilled, his hand on the door. The easygoing smile had dropped from his face, and his entire body seemed to go cold. "Listen, it wasn't my idea for you to come along for the ride. So do me a favor, and just let me pick up the feed without the barrage of questions."

Every time she tried to do her job, he threw up a road-block. Maybe she should just get back in her car, go home, and admit defeat. Except failure wasn't in her vocabulary, and the past month of . . . disasters was enough. She wasn't going to let this fall apart, too. One way or another, she'd get her story on Hunter McCoy written.

A part of her wondered, too, if Hunter's abrasiveness stemmed from whatever it was that Barbara Jean had refer-enced earlier. Some past history Elizabeth wasn't privy to. Heck, she had things in her past she didn't want to talk about and that she bristled at when someone brought them up. So she could hardly blame Hunter for being the same.

The interior of the feed store was dim, musty, yet charm-ing in a way, with metal walls painted a soft caramel that mimicked wood and a hundred rustic street signs posted here and there, like a map with attention deficit. Except for the counter at the front, it wasn't much of a store at all. A few shelves of supplies, then what looked like miles and miles of bags of feed on stainless steel shelves stretching deep into the cavernous building. A portly white-haired man in a red flannel shirt and jeans came out from behind the coun-ter as Hunter walked in. "Didn't think I'd ever see you in here again."

Hunter reached into his pocket and pulled out a slip of paper. "Got your check here, Johnny Ray. After I load up, I was hoping maybe we could talk—"

"Leave the money on the counter. I ain't in a talking mood, and especially not in a mood to talk to you." Johnny Ray turned away from Hunter and pushed through a swinging door. Just before the door swung shut, he called over his shoulder. "You know where your order is."

Hunter didn't say anything for a long moment. "Suppose I do," he muttered to himself, then dropped the check on the counter and headed toward the back of the store.

Elizabeth doubled her pace to keep up with Hunter as he strode down the long hall. An old rock station played on a radio up front, the sound muffled into bass notes in the back. Again she sensed an untold history behind those words. "Not exactly a friendly guy."

"He has his reasons for not liking me."

"Well, there goes my theory of a *Big Valley* remake here in Chatham Ridge." She smiled, trying to lighten the mood.

Hunter grabbed a wheeled flatbed cart and hefted a bag of feed onto the metal base. "Not everything is a television show, you know. And you're sure as hell not going to find Lee Majors skulking around back here. Or Linda Evans pulling up on a horse."

She grabbed the other end of the next bag and helped him load it. "You used to watch *Big Valley*?"

"It's pretty much required television for a kid who loves horses." He turned back for a third bag. "Let me guess. You dreamed of a horse when you were a little girl. Had a blanket with horses on it and everything on your bed. A whole collection of cheap plastic ponies on a shelf over your desk."

"I was never one of those girls." She hefted the end of the bag and then reached for another. "I was just a kid who watched a lot of TV. Especially reruns."

"Why?"

She shrugged, kept her gaze on the fifty-pound bag. How did this become a discussion about her life? "I had a lot of time alone. And I liked the world I saw in those reruns."

"The one with horses."

"The one with family." Damn. That had slipped out, and she hadn't intended it to. She'd just gotten so caught up in the breakfast and the big ranch house and the talk about *Big Valley* and the damned stoneware dishes. She reached for a fifth bag with Hunter and changed the subject. "How many of these are we buying?"

"Ten."

"And how long will that last?"

"A week."

"Really? Five hundred pounds of this stuff in a week?"

"Horses eat a lot." He grinned. "Kind of like men."

"That I saw at breakfast. It was like you guys vacuumed up all that food."

He hoisted bag six onto the cart with no help from her. "You should see the men at the monthly barbecue. I swear, we could roast an entire brontosaurus and it wouldn't be enough."

"Well one thing is for sure," she said, grabbing the tail end of bag number seven, "all that food isn't going to go to my hips if I keep helping you out."

He paused in reaching for the next bag. "I'd say when it comes to calories, you don't have anything to worry about, Miz Palmer."

She brushed her bangs off her forehead and let out a breath. "Every time you call me that, I feel like you're talking to my grandmother."

He chuckled. "You don't look anything like a grandma."

"I'll be sure to tell that to the lady at Lancôme who sold me that insanely expensive antiaging cream."

He chuckled and reached for the last bag. "Well, Grandma Palmer, let's get the truck loaded so I can get back to work."

Grandma Palmer? "Has anyone ever told you that you're not exactly a charmer?"

He came around to the handle end of the cart, and stopped a few inches from her. "Is that what you want? For me to charm you?"

"No." *Yes.*

"Good. Because I'm not planning on being charming. To you or to anyone else." His mood shifted again, as quick as flipping a switch. He grabbed the cart's handle and with a grunt, started tugging the cart toward the back door. Once outside, they hefted the bags into the back of the truck, a movement that required a lot more effort on Elizabeth's part just to keep up with Hunter.

And not just with the feed bags.

∞

Hunter could have left the cart where it was, sitting on the cracked pavement drive in the back of the feed store. He could have slipped it inside the wide back doors, leaving it for the next person. Instead, he told Elizabeth he'd be right back and he marched the cart all the way down the long center aisle, parking it where he'd found it, nestled in the corner between where the main store left off and the storage area picked up.

Johnny Ray Spencer stood behind the counter, in the same place he had occupied for the past forty years. Elizabeth had been right—there'd been a time when the Spencer and McCoy families had worked together for as long as anyone could remember, an alliance started back when the South was young and they were both new businesses, struggling to stay afloat. The two families had been neighbors and friends, jointly sharing barbecues and helping hands.

Until two years ago. When Johnny Ray punched Hunter in the parking lot of the funeral home, knocking him into the hearse and causing a scene that had Chatham Ridge buzzing for a good long time. Ever since, Hunter had steered clear of the feed store.

Until today.

"Forget something?" Johnny Ray said, with all the friendliness of a warthog on a hot day. There'd been a time when Johnny Ray had been like a second father to Hunter, when he would draw him into a hug and call him *son*.

Those days had ended the day Jenna drove into that ditch. Johnny Ray had blamed Hunter that night—and every day since. But not near as much as Hunter blamed himself.

Hunter took off his hat and held it between his fingers. He had been saying these words in his head for months now. Johnny Ray stood there, a smaller, grayer, sadder man than he'd ever been before. A man who had lost everything.

"I just wanted to apologize," Hunter said.

"You've done that enough. Doesn't change a goddamned thing. My daughter's still dead, my wife's still gone, and my life is still destroyed." Johnny Ray turned away, pretending to be busy straightening a pile of papers on the counter. His shoulders and back stayed tense, waiting for the retreating sound of Hunter's footsteps.

A thousand times Hunter had tried to have this conversation. Almost every single time he'd walked away, leaving Johnny Ray with his guilt and his anger. Hunter could take every ounce of that hatred and fury, take it square in his chest where it took up residence with his own crushing regrets. Truth be told, Hunter deserved every ounce of it. But Johnny Ray was a good man, a man who had never said a cross word to anyone in his life, until that day. He was a man who was slowly dissolving, inch by inch, as the toll of the last two years wore him down to almost nothing. Hunter could abide a lot of things, but he couldn't abide watching that happen to a man he loved like his own father.

"Doesn't mean I'm not sorry as hell, Johnny Ray. I've been sorry every minute of every damned day," Hunter said. "I never would have sent her out that night—"

Johnny Ray whirled around. His light blue eyes, once friendly and sparked with laughter were now icy and cold. His fists had clenched at his sides, and his features had gone stony. "Don't you dare talk about her. About my family. You have no right."

"Goddamit, I loved her, too, Johnny Ray." Hunter's throat jammed, and acid chased through his veins. Two years, and it was still damned hard to talk about. "I—"

"Don't tell me how you felt," Johnny Ray said. "If you loved her, you never would have sent her out on that fool's errand. In that storm, with that load on the back of the truck. I lost everything, Hunter. Everything that ever mattered a damn to me. You know what I have left? This store." Johnny Ray waved a hand at the walls, the roof, the shelves of inventory. "This cold, lifeless store. I would have sold it off or burned it to the ground long ago, if I could have. But I haven't. And you know why? Because I want to be here, every week when you place your order, when you drive by. I want to be here to remind you of what you cost me."

"I didn't mean—" Hunter cut off the words. "Damn it, Johnny Ray. I'm sorry. So damned sorry."

"Get the hell out of my store, Hunter." Johnny Ray pointed at the door, his arm shaking as much as his voice. "Just get the hell out."

Hunter lingered a second longer, then turned on his heel and headed out into the sunshine. Behind him he heard the sobs of a broken man. His steps faltered, but he didn't stop. He couldn't. He had no fix, no salve for the gaping wound in Johnny Ray Spencer's heart.

Chapter 5

Hunter said maybe three words the whole ride back to the ranch. The tension in the cab was as thick and impenetrable as the tension in his shoulders. Something had happened when he'd gone back inside with the cart. An argument over the price of the feed? A disagreement about cart placement? Or something to do with whatever no one was talking about?

I'm tired of letting things go on the way they have. It's time the winds shifted.

There were a thousand pieces to the puzzle of Hunter McCoy—the encounter at the feed store, the way Barbara Jean worried over him, the boots stored in a dusty, locked room.

She glanced down at the boots. Those damned boots. She never should have accepted them. First chance she got, she was going to run out and buy a pair of her own. In the pouring rain, she hadn't seen any kind of clothing or boot store in downtown Chatham Ridge, but surely there was something. She debated asking Hunter to turn around and take her back to town, but given the stony set of his jaw, she changed her mind. Instead, Elizabeth resorted to burying her nose in her phone, sending texts to Sophie.

He still refuses to talk to me, she wrote. How am I supposed to do this interview?

Find common ground, Sophie replied.

Common ground? I'm a bookkeeper from Jersey. He's a horse breeder from Georgia. About the only thing we have in common is that we're both human.

Sophie sent back a winky face. I'm sure there's more than that. Just give him time. He'll open up.

Elizabeth sighed. I hope so. My deadline is in six days.

Plenty of time. Don't sweat it.

LOL. I've spent my life sweating everything. That's what I do, Soph. From the minute she was old enough to know what the word *responsible* meant, Elizabeth had been the one to make the lists, set the alarms, prioritize the bills. Her mother had been firmly in the Scarlett O'Hara camp—worry about it tomorrow, or the next tomorrow, or the one after that.

Don't you think it's time you stopped? And learned to enjoy life a little? Sophie followed that with a smiley face and a heart. Take some time to soak up the landscape and RELAX, girlfriend. You need it. You deserve it.

Sophie's words tumbled around in Elizabeth's head as the truck bumped down the road. Outside her window a constant movie played, filled with rolling green landscape and vivid blue sky dotted with fluffy white clouds. She felt like Dorothy—leaving the black-and-white concrete world of New Jersey for this Technicolor world, so bright and beautiful, it looked almost fake.

"Is it always this beautiful here?" she asked Hunter.

"Pretty much."

"I've never seen so much green in one place," she kept talking, as if she could fill the tense space in the truck with babble. "Where I live, the color is gray. As in gray buildings, gray concrete, gray skies."

"I don't know how people live in places like that. A person needs room to stretch, to breathe."

"Have you ever been outside of Georgia?" She put up a hand to cut off his objection. "Before you say anything, I'm just making conversation, not quizzing you for the story."

"Hey, I wasn't going to say anything. I'm not that bad."

She arched a brow.

He chuckled. "Okay, then. I've lived here all my life. For a while, I thought I'd leave, go do something else, but my heart is in the ranch." He turned back onto the dirt road, which made the truck start bouncing again. "I don't want to sound all sentimental or anything, but it's like every inch of that ranch is part of my DNA. My grandpa loved it something fierce, and I got a lot of that love from him."

"You were close to your grandpa?"

Hunter nodded. "There was nothing I liked more than helping my grandpa out. I'd rush home from school, and head straight for the stables. I didn't care if he wanted help mucking out the stables or brushing down the horses. I just wanted to be with my grandpa and the horses in the warm Georgia sun. My dad, on the other hand, was never much of a ranch person, so I think my grandpa loved that I was so involved."

"But your dad ran it for a while."

"And his heart was never in it. I think that impacted his

decisions and in the end, almost destroyed the Silver Spur. He meant well, but he just never loved it." Hunter shrugged. "Maybe he had other dreams. If he did, he never told me. We weren't close. I don't think my dad understood me any better than I understood him."

The truck turned left and the landscape shifted. They passed a dairy farm, lumbering cows making their way from one end of a pasture to the other. "My mother was a dreamer," Elizabeth said, "but not the practical kind. She had a dream a minute, like a kid with a mile-high list for Santa. She'd cut out pictures of a boat or a car or a trip to Mexico, and tack them on the fridge. Eventually, the pictures would fade and fall to the floor. She never pursued any of those dreams, just talked about them. And I think that's kind of sad."

"I think not loving what you do every day is sad," Hunter said. "I couldn't work in an office or do sales calls or any of the stuff the rest of the world does. I'm the kind of man who needs to be outside, working with my hands, every day of the week."

"And I have spent most of my life working in an office. It's . . . suffocating." She breathed in deep, drawing in the fresh fall air drifting through the open windows. "I can see why you love this so much."

"I do love it. But there are also days when being here is, as you said . . . suffocating," he said in that quiet kind of voice that didn't offer any room for an explanation or a question.

If she had been a good journalist, she would have pushed it. Would have hammered at him until he told her what about this amazing place he could possibly dislike. But she wasn't that kind of person—never had been. She wasn't cutthroat, wasn't a story-at-all-costs girl. She knew all about not wanting to share and open up the wounds in your heart, and she sure as hell wasn't going to force Hunter to do that now.

Besides, her story was about the Silver Spur, on the legacy of champion quarter horses it had produced for four decades. The comeback being launched by Hunter McCoy, starting with the three-year-olds that were already showing great promise in reining competitions. That was what she should focus on, not what shadows crowded his blue eyes.

They turned onto the ranch, and Hunter swung the truck around to the back of the stable. He put it in park, then hopped out and opened the door for Elizabeth. Then he went around to the back and pulled down the tailgate. "If you want to go in, I'm going to unload this feed."

"I said I'd help, and I will." She wrestled the first bag onto the edge of the bed, and hoisted it herself, letting out a grunt as she did. Maybe if she did enough manual labor, she'd focus on why she was here instead of what pained a man she wasn't dating. A man she should have no interest in beyond the words she needed to write about him.

He grinned. "You're going to regret that in the morning."

"I'm not the kind of girl who does things I'm going to regret in the morning." Elizabeth dropped the bag on the stable floor with a grunt, then turned back for the next one. As she did, her feet tangled, and she stumbled into a pile of hay. The hay poofed up around her, launching her into a sneezing fit.

Hunter put out his hand and helped her up. Laughter played at the edge of his lips, but he didn't tease her for falling. "Never?"

"Never wha—" She sneezed again. "Never what?"

"Never do things you're going to regret?"

Was he flirting with her? Teasing her? Asking her if she wanted a one-night stand? Then she thought of the query letter, quitting her job, all the spontaneous decisions she'd made in the last few days. "Almost never."

"Good to know." He grinned, then turned away before she could decide what he meant by that. Hunter hefted the next bag and tossed it onto the pile with ease, as if it weighed no more than a bag of feathers. He lifted the end of the next bag with her, the two of them working in concert, just as they had back at the store, stacking the remaining feed near the hay bales at the back of the stable.

The whole time she was dying to ask him what had happened back at the feed store, and what made his moods shift as quickly as the winds. Because asking would mean getting personal, developing a relationship. She didn't need that to write her story. Didn't, in fact, need that at all.

She'd just ended a two-year relationship that had been as stale and dead-end as her bookkeeping job. Granted, from the day she met Roger, she'd never felt the kind of overwhelming electricity that raced through her body when she looked at Hunter. But Elizabeth wasn't a girl who wanted electricity and sparks. She'd seen too many people make crazy decisions because of a rush of hormones.

Steady, predictable, safe. That was the kind of relationship she wanted. Not the kind of insane one-day infatuations she'd watched her mother hop to, a different man every month, every week. The new love of her life, who was then blacklisted just as quickly, for reasons that seemed as mercurial as Elizabeth's mother's heart.

Except, a part of Elizabeth whispered, *what had been the result of steady and predictable?* Roger, upstairs with the cougar in 4B, and her, out in the middle of Georgia with an intriguing cowboy who drove her crazy.

"Last bag," Hunter said, dropping it onto the pile. The thud drew her back to the present. "Thanks for the help."

"Just pulling my own weight." She smiled. Damn, he looked good with a light sheen of sweat on his skin, his hat pulled down over his brow and that all-too-small glimpse of his skin beneath the undone buttons. So much for getting back on track.

"And buttering me up for this interview, I bet." He put up a hand, and she saw in his face that he wasn't being harsh, just teasing. "Before you start throwing questions at me, I have stalls to muck out. You can follow me, but I'm sure you don't want to be doing that."

"Will it earn me extra brownie points if I do?"

Damn, this woman was relentless. He recognized and respected that spirit in her—because he'd been the same way as a kid. Eager to do whatever it took to prove his worth to his grandfather. "If you're serious, then follow me."

"I'm always serious, Mr. McCoy."

He chuckled. "Please don't call me that. When you do, I go looking for the headstones in the Chatham Ridge Cemetery. Hunter is good. Or you could take a cue from my sister and call me PITA."

Elizabeth laughed. "I think I like that one best."

"You'll be using that word a lot in the next half hour." He crooked a finger and she followed him down the aisle of the stable. He stopped beside a wheelbarrow, a stack of work gloves, and a pair of pitchforks. "I think the green gloves are the smallest pair we have. So grab those and a pitchfork and let's go have fun."

"Fun?"

He grinned. "I'm just trying to put a positive spin on a shitty job."

"Oh, ha, ha, ha." But she laughed all the same.

Her light laughter echoed in his mind as they headed down to the first stall and started working. The leather gloves dwarfed Elizabeth's small hands and the pitchfork seemed to be two feet too long, but she didn't say a word.

She slid into the stall and started working alongside him. No complaints about the smell, not a word about how hard the work was. Hunter was impressed. He'd had experienced ranch hands who whined like little kids when they mucked out stalls.

He hoisted the worst of the soiled straw into the wheelbarrow, then gestured toward the perimeter of the stall. Elizabeth put the back of her hand against her nose as the worst of the smell was unleashed, but didn't complain. "You can leave the clean straw," he said. "We'll spread it out, then add fresh straw on top of that when we're done. It's not a tough job, just a smelly one."

"I grew up in Jersey. Smelly things don't bother me." But she grimaced as she said it.

He chuckled. "I'll remind you of that ten stalls from now."

They worked together for a little while, with just the sound of the pitchforks sliding against the wood and the faraway sound of horses in the pasture filling the time between them. When they had finished the first stall, Hunter hefted the wheelbarrow in his hands and headed out of the barn.

Elizabeth walked along beside him. She had tucked her gloves in her back pocket, and the leather fingers tapped against her shapely butt while she walked. *Damned distracting*, Hunter thought. Too damned distracting.

"Why do you do this?" Elizabeth asked.

"Because the horses can get sick if I don't clean out the stalls. It's important for them to have clean bedding for their hooves and—"

"I didn't mean why do you clean out the stalls. That's pretty obvious." She waved a hand at the smelly pile in the wheelbarrow. "I meant, why do you work with horses?"

He gave her a grin. "Always trying to sneak in those interview questions, aren't you?"

She shrugged. "You're doing your job; I'm trying to do mine."

"Fair enough." Not to mention she had helped him several times today without complaint. They'd made an agreement, and Hunter was a man who stood by his word. He considered his answer as he walked. "Horses are a lot like people, only better. They can be slow to trust, but once you earn that trust, they'll remember you forever. They'll work themselves to death for the people they love and never complain. But that's not really the half of it." He kept walking, the wheelbarrow hiccupping from time to time as the wheel skipped over a divot in the ground. "My dad was never around when I was a kid, and my mom got sick when I was eight. She was in and out of the hospital, and life here was . . . stressful. I'd go out to the stables with my grandpa and the horses would be there, every single day, steady and sure and strong. They were like . . ." He shook his head. "This is all sounding corny."

"No, it's not, not at all." Her smile seemed brighter in the sun.

He cleared his throat and started talking again. "The horses became my family. My foundation. I could talk to them, and they would listen, and when I needed to get away, they were there. They were"—his gaze went to the mares in the pasture, the colts and fillies ranging around their mothers, the entire herd serving as one loyal, happy family—"everything I wanted and didn't have."

"That sounds . . . awesome. Guess I should have grown up here instead of New Jersey."

"It was a hell of a childhood, I have to say. I just hope I do my grandfather proud in the years to come."

"From what I've read, the Silver Spur is really coming back and coming back strong. My editor sees it as one of those rising-from-the-ashes kind of stories."

Hunter dumped out the soiled straw and thought it was a pretty apropos move while they were talking about what the ranch had been through. Ten years ago, he couldn't have gotten a reporter to write a story on the Silver Spur if he'd offered up his first born as payment. "Well, we're still rising, so we'll see how it goes."

"Do you usually have this many horses and babies at once?" Elizabeth asked as they walked back to the barn.

"A successful breeding program means breeding regularly. Not all the mares have foals every year because breeding is really a matter of precise timing, but yes, we do try to keep an active program going here. Or at least we do now. It took us a while to get enough money to bring in a strong stud."

Elizabeth grinned at him. "I thought all cowboys were strong studs."

He laughed as he stowed the tools and gloves back in their spot. Was she referring to him as a strong stud? And why was it suddenly so damned important to have that information? "You're thinking of the men in Texas. Here in Georgia, we're just average men."

"Oh, I think some of the women in town might disagree with that. Noralee says you're the most eligible bachelor in Chatham Ridge." She arched a brow, clearly teasing him.

"Noralee has been reading too many of those romance novels in her store." Hunter whisked the hay off his jeans. "Let's get cleaned up. I'm starving, and I'm sure you are, too. It's almost lunchtime and Barbara Jean won't let anyone in the house who doesn't look like they're ready for church."

Elizabeth glanced down at her clothes. Her silky shirt was stained and matted to her damp skin, hay stuck to her jeans and her hair. She looked more like a scarecrow than the buttoned-up businesswoman she'd resembled this morning.

"God, look at me. I'm a disaster." She shook her head. "I think this is the part where I tell you that you were right about my attire choices."

He leaned forward and plucked a piece of hay out of her hair. "You are a mess, Miz Palmer."

"Just like you don't want to be called Mr. McCoy, I'm asking you to please not call me that, or *Grandma Palmer*, or anything else. It makes me sound like some old, shriveled-up lady in a bonnet."

"You are far from old and shriveled up." He was standing so close to her, he could see the flecks of gold that colored her green eyes. It made them seem to dance and sparkle in the dim light of the stable. "And I definitely don't think you're the bonnet type."

"I don't know. I think I could really rock a bonnet with the hay all over my shirt and pants." She turned and bent to wipe the hay off the back of her, completely unaware of how sexy the move was. Her shapely backside, thrust to one side, her hand slapping the hay off the denim. Her shirt peeked open, the silky panels parting just enough to reveal a lacy off-white bra.

Holy hell.

Hunter McCoy had been alone for two years. Two years he had filled with work, with mindless, endless days that left him so exhausted, the only thing he wanted was to eat and sleep. He hadn't dated, except for the occasional night out in the city where the dates were about as meaningful as cotton candy, and just as lasting. But when he saw that peek of lace, that little view of pale peach skin beneath the creamy silk, a fire erupted inside him, a fire he thought had died a long time ago.

"You could probably rock about anything," he said, then added, because it fit perfectly with the woman he had come to know, "Lizzie."

She straightened. "Lizzie?"

It was the perfect nickname for her. To him, Lizzie was a woman who was a little wild, a little undone, not the severe and structured Elizabeth she purported to be. "I think it suits you better than Miz Palmer, or Elizabeth."

"Hardly anyone has ever called me anything other than Elizabeth, and only my best friend calls me Liz. But never Lizzie."

"To me," he took a step closer, telling himself it was just to whisk another errant piece of hay away, not to inhale the sweet, dark notes of her perfume whispering above the smell of horses and hay. Not to narrow the space between himself and this woman who both tempted and infuriated him. "You are more of a Lizzie than anything else."

She raised her chin, green eyes flashing with a challenge, a slight smile playing on her lips. "And what exactly is a Lizzie like?"

He caught a piece of hay and tugged it out of her hair. "Determined." He tugged out another piece. "Sassy."

"Sassy?"

He caught a third piece, watched it tumble to the ground. "Annoying."

"Hey!" But the word lacked any punch. She was watching him, her eyes wider with every second. He shifted closer to her. Why was he so attracted to someone that he wanted so badly to leave?

"And most of all, strong-minded," he said, watching her jaw harden, while her eyes danced, "and resolute."

"That I'll agree with. Though I do think you cheated with two synonyms." She raised two fingers and waggled them in his direction.

He caught the fingers and brought them down between them. "Then I'll add aggravating."

She laughed. "Another double synonym. Have you already run out of adjectives?"

He shook his head, and saw one more piece of hay slipped in among her bangs like a stowaway. He pinched it between his fingers and drew it out slowly. She opened her mouth, then shut it again, and he swore he felt the temperature rise ten degrees. He thought of how she'd jumped right in and helped with the feed order, how she hadn't complained about it being too hot or too difficult. How she raved about the Silver Spur, making it sound like utopia. How she peppered him with questions even as she worked side by side with him. There was nothing more attractive, Hunter realized, than a woman who wasn't afraid to get her hands dirty. And a woman who loved this place as much as he did.

He'd tried, tried so hard, with Jenna, to get her to love his world, but she never had. She'd tolerated it, but that was as far as it had gone. He'd been foolish, thinking he could convince a girl with a city heart to love the country life. And maybe he was just as crazy for thinking he saw a little country in this Jersey native. All he knew was that he hadn't felt this . . . alive in a long, long time, and for now, he wanted to hold on to that feeling. Just a little longer.

He moved closer, his gaze dipping to her parted lips, lingering there. "Beautiful."

"What are we doing here?" she asked, a breathless quintet of words.

"I haven't figured that out yet." He trailed a path down her cheek, then splayed his fingers against her jaw, one touching the edge of her bottom lip. Her eyes widened and her breath quickened.

"This is supposed to be an interview," she said. "Just an interview."

Her words reminded him of why she was here. That this

wasn't a date or a flirtation. It was business, and business wasn't something he should screw up with sex. She was here for a couple days at most, then gone again, back to Trenton, far from here. "I think you're wasting your time. There's not a lot worth interviewing me about. You'll find that out soon enough, Miz Palmer."

Then he left the stable and headed out to the ring to work the long yearlings with Carlos. Until his blood cooled and his mind stopped haunting him with the image of a lacy scrap of fabric and a women with sparkling eyes.

Chapter 6

〰

Amberlee McCoy had loved horses from the minute she saw one. She'd been that girl with the horse bedspread, the horse curtains, the horse notebook tucked tight against her chest as she walked to the bus stop every morning. Growing up on the Silver Spur had meant she could see newborn foals, patient mares, and anxious stallions every single day.

For a long while, she'd thought she could be a trainer, working with Carlos in the corrals, running the young horses through their paces. Then she'd spent three days in the hospital, and the entire family had held a meeting that felt a hell of a lot like some kind of crazy intervention and said the only way she could enjoy the horses was from afar.

So she sat in her dorm room, reading about Plato and Socrates for a liberal arts degree she didn't even want. Her heart, her passion, was back on the Silver Spur.

The problem was getting her brother and aunt to agree. Amberlee had had a thousand arguments with Hunter, then another two thousand after Jenna died. She loved her brother, she really did, but he seemed ten times more protective now and ten times more determined that she do anything *but* live on the ranch.

She glanced at the top right dresser drawer, the one that held the secret she'd been keeping from her family. To finally get what she wanted, to finally be where she wanted, she was going to have to keep that secret close.

In the meantime, she buried her head in philosophy and doodled horses in the margins of her notes. Dreaming of one while focusing on the other. Maybe one day it would be reversed.

∽

Elizabeth avoided Hunter for the rest of the morning. When he'd almost kissed her—was that what that had been?—she'd felt a surge of desire so powerful, NASA could have launched a rocket in her gut. This was wrong, so wrong.

But God help her, for a few minutes there in the stables, it had felt pretty damned right. She'd been looking into his blue eyes, hearing him call her *Lizzie*, feeling the dance of his fingers against her chin, the tension between them a living thing, and she had wanted him to kiss her. To do a lot more than kiss her, actually. A few fantasies involving her against the wall and him against her might have flitted through her mind. In color.

She'd headed up to her room—another bad sign, she was already considering space in his house as hers—and googled everything she could about quarter horses and breeding and ranches. And Hunter McCoy.

She'd done a preliminary search before she'd written her query, of course, but at that time, she hadn't been interested in him personally. Like whether he was married or dating or—

No. She was looking for horse info. That was all. She couldn't help that her mouse froze on a page with a wedding announcement, featuring a beautiful blonde with short hair and the kind of smile that said spunky, beside a beaming Hunter, wearing his trademark cowboy hat, the brim casting a slight shadow over those eyes. It was the same woman from the picture in the hall, the same woman who had looked at Hunter with love in her eyes.

> Johnny Ray and Wanda Marie Spencer are thrilled to announce the engagement of their daughter, Jenna Lee, to Hunter McCoy, son of Jack and Mary Sue (deceased) McCoy of Chatham Ridge, Georgia. Miss Spencer is a graduate of the University of Georgia and works as a fashion merchandiser at Bloomingdale's in Atlanta. Mr. McCoy works at the family ranch, the Silver Spur, raising quarter horses. A June wedding is planned.

Two years ago. What had happened? Because if Hunter was married, he was doing a good job concealing the wife. Johnny Ray Spencer . . . that was the man who owned the feed store. The man who seemed to hate Hunter.

Elizabeth clicked through the next few links, then stopped cold.

The picture filled the frame of her computer screen in stark black and white. An overturned pickup truck, a detached horse trailer a few feet back, lying in a ditch. And a tree, broken at the base, thrust through the truck's windshield like an angry fist.

LOCAL WOMAN KILLED IN CRASH;
PRIZE HORSE DIES

The headline seemed harsh and cold beneath the picture. Elizabeth skimmed the article, skipping words here and there. It almost felt like peeking into Hunter's diary to read this, to delve into personal details that would probably have no bearing on her article. But, oh, how much it explained about the tortured man she had met. Her heart broke for him.

Slick roads . . . heavy downpour . . . high rate of speed . . . swerved off road . . . died on scene . . .

Elizabeth shut the top of her laptop and sat back in her seat, her stomach in knots. That had to have been horrible for Hunter, losing his fiancée just a few months before they were supposed to get married. And a young horse, worth tens of thousands of dollars, when he was still trying to bring the ranch back to life.

Then she thought of that bedroom, the one that had been dusty and unused, the one Hunter had refused to enter. The one holding a woman's clothes. And boots.

Oh, damn. Damn, damn, damn. She should have been more prepared. Should have known better than to show up here without boots and without the facts. Now she'd gone and found out that not only was the man widowed before he could become a groom, but she was wearing his late fiancée's boots. No wonder he had looked at her like that in the barn.

Best thing to do was get done and get gone. Except . . .

Noralee had invited her to the book club and Barbara Jean had invited her to supper and all of that sounded like something so good, so wonderful. Elizabeth had told herself she wouldn't go to either, but the craving to be there, to be included, part of the . . . family, as it were, had grown in her with every minute she spent at the ranch. Book clubs and family dinners were the kinds of things Elizabeth had missed in childhood, because where she'd grown up, she'd have been lucky to find half a loaf of bread in the wooden bin. Her mother worked nights, and slept days, and more often than not, Elizabeth fended for herself. There were no Sunday family dinners or cozy chats in wingback chairs beside a fireplace. Elizabeth twisted the faux ruby ring on her right hand, worn there every day since her mother died as a reminder to be responsible, smart, and not go chasing after some harebrained whim. But wasn't that the exact opposite of what she was doing here? Getting caught up in thoughts about Hunter McCoy, lingering when she really should have just done the interview and been back on the road in the same day?

Elizabeth should have been strategizing how to get out of here as soon as possible, but a part of her really wanted those cozy chats and Sunday dinners. And to find out more about what made Hunter McCoy tick.

∞

"Yes, she's still here. You haven't driven her off yet," Barbara Jean said when Hunter came in for lunch. "A minor miracle, if you ask me, considering you've been about as nice as a late summer hurricane."

"How did you know I was going to ask about the reporter?" Hunter said. Calling Lizzie *the reporter* made it less intimate, as if two words could make him forget how close he'd come to kissing her back in the stables.

"Because I saw you looking for her as soon as you walked in that door."

He scowled as he headed to the sink to wash his hands. He refused to tell his aunt that she was right. Or admit it to himself. "I was looking for a sandwich. I have to get back out there and—"

"Do this interview you keep pretending doesn't exist."

"I do not have time for this. I have a ranch to run, horses to breed, and the foals to train, plus there's Dakota . . ." He dried his hands and draped the towel over the sink. Then he opened the fridge and looked inside for something that he could eat fast so he could get out of here before his aunt called his bluff. The magazine should have sent one of those grizzled old man reporters. Someone who wore a fedora and smoked cigars. Someone who didn't distract him with something as simple as a smile. "That's not even adding in the call I need to make to the vet or the fence in the back pasture that needs repaired or—"

"All those ors, buts, and excuses could fill a bushel and a half," Barbara Jean said. She put a hand on the fridge door and shut it. "And they can all wait till tomorrow. You go on into the dining room and talk with that girl."

"Why the dining room?"

Barbara Jean put a hand on her hip and raised her chin with the kind of confidence of someone who'd just played a trump card. "Because I made my famous steak quesadillas for lunch and the only place you're going to find your plate of them is right next to that lovely Elizabeth."

Damn, his aunt knew him well. He never could lie to her. Maybe it was because Barbara Jean had lived off the ranch for part of her life, traveling the world, meeting new people, doing new things, or maybe because he'd grown as close to her as he had been to his mother and grandfather. He remembered long summer nights after Aunt Barbara Jean came to live with them, where they'd sit outside on the porch and

watch the sun go down and talk about everything from fire-
flies to girls.

After Mama died, Aunt Barbara Jean had stepped in and
loved him and Amberlee as if they were her own children,
and try as he might to be irritated with his aunt for trying
to push him together with the reporter, he couldn't hold the
emotion for longer than a millisecond.

Hunter grinned. "Would you be trying to bribe me?"

"Let's just call it incentive." Barbara Jean patted him on
the cheek. She was a good foot and a half shorter than him,
but when she looked up at her tall nephew, she seemed to
reach eye level. "Because I love you and worry about you."

"I'm fine."

Barbara Jean harrumphed. "Keep on telling me that, and
maybe I'll believe it. I swear, all I do is worry about you and
Amberlee."

"Why? Is Amberlee sick again?" The notes in Barbara
Jean's voice sent a ripple through Hunter's chest. He didn't
bother to tell his aunt she didn't need to worry about him.
He had a feeling his aunt would do that till the day she died.
It was comforting, in a way, to know someone always had
his back. But his sister—that was a person both of them
worried about. Had ever since she'd been a little girl and
been wracked with asthma so bad, she barely left the house.
She was eighteen now, and determined to live her own life.
Stubborn as a tick on a dog, she was, but that didn't stop
them both from worrying about her.

"She says she's not, but she looks a little pale to me. I'm
going to try to get her to come for the weekend. Take some
time off. She works too hard."

"You're just overprotective." He pressed a kiss to her
cheek. "And we still love you anyway."

She waved him off, but with a smile that was filled with

love. "You worry about the people in this family more than you worry about yourself. The rest of us will be just fine, so you concentrate on the ranch. Especially that Dakota. I know that horse is important for a lot of reasons. Maybe you're hoping saving her will help right some wrongs?"

Hunter's eyes filled, but he shook it off. "She's just a horse."

"And I'm just an aunt who worries too much. Promise me, Hunter, you'll take care of yourself better. The horses will be fine. Horses have been living without human help for centuries." She patted his cheek again. "Right now, your job is to spread the word about the amazing things you're doing at the Silver Spur. So stop delaying and get in there."

Hunter grumbled, but Barbara Jean just gave him a not-so-gentle nudge in the direction of the dining room, reminding him to be nice to Elizabeth. She meant well, and he knew it. Barbara Jean had been the one to drag him out of his self-imposed cave after Jenna died. The one who made sure he got back to the horses, to the ranch, to living. She'd fed him and badgered him and loved him until he stopped needing to be reminded to get out of bed in the morning and to breathe again.

The large dining room had barely changed in the years since his mother passed away. A long walnut table with claw feet dominated the room, married to a matching hutch and scuffed buffet—scratches put there one Christmas day by Hunter and his cousins turning it into a Matchbox race track. His mother's blue flower-patterned china, a wedding gift from more than thirty-five years past, still sat behind the glass doors of the hutch, never used anymore.

Long white pleated drapes hung to the floor, severe against the dark woodwork and pale blue walls of the room, but cheery when decorated with big red bows at Christmas, something that had also stopped once Mama was gone. It seemed the entire house had come to a standstill all those years ago. When his mother died, his father didn't want Barbara Jean to move or change a thing, so the entire house was caught in a time warp. For a long time Hunter had thought about moving out, moving on, then Jenna came along and he'd begun to see signs of life in the house—a vase of flowers here, a new rug there, a parade of freshened pictures along the top of the upright piano.

Then Jenna had died, and all that had died with her. He hadn't sat in this dining room in months, and wondered if Barbara Jean had chosen this location on purpose. Because if there was one thing Hunter excelled at, it was staying in the same place, every single day of his life. There was comfort there, predictability.

Lizzie was sitting at the head of the table, with a laptop to her right and a pad of paper and stack of pens in front of her. A tiny digital recorder sat in front of the seat to her left, presumably where she wanted him to sit. She looked up when he entered, and a smile . . . blossomed on her face.

Blossomed was the only word for it. The smile started slow, edging away from one corner of her mouth, then spreading across her face and brightening her eyes, like a daisy opening its petals. It unfurled in the room, filling the empty spaces in his gut, causing his own lips to curve upward, as if the smile were contagious.

She had changed out of Jenna's jeans and boots, and put on another silky shirt, this one a lilac color, and gray dress pants. She looked like an attorney, not a reporter, and sure as shootin' not like a woman who had just helped him load and unload a week's worth of feed. She looked beautiful, and the cold places in his chest began to warm.

"Mr. McCoy," she began, "thank you for agreeing to do the interview this afternoon."

So, they were back to Mr. McCoy and Miz Palmer now. Seemed he wasn't the only one who wanted to forget what almost happened earlier today. Except every time he looked at her, he could only think of her as Lizzie. And how much he still wanted to kiss her.

And that was what had him resisting this interview like a mule being put to work on a hot summer day. For the hundredth time, he wished for a grizzled old man reporter instead of this intoxicating blonde.

"Barbara Jean says the only way I'm going to get fed is if I sit in here and talk to you." Well, that wasn't his most friendly how-do-you-do. He could almost feel the ghost of his mama sending him a glare. He cleared his throat, tried again. "I mean to say, I think sitting down over lunch and talking is a good idea."

"Barbara Jean told me to tell you there's pie if you make it all the way to the end." Lizzie wagged a pen at him. "But I'm the one who gets to decide if you earned your pie or not."

He liked the way Lizzie teased him. She had this little twitch to her nose, like she was about to burst into laughter. "I'd do about anything for pie, and Barbara Jean knows it."

"Good to know," she said.

An echo of his words earlier when he'd asked her about things she'd regret in the morning. Every time he looked at her, his mind created a whole list of things he'd like to do with her—things they would surely regret. Didn't mean he didn't still think about them, or wonder about them.

Lizzie dipped her head to study the pad of paper before her. A blank pad of paper, so he wasn't sure what she was studying except maybe how to keep him from wondering

what she meant by that or if she was thinking the same
things he was. She wasn't staying, he knew that. She was
heading back to Trenton, or on to the next interview. So he
needed to stop getting used to having her around.

Might want to start with not thinking about her every
five seconds. Wondering what she was doing. If she was
thinking about him. If she wished they'd finished that almost
kiss as much as he wished they had.

Hunter reached for the dish of quesadillas, put three pie-
shaped cheese-oozing pieces on his plate, then topped them
with heaping scoops of extra guacamole and a dollop of sour
cream. He spooned on more salsa, and added some Tabasco
on top of that. Instead of going after the whole thing with
his hands—which is what he'd do if he were at the kitchen
table with the guys—he opted for the fork and knife. It was
his mama's dining room, after all, and he figured he could
put his heathen ways to the side for at least an hour.

He glanced over at Lizzie and saw her empty plate to the
right of her elbow. "You're not eating?"

"Oh, I'm not much for Mexican food."

"If what you refer to as Mexican food is the stuff that comes
out of a box or from a drive-through, then that's not anything
close to this. You haven't lived until you've tasted Barbara
Jean's steak quesadillas. She marinates that steak overnight,
mixes up fresh guacamole and salsa for the insides, and adds
three kinds of cheese. Not to mention the sautéed peppers and
onions, and cilantro she cuts from the garden out back. They're
a whole project, which is why she makes them so rarely, and
why she successfully uses them as bargaining chips."

Lizzie laughed. "Quesadillas that double as bargaining
chips? Maybe I have been missing something."

"Oh, you are. Trust me."

Her gaze met his, her green eyes wide and curious. Tension knotted between them, already threaded earlier when he'd dubbed her Lizzie and come close—so close—to kissing her. She had her hand on the table, inches away from his. He ached to reach out and touch her, to close the gap. But he didn't move.

"Trust you?" she said, with half a laugh. "I hardly know you."

"If it helps, I can get a reference from my third grade teacher. Mrs. Henley always did like me." He grinned. "Though I wouldn't recommend contacting my sixth grade science teacher. Mr. Spinale called me *rambunctious* on my report card. I'm still disputing the charge."

That made her laugh. He liked her laugh. It seemed to come from some well deep inside her, and made him feel like he'd opened a door that no one else had access to.

"I was the one who was always called *studious* and *well-mannered*," she said.

"Let me guess. Honor Society and teacher's pet? Homecoming queen and class president?"

"Honor Society, yes, but never the teacher's pet. And definitely never homecoming queen or class president." She fiddled with the pen. "I never really had time for those kinds of extracurricular activities. I concentrated on my grades."

He wondered about what she was leaving unsaid, what was in the shadows behind her eyes. But asking questions that delved deep meant doing the same with his own life, and right now, he was happy to keep it light. No questions about the last two years of his life, the mistakes he had made, the guilt that plagued his nights, haunted the edge of every day. "I played football a couple years, but mostly, I was here. A ranch is a full-time-plus job. No vacations, no days off." He shrugged. "Good thing I love it."

"Hardworking, no vacations? The rambunctious thing must have been a fluke."

He chuckled. "No, that part was true. My mama used to say I had more energy than a roomful of puppies. Guess that's why my grandpa was always putting me to work." His gaze went to the acres beyond the window, the horses standing tall and proud in the green, green grass, the flowers at the edge of his land. "This ranch has saved me, in more ways than one."

"I can see how it would do that," she said quietly.

He turned back to Lizzie. "Don't get much of this in your land of gray, do you?"

"I never had anything like this." She fiddled with the pen again, her gaze averted. "Uh, why don't we start with the interview now? I know your time is limited and—"

"I'll answer your questions if you try one bite," he said, gesturing toward the quesadilla. He might not be able to give Lizzie the experiences he'd had on this ranch, but he could start with the quesadilla. "Just one, and you'll be sold for life."

"Sold for life? That's a pretty big job for a little quesadilla."

"Not these ones." He cut a section out of the center of the quesadilla, and held his fork out to her. "I'm making a huge sacrifice here and giving you part of the nucleus. So I hope that works in my favor when you're writing."

"The nucleus?"

"It's the part where all the goodness comes together. The most cheese, the biggest chunks of guacamole and salsa, and most of all, the tenderest morsels of that steak. Barbara Jean's secret marinade is amazing. Try it and see."

The fork was inches away from her mouth. In his large, strong hands, the silverware was dwarfed. Lizzie put her hand on top of his, only to guide the fork, but when her

WHEN SOMEBODY LOVES YOU

fingers brushed against his, his pulse tripped, and he nearly dropped the fork.

Then she opened her mouth and closed her eyes. And he damned near had a heart attack.

He knew the instant the bite of quesadilla hit her palate. He could see the taste sensations wash over her features. He'd had these quesadillas so many times, he could describe them without even eating them. The warm, gooey insides hitting her palate like a song, tangy and smooth at the same time, with the salsa and the queso marrying happily on her tongue.

She chewed, then swallowed, and an honest-to-god moan slipped past her lips. He had to force himself to stay in his chair and not lean over and try to make her moan in other ways. Holy hell, that sounded sexy. If she was that way about lunch, he couldn't wait to get to dessert.

Lizzie opened her eyes. Crimson flushed her cheeks. "You weren't kidding. That was . . . incredible."

"Told you so." He nodded toward her plate. "Let me load you up."

She put up a hand, warding him off. The blush faded from her cheeks and she seemed to shift to a businesslike demeanor, one that fit the dress pants and shirt. "Oh, I shouldn't."

"Don't tell me you're one of those girls who only eats a stalk of celery a day."

"I love food." She gestured toward the notepad and the pens and the tape recorder. "I'm just trying to concentrate on my job here."

"Okay, then how about this? You eat for a bit and I'll interview you. If you don't eat, Barbara Jean's feelings will be hurt." He scooped up two pieces, and put them on her plate.

She hesitated. "Somehow, this seems like another way for you to get out of talking to me."

"And why would I want to do that?"

"Because you are rambunctious and difficult." She inhaled, and smiled. "Damn, those do smell good, though. Okay, just a few bites, then it's your turn. Deal?"

"Deal." If he thought dining on the quesadillas was pleasurable for him, it was ten times more enjoyable to watch Lizzie eat them. Every bite made her smile, and that warmed him in a thousand ways. He crossed his hands on the table. "Okay, first question. Why?"

"Why what?" She cut off a piece of the next triangle.

"Why my ranch? Why now?"

She took a bite, chewed, and swallowed. "I came across the page for the Silver Spur on Facebook one night, and I was intrigued. I loved the story you had on there about it coming back from the edge of bankruptcy, how you were trying to keep the dream alive with the fourth-generation ownership. It was . . . hopeful. Sweet."

"And written by my aunt." He shook his head. Barbara Jean, the master marketer. Maybe it was her optimistic spirit, but she'd always painted the ranch and his family with a positive brush. "She always did believe in fairy-tale endings."

"My mother was like that. But her fairy tales always ended in disaster, as in us being broke. She also played the lottery every day, and totally believed in psychics and horoscopes." Lizzie rolled her eyes. "If there was someone with a prediction, my mother was right there with her ten bucks to hear it."

"And you're more of a realist?"

"Definitely." She picked at her food. "I was a bookkeeper before this, and everything in my world always added up just right."

He couldn't imagine her as a bookkeeper, though he did like the mental image of Lizzie with her blond hair piled atop her head and a pair of glasses perched on her nose. "A bookkeeper? How'd you end up as a writer?"

"Well, that's, uh, kind of a funny story." She took another bite, really fast, and swallowed it just as quickly. "There, I'm done. Let's get started on—"

His Spidey sense started tingling. There'd been some-thing about Lizzie ever since she'd arrived that wasn't what he expected—not just as a woman, because she sure as hell wasn't like any other woman he'd met—but as a reporter. She'd been . . . unconventional, unexpected. He thought it was because she was a city girl from Jersey, and not used to the country life.

But now he was beginning to get a bad feeling about the bookkeeper turned journalist sitting across from him. "What do you mean, kind of a funny story? Funny . . . how?"

"You're, uh, actually my first article." She gave him a bright smile, as if to offset the words. "Well, first official article. I've written for—"

"*First* article?" He pushed his plate away. The quesadillas had gone cold. The sick, worried feeling in the pit of his stomach quadrupled. "As in first ever?"

"Sort of. I've got writing experience."

"Writing what?"

"I wrote the company newsletter for several years, and when they decided to shut that down, I realized I was going to be stuck adding numbers the rest of my life if I didn't do something about it. Then an editor decided to give me a chance on the query about your ranch so . . . here I am."

"Just like that." Hunter ran a hand through his hair. He was putting the fate of the Silver Spur in the hands of someone who had almost no experience. "I can't do this interview."

He started to get to his feet, but she put out a hand to stop him. "I assure you, I'll do a great job."

"You don't understand. This ranch is my life. Every one of these horses, every inch of this land, is part of me. It's all I have, I can't just—"

"Trust me."

"Well, yeah, exactly. I don't trust you. I've seen what bad publicity can do. Joey Bishop's ranch was caught up in some 'investigative reporter's'"—he put air quotes around the word—"story on doping. Joey's never doped a horse in his life, and sure as hell wasn't doping the horses he had in the ring. It was just some idiot's attempt to make a buck by creating a story that didn't exist. Joey lost everything he had, all because of one bad reporter."

"You think I'm going to do something like that?"

"I don't know what you're going to do, and that scares me. I won't go in the ring with an untried horse, and I'm sure as hell not handing over my ranch's reputation to someone with no track record." He got to his feet and picked up his still-full plate. "And you can quote me on that."

∞

Barbara Jean was not the kind of woman to let things go unsaid, tasks go undone, questions go unanswered. But as she readied a helping of her quesadillas and headed over to the stable, a flutter of nerves had her slowing her steps and wondering if she had read that moment in the kitchen wrong.

She had a thousand other things she could be doing right now, of course. She could be paying the bills, balancing the books, starting dinner. She was pretty much a jack-of-all-trades around the Silver Spur and that meant whatever needed doing, Barbara Jean would probably do it. She loved this place like it was her right arm, and loved every last person who lived here.

She found Carlos sitting on a bench in the shade outside

the cabin he sometimes slept in when the workdays grew too long. He was repairing a saddle, stitching up the leather with a giant, thick needle that looked like a splinter in his big, strong hands. He looked up when she approached, and she swore she caught a glimpse of a smile before the brim of his hat blocked her view.

"I, uh, thought you might want some lunch." She held up the plate and lifted off the plastic cover.

"Thank you, Miss Barbara. I brought my own today, but haven't got to it yet."

"Oh, okay." She lowered the lid. "Well, just thought I'd ask."

"Is that your famous quesadillas I smell?"

A flush filled her cheeks. "I don't know if they're famous, but yes, it's my steak quesadillas."

"Hell, yes, they're famous. Best damned quesadillas in five counties, maybe six. That's what I hear, anyway."

She giggled—actually giggled—at the compliment. "Well, thank you."

"I figure they're a whole lot better than the sandwich I brought. A man cooking for himself usually doesn't make anything too complicated. Just a couple slices of bread and some ham." He gestured toward the cabin. "If you don't mind coming in for a minute and sharing with me, I'd sure like that."

"Oh, well, I don't know. I mean—"

"It's okay if you have to get right back. I just don't much like eating alone."

So it wasn't like a date or anything. Just keeping him company. Letting her gaze drink in the sight of him, with the first two buttons of his shirt undone and that smile that appeared every few seconds just to send her pulse soaring. "I might have a minute or two."

"Come on in, then." He put the saddle on the bench, then opened the door and ushered her in. "It ain't much, but it does the trick on those nights I'm too bone tired to do anything but stumble into bed."

He was right. The cabin wasn't much of anything, more utilitarian than anything. A single twin bed flanked one wall, a small table with two chairs against the other, beside a sink and a row of cabinets. A portable air conditioner hung in the window. Carlos switched to turn it on, then pulled out one of the chairs. "Have a seat. I think I have some forks and stuff here."

She did as he asked, feeling like an interloper, sitting in Carlos's kitchen/bedroom. The sheets on the bed were barely rumpled, which meant he'd probably been too tired to do anything more than sleep on top of the covers before getting up early to get back to work. She thought of him there and wondered what he'd look like if he was out of those jeans and shirts, and sliding between a cool pair of sheets.

Goodness. She was too old for those kinds of thoughts. But when Carlos handed her a fork and his fingers once again brushed hers, she wondered if maybe she wasn't the only one thinking like that.

He grinned as he sat across from her. "I don't have any clean plates, because I'm not much good at cleaning up after myself. Seems there's always work to do instead. But we can share like this, if you don't mind."

A part of her wanted the plates and the distance they would bring. Another part of her really wanted the intimate act of sharing a meal with a man who made her heart race. She looked up into his big brown eyes, and something melted deep inside her. Something that hadn't melted in so long, she'd begun to think she'd spend all her days alone. "I, uh, have some work to do in the house." She laid her fork on the table, then got to her feet. "Enjoy the . . . the . . . quesadillas. And just bring back the plate whenever."

He nodded at her, a smile playing on his lips. "I will. Thank you, Miss Barbara."

"You're welcome, Carlos. Anytime." Then she hurried out of there and back to the main house, before she started something she wasn't so sure she knew how to finish.

∽

Elizabeth muttered a lot of very unflattering things about Hunter McCoy as she shoved her clothes back into her bag, gathered up her toiletries and her laptop, then headed down the stairs. The man was intolerable. Simply intolerable.

She almost stomped right out the front door, but then she thought of Barbara Jean, and realized no matter how angry she was with Hunter, Elizabeth couldn't be rude to his aunt. She stowed her things by the door, then headed down the hall and into the kitchen. "I'm saying good-bye."

Barbara Jean looked up from the vegetables she was chopping. Her face was flushed, as if she'd just rushed in the door. "Giving up so soon?"

"I'm not giving up," Elizabeth said. "I'll get my editor to send another writer and—"

Barbara Jean shook her head. "No, you can't do that." She reached for a towel, and cleaned her hands, then crossed to Elizabeth. "You are the right one for this story. I know it."

Whether that was so or not, there was the pesky problem of the man who refused to talk to her. "Hunter wants someone he can trust, someone with experience. I'm neither of those."

"Hunter doesn't always know what's good for him. Heck, maybe most of us don't." Barbara Jean drew Elizabeth over to the island, and sat her down on one of the bar stools. "You know that horse he has in the stable? The skittish one?"

Elizabeth nodded. "Dakota."

"Well, Hunter is a lot like that mare. He's been hurt a lot, burned by some bad business deals his father made, and that's made him very guarded about anything to do with the Silver Spur. This ranch is his life, those horses are his family, especially that one, and when anything threatens that, he turns into a porcupine."

It was almost exactly what Hunter had told Elizabeth before. She'd never lived in any one place long enough to love it like Hunter loved this place, but just being here for a little over a day had Elizabeth wanting to protect this place, with its magic spell wrapped in its deep green acres and majestic horses. "I'm not threatening the ranch. I want to do a good story on it. I think the work he is doing here is amazing. So few ranches come back after the kind of devastating losses the Silver Spur has endured."

Barbara Jean smiled, as if Elizabeth had passed some kind of test. "That's exactly right. And if you want Hunter to know you feel that way, you need to show him that your heart is in the right place."

"Show him? How?"

Barbara Jean reached into the fruit bowl and plucked out a shiny red apple. She plopped it into Elizabeth's hand. "By making friends with the other skittish animal at the Silver Spur."

Chapter 7

Hunter watched Carlos working one of the three-year-olds through a reining exercise. The horse showed strong promise. Loaded Gun's timing was good, his body moving without hesitation at Carlos's lightest touch. The eager horse made quick lead changes, had a blazing-fast rundown and long, smooth stops. When Loaded Gun stopped, Carlos turned, looked back at the horse's rump, checking his position on the ground. Perfect.

Loaded Gun needed some work on his spins, but he was already one hell of a reining competitor. The last few futurity events, Loaded Gun had put in a strong showing, winning more than once. There was buzz about the horse, and anticipation for his next event. That was what had people excited about the Silver Spur, and what had made Hunter optimistic about the future. After his father had sold off their best stallion and mares to pay down bad debts, Hunter hadn't been so sure he could rebuild the ranch to its former glory. But one horse at a time, one foal at a time, he was doing it.

Carlos drew up beside the corral gate. He leaned forward and gave Loaded Gun a good-job pat. The horse pranced a bit, anxious to get back to the ring. "He's doing great, boss."

"You think he'll be ready for Oklahoma?" Making a strong showing at the National Reining Horse Association event was something Hunter had been working toward for a long time. It was the biggest reining event in North America, and having the Silver Spur horses do well would prove the ranch was back in business. It had been years since they'd had a champion at Oklahoma, and taken him a long time to build up a strong breeding program again. Last two NRHA events, Hunter had had several horses do well, but this year, he wanted them to place. Or even better, win. Loaded Gun had one hell of a good chance at that.

Carlos nodded. "He's gonna wow them. People will be lining up to have him sire their own winners."

"And that is exactly what we need. A stallion that gets everyone talking about our breeding program, and some mares that are just as good as Dakota's mother and grand-mother were."

Carlos gestured toward the stable. "You thinking of breeding her again?"

"Maybe. She's only ten. She's got some good years left in her. It all depends on whether she decides to trust me."

Saying those words made Hunter think of Lizzie. He hadn't handled lunch well, at all. He'd reacted like a nervous colt stung by a wasp. It wasn't her fault that just being around her set him on edge, made him think about things he had no business thinking about. She was here for a job, and she was determined to do her job, something he respected. Okay, so she didn't have experience. Didn't mean she couldn't write one hell of a story. Maybe he should give her a chance. After all, she seemed to really love this place already and for Hunter, the first—and best—place to start was with loving this rich earth and all the blessings it could bring to everything with a heartbeat.

Hunter leaned over and patted Loaded Gun. The horse sure was showing well, and that was a real good portent for the future. "You put this one with Dakota's blood line and we'll have one hell of a powerful combination." That had been part of his plan when he'd bought Dakota, though he still wasn't sure it was executable. Dakota was still skittish, still scarred by what had happened to her. Just getting close to her was almost impossible—breeding her wasn't even on his radar yet.

"How's your aunt this morning?" Carlos asked, in a casual tone that feigned small talk.

Hunter knew better. He'd seen the way Carlos looked at Barbara Jean. The two of them were like forlorn teenagers watching each other from afar. In all these years, neither one of them had made a move. "She's doing fine. Though you can just go in the house and ask her yourself."

"She's busy. I don't want to bother her." Carlos gave Loaded Gun another pat. "Though she did bring me quesadillas for lunch."

Hunter let out a low whistle. "That, my friend, is a sign. Barbara Jean doesn't share those with just anybody."

A smile filled Carlos's face, then just as quick, it disappeared. He nodded toward the stable. "Hey, isn't that the reporter over there?"

Hunter glanced over and saw Lizzie heading through the big stable doors. She was probably looking for him. And if he knew her, it was most likely to give him a piece of her mind about the way he'd handled their lunch meeting. "Guess I better go talk to her."

Carlos chuckled. "She looks mad. You might want to wait a few minutes. My ex-wife, she used to get so mad at me, the best thing I could do was steer clear until the storm passed."

"How long did that take?"

"Depends on how much I'd screwed up. A few hours. Or"—he clicked to the horse and Loaded Gun started off again at a canter—"a few days!"

Hunter didn't have a few days. Or a few hours. The longer Elizabeth Palmer hung around the Silver Spur, the longer she was going to distract him. He'd spent enough time in the last two years being distracted. He couldn't afford any more.

But he did take Carlos's advice and lingered long enough to watch Carlos run Loaded Gun through a few more exercises, then he gave the trainer a wave and headed off to the stable. Foster roused himself from his usual place in the sunny corner of the porch, and trotted along behind his master.

Hunter ducked inside the stable door and waited for his eyes to adjust to the dimmer light. The rest of the horses were out in the pasture, mares with their foals, with the yearlings and three-year-olds in a paddock of their own. But at the far end of the stable, he heard a nicker, then Lizzie's voice.

"I'm sorry about that cell phone ringer before. I just haven't been around horses much, and I didn't know it would scare you." Her tone was almost a sing-song, just a hair above a whisper. "The only horses I've seen were ponies at the zoo. And they were pretty grumpy. I was always afraid one would bite me."

The only horse in the stable right now was Dakota. She'd refused to go out this morning when he'd let the others out, just as she had refused every day since she arrived. He increased his pace and headed down the wooden aisle.

"You're a pretty horse. Real pretty," Lizzie said.

It took Hunter a second to realize why he didn't see anyone standing in the aisle outside Dakota's stall. Because Lizzie was *inside* the stall, with Dakota. He bit back the urge to yell at Lizzie—because doing that would only scare the horse more, and end badly, he was sure. Instead, he approached the stall, and leaned over the gate. "I wouldn't recommend—"

His words cut off when he saw Dakota nuzzling at Lizzie's hand. Lizzie giggled, then turned to look at Hunter over her shoulder. "She's eating that apple slice right out of my hand."

The look on Lizzie's face was sheer, unadulterated wonder. He knew that feeling, knew how the first time a horse became a friend, it sent a sweet tickle through your gut. If that giant, powerful animal could trust, even love, a human, it made anything seem possible.

And right now, with Dakota chomping on apple slices, as easy as a summer breeze, Hunter was starting to believe anything was possible, too.

Foster dropped down beside Hunter and stared up at his master, as if he was just as surprised as Hunter. "Stay here," he whispered to the dog, then, very, very slowly, he opened the gate and slipped inside.

Dakota's ears flickered, but she kept on eating the pieces of apple in Lizzie's palm. Dakota's tail swung back and forth in a lazy, content arc. "Well, I'll be damned," Hunter said. "She let you get that close?"

"It took some time. I talked to her and talked to her, and kept on handing her apple slices. Every one brought me a little closer." Lizzie pulled her hand back. "That's it, Dakota. All gone."

The horse nudged at Lizzie's shoulder. Lizzie reached up and ran a hand down Dakota's muzzle. "Sorry, honey. I'll bring more later. I promise."

The horse seemed to lean into the touch, content, secure. Hunter could swear he heard Dakota sigh.

He took another couple steps closer. Dakota tensed, so Hunter stopped moving. When he froze, Dakota went back to nuzzling Lizzie for more attention.

"Well, I'll be damned. Seems my horse only likes you."

"Maybe because we're both girls." She tossed him a triumphant smile. "Maybe she doesn't like men."

"I thought she didn't like anyone."

"Well, you thought wrong." Lizzie gave Dakota one final pat, then turned back to Hunter. The two of them slipped out of the stall, and leaned over the gate, watching Dakota. The horse still hung close to the back of the stall, but she seemed more at ease, less stressed. The scars on her legs had healed, though there was still a big divot on her right foreleg and another on her back that would never go away. "She's a beautiful horse. What happened to her?"

"She was in an accident a couple years ago. Cut the hell out of her legs and scared her. She's been skittish and nippy ever since."

"Not the same accident that killed . . ." Lizzie lowered her gaze. "Sorry. It came up in my research."

And just like that, the victory with Dakota, the hope he'd felt in his heart, evaporated. He didn't know why it bothered him that Lizzie knew about Jenna. Maybe it was better that she knew, realized who she was dealing with here. Not some superstar rancher, but a man who made mistakes. "No, not the same accident. That horse died. And so did Jenna."

Saying it didn't make it hurt less. Saying it didn't ease his guilt. Saying it didn't undo the mistakes of that night.

"I'm sorry," Lizzie said softly.

"Yeah. Me, too." He turned away, busying himself with straightening tackle that didn't need straightening. Avoiding.

Seemed that was his specialty. Foster laid on the floor, put his head on his paws and let out a doggie sigh.

Outside, a tractor chugged, and the horses whinnied. The breeze carried the scents of fall, crisp leaves and cut hay. Like a utopia that lay just out of Hunter's reach. Time passed, while dust motes floated in the sunny rays peeking through the slats of the stable walls.

"So, tell me about Dakota," Lizzie said after a while, in a brighter tone. "Like . . . where'd she get her name?"

Anyone else would have pressed him to explain his feelings or some such crap. But Lizzie had simply changed the subject to one about his horse, the kind of safe ground where Hunter felt most comfortable. They may have only met yesterday, but she seemed to know him well.

"Actually, her whole name is Diamond Heel Dakota," he said. "She's descended from one of the first and best broodmares my grandpa had on the Silver Spur. Her grandma was Diamond Girl, then we named her daughter Diamond Heel, and we carried that forward with Diamond Heel Dakota."

"It's a nice name. And goes with the teeny tiny bit of white on her back legs."

He pointed at the small white triangles above Dakota's rear hooves. "That's called a partial pastern. If it went further up, it would be called a sock; halfway up is called a stocking. Her grandma, mother, and she all have that same little patch of white on the pastern, hence the Diamond name."

"So why is this horse so important to you?" Lizzie asked, then added, "When my cell phone went off, you said I shouldn't scare a horse who has been through as much as this one, or is as important as this one. And I am still sorry about that, by the way. I didn't mean to scare her."

Hunter leaned an elbow on the gate. Lizzie did the same. Dakota loped over, a wary eye on Hunter, and nudged at

Lizzie's hand. She rubbed the horse's muzzle, and the horse seemed to become putty in her hands. Hunter knew that feeling. Every time he was around this intriguing, infuriating, incredible woman, he felt the same way.

"Dakota was sold off to another breeder eight years ago, before I took over the ranch. My father sold her, and our best stallion, to pay off some debts." Hunter shook his head, thinking of all his father's actions had cost the Silver Spur. "Gambling debts. My father was always a risk taker, but not the kind that made good decisions. Know what I mean?"

"You're talking to the woman whose mother spent twenty dollars on lottery tickets every week, even if it meant she didn't go grocery shopping. Yeah, I know exactly what you mean." She scoffed, then tossed an errant piece of hay onto the floor. "Personally, I would have rather bought peanut butter and jelly than wishes and dreams."

How he could relate to that. He'd watched the Silver Spur die a little bit more each year under his father's tutelage, withering away like a garden left to rot in the sun. "I never understood why my dad kept on gambling instead of keeping what we had and building it up. I know he never really wanted to run the ranch, so I wonder if part of that was some unconscious way of destroying it."

Lizzie leaned her back against the gate and faced him. "I never thought of it that way. My mom hated her job—she was a waitress at a diner for pretty much her whole life—and kept thinking that if she just hit the number, she'd be rich and could walk away from our crappy apartment and empty fridge and piles of bills. But gambling away her paycheck did the opposite."

He cocked a grin at her. "Well, would you look at that. We have something in common."

She grinned right back. "Might even make us friends."

"Friends?" He shifted until he was facing her, and the air between them tensed with all those half-started kisses and unanswered questions. "I think we are way past friends."

"True. And besides, I already have a lot of friends," she said, a tease dancing in her eyes. She cocked her hip to one side, almost touching him. He wondered if she realized that when she flirted with him, she always edged closer. He liked that. A lot. "I don't think I need any more."

Hunter's gaze dropped to her lips, then down the curves outlined beneath her shirt and pants. Another one of those damnable business casual ensembles that didn't do much to hide her innate sexiness. He wanted her just as much in the silky shirts as he did when she had on jeans. "What about lovers? Have a lot of those?"

She laughed, a soft throaty laugh that warmed him. Then she put a finger to her lips, feigning deep thought. "No, I don't. What about you?"

"My list could be written on a grain of rice."

She laughed again, then took a step that swayed her hip into his. He caught her, and she looked up at him, wide-eyed and breathless. "I was going to leave today, you know."

The image of her driving away made something in his chest ache. "I'm glad you didn't. If I promise to play nice, will you stay one more day?"

"Will you give me my interview?"

I'll give you anything you want if you keep on looking at me like that. "Tomorrow, I'm all yours. I promise."

"That, Mr. McCoy, is a promise I'm banking on." Then she tossed a smile at him, and headed out into the sunshine.

∽

Barbara Jean had been a part of the stubborn McCoy family for most of her life. She'd always been headstrong and stubborn, as her mother called her, but being part of the McCoys—related by marriage through her sister—had taken all that up a notch. And when Barbara Jean had a plan, she'd pull out all the stops to make sure it came to fruition. Especially when it involved the two McCoys she loved most in the world—Amberlee and Hunter.

So when it became clear earlier today that Elizabeth Palmer had her foot halfway out the door and back to New Jersey, Barbara Jean had called in reinforcements. Not that Barbara Jean could blame poor Elizabeth. So far, Hunter had been about as friendly as a wolverine in a steel cage. He was still such a wounded animal, lashing out at anyone who came near. There were nights when she'd lie in her bed and pray that someday Hunter would learn to love himself as much as he loved those horses. Maybe then the unbearable weight would ease from his shoulders.

She could only hope that her idea with the apple and the horse would work. Hunter had put a lot of hope into bringing Dakota back from whatever edge she'd been lingering on ever since she'd been sold to Billie Ray. If Elizabeth could win Dakota over, it was only a matter of time before she won Hunter over, too, by default.

Barbara Jean watched her nephew leave Carlos and Loaded Gun in the training corral, then stride toward the stables, his head down, his steps firm and decisive, every ounce of him radiating *keep away*. Her fingers fluttered against the glass, as if she could send him a hug, a comforting touch, all the way from the kitchen. He'd been through so much in the last two years—too much, some would say—and all Barbara Jean wanted was to see him smile again. No, see him *live* again.

Hunter was existing and that wasn't the same thing, not at all.

But every time he'd looked at that reporter, Barbara Jean had seen a spark in his eyes again. A flash, really, gone just as fast as it appeared, but it gave her hope. Enough to build on—with a little help. Hopefully that apple was doing the trick right now, not just for the stubborn, injured horse, but for the two willful, wounded people in the stable.

Barbara Jean glanced back at the corral, watching Carlos for a few minutes as he led the horse through a few more exercises. Heat filled her belly. What would have happened if she had stayed for lunch with him? If she had shared that plate of food and maybe stayed a little longer, lingering over conversation?

She was probably reading into it too much. The man hadn't invited her in to get to know her. He hadn't wanted to eat alone, nothing more. She needed to quit seeing things that weren't there. Barbara Jean turned away from the window, picked up a spatula, and started mixing a double batch of cornbread dough. Just then, the front door opened and Amberlee's voice carried down the hall. "I smell pie. I think I came at just the right time."

"It's always just the right time when you arrive." Barbara Jean drew Amberlee into a tight hug. Her niece felt small and frail. Barbara Jean drew back and caught Amberlee's chin in her palm. "How are you feeling?"

"I'm fine, Auntie Barb. I swear." She pulled away and crossed to the sink. "Would you look at all these dirty dishes? I'll get these washed up right quick for you."

Barbara Jean bit her tongue. She wanted to quiz her niece, but worried that she'd be hovering again, something that drove Amberlee crazy. It was just that Amberlee had been so sick for so long, the asthma that plagued her sending her to the hospital time and time again when she was young. Even now, six years after her last hospitalization, Barbara

Jean worried. Was Amberlee working too hard? Studying too much? Exercising too much? Getting enough rest? Barbara Jean's worries multiplied and intertwined with her every thought about her niece, like mineral veins spidering into the earth. But she affected a bright tone and pretended she didn't carry a constant weight in her chest whenever she looked at Amberlee.

"I sure appreciate your help with dinner tonight, Amberlee," she said, as she gave the simmering pot of chili on the stove a stir. The recipe had been handed down in Barbara Jean's family for so many generations, everyone had lost count and just called it Family Chili. It was nice, Barbara Jean thought, working side by side with Amberlee, especially on something with so many roots and memories. "It's been too long since you've been over."

"Well, when you said there was pecan pie, Auntie Barbara Jean, how could I say no?" Amberlee grinned. A little twig of a thing, Amberlee was a hundred percent her mama's girl, all curly hair and fancy dresses and pretty little shoes with bows on them, even though Amberlee's mama had died when the girl was six and Hunter was only eighteen. A few weeks after that, Barbara Jean moved in and started helping her brother-in-law raise the two kids.

It was ironic, Barbara Jean thought, that the very thing she'd never wanted to become she'd ended up voluntarily doing. All it had taken was one look at Amberlee's shattered face, still stained with tears hours after her mama had succumbed to a quick-moving cancer, and Barbara Jean had upended her life to move in here.

Her brother-in-law had never been very plugged in to his kids, and withdrew even more after his wife died. He'd taken to hitting the track first thing in the morning, or one of those offtrack betting sites, always banking on the next get-rich-quick race. Barbara Jean, the one who had never thought she'd be a mother, had been the one picking up Amberlee from school, the one consoling Amberlee after her first heartbreak, and the one nudging Hunter to do his homework, to go to college for a business degree, to concentrate on school instead of just the horses.

In the years since Barbara Jean had moved her boots into the bedroom at the end of the hall, she and Amberlee had become close as peas in a pod. The house had felt a little more empty since Amberlee had moved into a dorm and started going to college, but every time she was back, the two of them stepped into their well-rehearsed routine of working side by side in the kitchen. They'd cooked dinner together in this kitchen more times than there were stars in the sky.

Barbara Jean poured the cornbread batter into a buttered pan, then set the bowl on the counter. Amberlee scooped up the empty glass bowl and plunged it into the soapy water. "So, how's the new boyfriend?"

Amberlee sighed. "Another resident of Loserville. I think the statistics are right—all the good men are taken by the time you're twenty-five."

"Good men are out there, even if they're as hard to find as bees in a snowstorm. And you're just barely eighteen so you have plenty of years ahead of you before you have a thing to worry about." She put the cornbread into the oven, then set the timer. "All in good time, Amberlee. All in good time."

Amberlee sighed, as she put a clean breadboard into the strainer. "You're right, as usual."

"That's why I'm your favorite aunt."

"You're my only aunt." Amberlee smiled. "But even if I had a dozen others, you'd still be my favorite."

That warmed Barbara Jean's heart, warmed it in ways

she couldn't even tell Amberlee. It was what kept her here, had kept her here for twelve years now. And it was enough. "It's the pecan pie that works in my favor, isn't it?"

"You know it." Amberlee scrubbed the batter bowl and set it in the strainer. "So when are you going to find your own good man? It's about time you settled down."

Barbara Jean laughed. "I'm not the settling-down type. Besides, I have plenty to keep my life filled, between you and Hunter and the ranch—"

"That's all about other people, not about you." Amberlee pulled the plug, then put her back to the sink and reached for a towel to dry her hands. "You deserve happiness as much, or even more, than anyone else in this house."

Barbara Jean cupped Amberlee's cheek, and gave her a tender touch. "I am happy, being here."

Amberlee's hand covered Barbara Jean's. The water had warmed her hands, softened her palms. "But you deserve so much more."

"I've got everything I want right here." There was so much more in that sentence than Barbara Jean could say, so she backed up, put a smile on her face, and turned to the stove. She gave the chili a stir, watching it bubble away. The pies were cooling on the counter, the cornbread baking in the oven. "So, how has school been? You're not overdoing it, are you?"

"No, worrywart, I'm not." Amberlee grinned and gave her aunt a kiss. "In fact, I feel great. Not one little problem being here."

Barbara Jean arched a brow.

"Really. I'm fine. Taking care of myself. And I'm staying far from the horses, even though I'm pretty sure I have out-grown all that silly asthma stuff." Amberlee grinned. "What kind of daughter of a ranch owner is allergic to horses?"

"Only the most special ones." Barbara Jean smiled. She

should have been relieved, but that little tickle of worry stayed in her gut.

The back door opened and Carlos came in, with an apologetic smile. "Sorry to interrupt, but I was bringing back your plate."

"Oh, thank you. You didn't have to do that. I could have gone out there and gotten it." Good Lord, she was babbling. What was she offering to do? Stop by in the middle of the night and get the plate from his bedroom/kitchen space?

"Those quesadillas are mighty good," Carlos said. He doffed his hat and gave her another smile. The man smiled. A lot. She liked that. "I ate every last bite."

"Oh, why thank you." Another giggle. What was happening to her? She was a schoolgirl every time he came near.

Carlos looked like he wanted to say something else, but instead, he just plopped his hat back on his head. "Guess I better get back to work."

She took a step forward just as he reached for the door handle. "Uh, Carlos?"

He turned back. "Yes, ma'am?"

"We're, uh, having chili for dinner. If you want some. At six."

He considered her for a moment, his big brown eyes hidden by the hat. "Are you inviting me or just informing me?"

Barbara Jean glanced over at Amberlee, who had her arms crossed over her chest and was watching the whole thing with amusement. Probably thinking it was funny to see two old people dancing around something as simple as a dinner invitation. She wasn't asking the man out, for goodness sake, just feeding him a hot meal at the end of the day. Carlos had been divorced for a long time, chances were good that he would like that. "Inviting you. Unless you have somewhere to go after work."

Was that her roundabout way of asking if he had a girlfriend?

"Nowhere I want to go but right here," Carlos said. Then he tipped his hat and nodded at her. "See you at six."

"On the dot," she said.

"Looking forward to it." Then he was gone, back out the door and striding across the lawn with fast, purposeful steps.

"And what was that?" Amberlee asked.

"Nothing. Nothing at all. Just me inviting Carlos to dinner. He's been working a lot of hours lately and it's a nice way to thank him."

"I didn't see you inviting any of the other hands to dinner."

"Oh, well, it just sort of slipped out." Barbara Jean picked up the spoon and stirred the chili, if only so she could tear her gaze away from her niece's inquisitive eyes.

"Uh-huh. Sure. Lots going on here that I seem to be missing since I'm in college. Like whose car is in the driveway?" Amberlee asked, nodding toward the window, changing the subject, thank goodness.

"There's a reporter from New Jersey in town to interview Hunter. She's been trying all day to get him to talk to her, but he's being . . ."

"Hunter."

"Exactly." Barbara Jean dipped a spoon into the chili, then cupped a hand beneath it and held it up to taste. "Elizabeth is a little out of her element here, so I was hoping you could take her into town after dinner. Take her shopping, bring her along to the book club. I know you're not really a member of it, but you know all the other ladies in it, and it might help Elizabeth if someone she knows is there with her."

"Mmm . . . maybe a tiny bit more salt," Amberlee said,

her hands still immersed in the soapy water. "Shopping? You said the magic word."

Through the kitchen window, Barbara Jean saw Elizabeth heading up the back walkway, a triumphant smile on her face. That was good, Barbara Jean thought, very good.

The back door opened. "Hi, Barbara Jean. I wanted to ask you—" Elizabeth said, then she stopped. "Sorry. I didn't realize you had company."

Barbara Jean drew Elizabeth inside. "Stay, sweetie. Meet my amazing niece, Amberlee. Hunter's sister."

Amberlee wiped her damp hands on a dishtowel, then shook with Elizabeth. "Don't believe a word Barbara Jean says. She's my most biased aunt."

"Only because I have the best niece in five counties."

"See? Biased." Amberlee laughed, then turned to Elizabeth. "My aunt says you're new in town."

"Oh, I'm only here for a few days. I'm interviewing Hunter for a magazine article, or trying to."

"And he's cooperating?"

"Well . . . he wasn't, until I talked to him just now." A smile brightened her face before she turned to Barbara Jean. "You were right about the apples and the horse. Worked like a charm. Hunter has promised to clear his schedule tomorrow for me."

"That's wonderful!" Barbara Jean clapped her hands. "And about time, too."

Elizabeth scoffed. "You're telling me. I was halfway to New Jersey this afternoon."

"Hunter can be a total pain in the ass." Amberlee laughed. "And I can say that because I'm his sister."

"Amberlee McCoy!" Barbara Jean flicked the towel at her. "A lady doesn't use that kind of language."

"She does if it's true." Amberlee took Elizabeth's hand and drew her over to the bar stools. Amberlee perched on one of them, propping one dark blue heel on the rung. She leaned an elbow on the counter, looking for all the world like Elizabeth's new best friend. "He wasn't always that way, though. Just give him time and a little distance."

"That's what your aunt was saying. Time, I don't have much of, and as for distance . . ." She put up her hands.

"Elizabeth is staying here. So Hunter hasn't even had a chance to miss her." Which was a good thing, in Barbara Jean's opinion, because the pretty little reporter was also always in Hunter's thoughts and Lord knew that man could use something sweet to occupy his thoughts.

Elizabeth scoffed. "He's not going to miss me at all when I leave. He'll probably throw a party."

"Oh, I don't know about that. I think you're growing on him." Barbara Jean put a hand on Elizabeth's shoulder. "What you need is some time to have fun. Relax a little. You drove clear down here, barely taking a breath since. Since you have to be here until tomorrow anyway, why don't you go into town with Amberlee tonight and do a little shopping, maybe visit Noralee's book club?"

"My best friend Sophie told me the same thing. She reminded me that I almost never take vacations and I should look at my time here as an opportunity to relax, take a breath. But I can't impose . . ."

"It wouldn't be an imposition at all," Amberlee said. "For one, I love to shop, and love any excuse I can find to shop."

"You and Sophie would get along like gangbusters." Elizabeth laughed. "I'm so shopping challenged. I own about five hundred of the same outfit."

Which explained all those silky shirts and dress pants

she'd been wearing, Barbara Jean thought. The girl needed some dresses and skirts, and definitely some jeans. Spending time with Amberlee, who made shopping a sport, would be good for her.

"Girl, I can hook you up," Amberlee said. "You have come to the right person for shopping advice."

Elizabeth waved a hand in dismissal. "I shouldn't invade the book club. Whatever they're all reading, I'm sure I haven't read it and—"

"I saw the sign on the door the other day," Amberlee said. "This week it's Open Book Night. Which means anyone can go and bring anything they want. I'm not really a part of the group, but I do stop in once in a while. There's nothing like asking a book club about their opinions on *Hamlet* when you have a term paper due." Amberlee winked.

"Amberlee McCoy. You did not use those nice ladies at the book club to cheat on a paper."

"Of course not, Auntie." She pressed a kiss to her aunt's cheek. "I use them for test review."

Barbara Jean just rolled her eyes.

"Anyway, Elizabeth, anyone can come tonight," Amberlee said. "Just bring along your favorite book, or if you don't have it with you, chances are Noralee has it in stock. You'll meet the girls, you'll have fun, you'll get away from Mr. Grumpyface—"

The back door opened and Hunter walked in, as if conjured up merely by the conversation. He doffed his hat and cast an amused glance at his sister. "Did you just call me Grumpyface?"

"You're my brother. I can call you anything I want." Amberlee bounded over to Hunter in three quick steps and gave him a loud smacking kiss on the cheek. He just rolled his eyes and feigned swiping off the kiss. "And if you don't start being nice to Elizabeth here," Amberlee said, "I'm going to call you far worse things."

"You have been talking to our aunt. And she has been filling your head with all kinds of nonsense. I'm nice to Miz Palmer. Aren't I?" He raised his gaze to Elizabeth's.

It was as if someone had turned on an electric generator. When the two of them looked at each other, there was a hum in the air, an unspoken tension that Barbara Jean would bet a million dollars neither one of them realized existed.

Elizabeth was the first to break eye contact. "I, uh, think I'll freshen up before dinner." She dashed out of the kitchen, like a woman with her hair on fire.

Barbara Jean sighed and went back to the chili. It had only been a little under twenty-four hours since Elizabeth Palmer arrived at the Silver Spur. Barbara Jean couldn't expect a miracle that fast. Though she sure did wish for one all the same.

Hunter sidled up beside his aunt and dipped a tablespoon into the pot. "When's dinner ready?"

She smacked his hand away when he tried for a second tasting. "In about thirty minutes. I'm waiting on the cornbread."

"Did you put the little pieces of jalapeño in it? And the cheddar cheese?"

Barbara Jean propped a fist on her hip and just gave him the Eye. Which was her usual look whenever Hunter broke a rule or drove her crazy. Even though he was thirty, his aunt was still giving him the Eye on a regular basis. "I've been cooking since before you had teeth, what makes you think I'd forget anything?"

"I just like teasing you." He grinned. "You get all flustered, and that gives me a second to"—he dipped the spoon in again and stuck the bite in his mouth—"eat."

She tugged the spoon out of his hand and dropped it in the sink. "You are incorrigible. Now go wash up for dinner. You might even want to change your shirt."

"What's wrong with what I'm wearing?"

"You smell like a manure factory. And we have company, so that means looking your best."

"Amberlee doesn't care if I smell like horse crap. Do ya, sis?" Before she could answer, he reached out and drew her into a tight hug against his side. He ruffled her hair, and she smacked at his chest until he let go.

"Any woman with a working nose cares," Amberlee said. "You are disgusting."

"But you love me anyway." He glanced between the two women, then threw up his hands. "Okay, okay, I'll change."

Once he was out of the room, Barbara Jean tugged Amberlee over to the sink. "Did you notice what I noticed?"

Amberlee raised her brows and nodded. "That there's a storm brewing between those two? You'd have to be on the space station not to see it."

"Exactly. And after everything Hunter's been through, I think this Elizabeth might be good for him. I don't know her well, but I get the feeling being here is good for her, too."

Amberlee smiled. "Always trying to fix everything that's broken, Aunt Barbara Jean."

Barbara Jean drew Amberlee into a hug, to hide the tears in her eyes. "I can't fix everything, Amberlee. But I'm doing my best."

∞

Hunter tore off the dirt-encrusted shirt and jeans he was wearing, balled them up, then tossed the clothes at the hamper in the corner. They landed with a thud a few inches shy of the plastic basket. He just left them there, atop a growing pile of dirty clothes. There'd been a day when everything in Hunter's life had been neat as a pin, all organized and labeled. He'd been on an upward path, his business plans as sure as his personal plans.

Yeah, not so much anymore. Most days, he felt like he was barely treading water. Just one big wave, and wham, he'd drown.

But there was hope now, with the ranch, with Dakota, with Lizzie and that made him smile. Lizzie. Just the thought of her made his smile widen and filled his heart in ways it hadn't been filled in a long time. The way she'd won over Dakota, the way she looked at him with that tease in her eyes—it all made him feel . . .

Light. Yes, that was the perfect word for it.

He reached for a fresh pair of jeans from the basket of clean laundry Barbara Jean had parked in his room a week ago. Thank God someone was taking care of things like laundry and dinner because, Lord knew, Hunter was barely taking care of himself.

As he pulled on the jeans, his gaze caught on the framed picture sitting on top of his dresser. Jenna, smiling into the camera, her hair lit from the sun above, almost like a halo. It was one of those pictures he'd taken just because. Just because it was a great day. Just because he'd made her laugh. Just because he'd wanted to preserve the moment.

Guilt poured over him. He'd taken that picture the day he'd proposed to her, so sure that she was going to love living on the Silver Spur, love living the life that he held so dear. She'd tried it, even quitting her job in retail and moving in with him. For a week, maybe two, she'd been happy, then he'd noticed the cloud.

That's what he'd taken to calling it in his mind—the cloud. Jenna's smile was dimmer, her eyes a little less bright.

But she'd pitched in and helped on the ranch, and he kept telling himself it would pass. That she would grow to love the place as much as they loved each other.

But she hadn't. And the night of the accident, she'd told him she was done, that as soon as she got back from delivering the foal to a ranch twenty miles away, she was done, and moving out. They'd had a fight, she'd stormed out into the rain—

And never come back.

Her picture stared back at him, smiling, laughing, happy. A moment in time when maybe she had been happy, before he'd tried to force her into a world she hated. If only he'd listened, if only—

His right arm came out in a sweeping arc, sending the picture crashing to the floor. The glass shattered, puncturing the image, marring that smile.

"Are you okay, Hunter?" Aunt Barbara Jean's voice from down below. "I heard a crash."

"I'm fine," he told her, repeating the same lie he'd told himself and everyone around him for so long, even he was starting to believe it.

But the broken picture on the floor told the truth. Hunter picked it up, laid it on top of the dresser, and left the room. He was halfway downstairs before he noticed the blood pulsing out of his finger. A deep cut he hadn't even felt.

Chapter 8

Elizabeth had never had a little sister. But if she'd had one, she imagined she would be a lot like Amberlee McCoy. Amberlee was bubbly and funny, pretty and sweet. When Hunter went back to work instead of sitting down to dinner, Amberlee had quipped that he was probably running from the estrogen overload in the kitchen. It had made his absence easier to bear. She still missed him, which was all the more reason for a girls' night on the town, to take her mind off that frustrating cowboy.

Carlos had been at dinner, but neither he nor Barbara Jean said more than a handful of words, which was weird. Amberlee, though, had talked enough to fill the whole room with sound.

Amberlee had kept on talking, almost the whole way into town, telling Elizabeth all about Chatham Ridge and giving the history of, as far as Elizabeth could tell, every single resident. "That's George Markham's house. He's retired from the police force, but he still shows up at all the town events, standing guard at the door, just in case we have a zombie invasion or something. And that over there, that's the oldest house in Chatham Ridge. Built in the early 1700s. Don't ask me the date, because I never remember it, but I do know that there was a rumor when I was a little girl that the house was haunted. Maybe because Claire Teahan lived there, all by herself, and she was so old, half the town was convinced she was a ghost."

"I think this is the smallest town I've ever been in."

"It is smaller than a shoebox, and most of the families that are here have lived here since the beginning of time, so most days it feels like going to a family reunion. And don't even ask me about the dating pool here. It's so shallow, it's a tidal pool."

Elizabeth laughed. "You'll have to come up and visit me in Trenton sometime. You can't sneeze without running into a man."

"Lots of eligible ones?"

"I don't know about that. I didn't date a whole lot." And not at all since her fiancé fell in love with the woman who lived upstairs. Maybe she needed to move to another apartment building. One where there were no eligible and predatory females in the hallways.

"Well, don't tell the book club that. Noralee will have you fixed up faster than you can scratch a cat. She just loves a happy ending." Amberlee grinned. "Now, let's go shopping before book club. If there's one thing I can do well, it's shop."

They parked outside a little shop with a bright pink awning. Ten minutes later, Amberlee had taken Elizabeth on a whirlwind tour of the store, and piled her arms high with jeans, chambray shirts and two pairs of boots. She'd added a cowboy hat at the last second, feeling silly even as she plopped it on her head.

"Hunter will have to take you seriously now." Amberlee flicked the brim of the hat. "I bet it was hard for him to see you in your city clothes."

"Why? I mean, they weren't anything unusual." She glanced down at the gray pants and silky lilac shirt she'd worn. Sophie was right, Elizabeth realized. Her entire wardrobe was a mimeograph of the one the day before.

"Hunter is just not too keen on . . . city girls," Amberlee said.

"Well, I'm not trying to date him, just interview him. But he's impossible to talk to."

"Give him time." Amberlee laid a hand on Elizabeth's arm. "He's a good man, who's been through more than one man should have to endure."

"What happened? I read about his fiancée—"

Amberlee put up a hand. "Hunter should be the one to tell you that. I was away at the time it happened, on a trip for school. I don't know all the details, but I do know it was a pretty awful accident and Hunter still blames himself. I tried to get him to talk about it a couple times, but Hunter is . . . a private person, especially about his private life. He's always been that way, and as much as my brother drives me crazy, it's one thing about him I respect."

"I understand that, and I wasn't asking you to spill the beans or anything. I'm just curious about him."

Amberlee paused in flicking through clothes and turned to Elizabeth. "For the interview or for you personally?"

"For . . ." Elizabeth paused. "Okay, maybe a little of both."

Amberlee's face broke into a wide grin. "I knew you liked him. I think he likes you, too, though he won't show it. He's the most stubborn man I've ever known, besides our dad, who was the king of stubborn. But at his core, he's also the best man I know. And don't tell him I said that. I have to keep my pesky little sister image up somehow."

Elizabeth laughed. "Your secret's safe with me."

"I think you need one more thing," Amberlee said. She leaned back, and put a finger to her lips. "You're a size six, right?"

"Yes, but I have plenty—"

"Of boring things. What you need is a great dress." She grabbed a white cotton dress, then a yellow one. "Get these, too."

Elizabeth tried on the outfits, which elicited lots of excited responses from Amberlee with each clothing change. Finally, Elizabeth emerged from the dressing room, her arms overloaded. "I don't need all this. I'm only here for a couple of days, at the most."

"And that means you need options. Lots of them." Amberlee grinned, and waved toward the register. "Buy them before you talk yourself out of it."

Elizabeth plunked down a credit card and tried not to think how she was spending five times more than she was making for this article. And the fact that she was unemployed after this. That she'd done something so insane, she needed a trip to a psychiatrist, not a shopping spree.

As she headed out of the store with two bulging bags and a receipt as long as her arm, she had to admit that the shopping had been way more fun than she'd expected. She could always return what she didn't wear on her way out of town. Or keep it all as a fabulous memory. Of course, in New Jersey, there wouldn't be much need for the cowboy boots or dresses, and especially not for the hat. But maybe she'd just store it on a shelf, and from time to time, remember the town with the Three Buck Bundle—

And Hunter McCoy.

The sun had dropped behind the trees, leaving the sky with a dark gold wash. The few remaining clouds pressed like fingers against the sky, as if peeling back the sunset to reveal the night yet to come. Chatham Ridge was settling in for the night, shop lights flicking off as street lights shimmered to life, and the traffic slowed to a car or two. Someone was barbecuing, the scent of fresh hamburgers carrying on the air, chased by the sound of children laughing.

On her way out of town. The words left an empty ache in Elizabeth's gut. The reality was that her life wasn't here, it was in New Jersey, among the concrete and congestion. She glanced away from the sunset and climbed back into the car.

"You okay?" Amberlee asked.

"Just reorienting myself," Elizabeth said. "I forgot where I was for a moment."

"Sounds like what happens to me after too many late-night study sessions." She laughed, then put the car in gear and drove the two blocks to the bookstore. Just like the first night, the façade of the Happy Endings Bookstore seemed to beckon Elizabeth in. The lights glowed warm in the windows, and the front door was open, as if waiting for them to arrive.

Amberlee turned off the car, then hesitated, her hand on the wheel. "My brother says you just quit your job and came down here."

"Probably not the sanest thing I've ever done, but yes, I did." Elizabeth looked out at the night sky. She'd given up everything for this article. Was she going to regret it later?

"Were you scared to do it?" Amberlee asked. She turned in her seat, and her eyes looked like big pools. "Scared to just up and take a big leap like that?"

"Terrified. But I decided the only way to not be scared anymore was to just do it." Elizabeth shifted to lean against the door. "That's kind of the New Jersey motto. Do it even if it scares you."

Amberlee laughed. "I like that. I think I'll have to follow it."

"You should. It's a good one."

"Well, even if I wanted to do something that scared me, Hunter would get in my way. Sometimes he takes the big brother role too literally and forgets I'm eighteen."

Elizabeth covered Amberlee's hand with her own. "My grandma used to say that Jersey girls aren't afraid of anything and will stand up to anyone who tells them different. Though you put a snake in front of me and I'm running for the door."

"Me, too." Amberlee thought about it for a moment, then nodded. "That's just what I'm going to do. Act like a Jersey girl, regardless of what Grumpyface Hunter says. Now, let's go get some cookies."

Elizabeth's hand hesitated on the door handle. "Cookies? I thought we were here for book club."

"That's what the women all tell each other, but really, pretty much everyone goes to the bookstore for Noralee's cookies. You'll understand why once you taste them. They're like a little slice of heaven."

Amberlee hadn't lied. As soon as Elizabeth walked into the bookstore, Noralee rushed to envelop both girls in a hug, then hand them a platter of cookies. Noralee peppered her with questions about how she liked Chatham Ridge so far, how she was enjoying staying at Hunter's ranch, all of which Elizabeth demurred from answering too honestly. She wasn't about to tell the bookstore owner about the complicated hot-cold encounters she'd had with Hunter so far. Or how the town was growing on her, even if its most eligible resident wasn't.

Elizabeth sank her teeth into the most delicious chocolate chip cookie she'd ever had in her life, the perfect combination of chewy and crispy and melt-in-your-mouth goodness. "Heaven."

Amberlee grinned. "Told you so. Now come meet the women in the book club."

A moment later, Elizabeth was sitting in one of those wingback chairs by the fireplace while she met the four women she'd seen the other night, now surrounding her in a flurry of names and introductions. Rachel, the only married one in the group, still glowing after her recent wedding. Susie, who was shyer than the others, but a sweet and pretty blonde. Katie Ann, a perky girl who was quick with a quip. Then Charlotte, who was lean and model-gorgeous, with long brown hair, and who was the first to greet Elizabeth like a long-lost friend. All of the women wore pastel dresses that belled at their waists and high heels, forming a quartet of flowers in the middle of the room. The Southern Belle Book Club was indeed filled with women who fit that description. Elizabeth half expected them to pull on white gloves and serve sweet tea or whatever a Southern belle drank.

"Welcome to the Southern Belle Book Club! We're always happy to have newcomers." Charlotte drew Elizabeth into a quick, warm hug. She wore a light floral perfume that seemed to perfectly match the beautiful brunette. She was taller than the others, with perfect makeup and a yellow cotton print dress that had barely a wrinkle. "So, have a seat and tell us all about where you come from, what you like to read, and—"

"What your secret is for looking so beautiful after spending a day working on Hunter's ranch." Susie grinned. "I'm glad I work in an office. I couldn't handle the heat out there today." She waved a hand at her face.

"And what's your secret for being around that hunk of a hottie man all day and not ravaging him right there in the barn," Charlotte added. She fanned herself, too, as if the mere thought of Hunter McCoy made her temperature rise ten degrees.

"Hey, that hunk of hottie man is my brother," Amberlee said, dropping into the seat closest to the fireplace. "Can y'all not use the words *ravaging* and *Hunter* in the same sentence?"

"Is it okay if we think it?" Charlotte grinned at Amberlee. "Okay, okay, I'll keep my hottie thoughts about Hunter to myself."

"Thank you." Amberlee took a sip of iced tea.

Katie Ann leaned toward Elizabeth. "So, what do you think of our resident hunk?"

"Katie Ann!"

"What? I didn't use the word *ravage*. Though if Elizabeth did ravage him, she'd surely give us all the details, wouldn't you?" Katie Ann propped her chin on her hands. "Out of earshot of Amberlee, of course."

Elizabeth put up her hands. Whatever these women were thinking about her and Hunter, they had the wrong idea. Not that Elizabeth hadn't had a thousand of those ravaging thoughts herself since she'd arrived in Chatham Ridge. The others were right—Hunter was a hottie. An intriguing, mystifying, frustrating man who made her want to do things she hadn't thought about in way too long. "I'm not doing any ravaging of Hunter McCoy. I'm here to interview him for a magazine article. Nothing more."

Charlotte sat back in her seat. "Well, damn. I really thought we'd have something juicy to discuss tonight."

"We do. They're called books." Susie held one aloft, a

romance novel featuring a bare-chested man wearing dog tags. "We can talk about men afterward. Books before brawn, remember?"

Amberlee sighed. "One of these days we'll have the books *with* the brawn."

"Sexy men to read to us. Now that's a club I'd join!" Charlotte laughed.

"That, my dear, would be a whole other kind of bookstore." Noralee laid the last platter of desserts on the table and took the lone empty seat. "So, shall we get started?"

∞

By the time they had finished discussing Charlotte's book selection—a historical novel about a WWII nurse—Elizabeth felt like she'd been part of the book club all her life. There was just something about these women, something warm and inclusive. Not to mention the fabulous books they had all chosen, which had Elizabeth starting a long mental to-be-read list in her head for when she got back to New Jersey.

Just thinking about returning to Trenton left her feeling empty and sad, though. She was going to miss these women. This town. Already, it had grown on her.

"So tell us about yourself," Susie said to Elizabeth in between books while they were standing at the counter, indulging in more cookies and sweet tea. Noralee seemed to have an endless supply of baked incredibleness, each cookie better than the one before.

"Not much to tell, really. Born and raised in New Jersey, pretty much lived there my whole life. Worked as a bookkeeper before I became a writer." And that was kinda sad, Elizabeth thought, that her entire history could be boiled down to a pair of dull sentences.

"So . . .," Rachel said, "is there a Mr. Palmer back in Jersey?"

Elizabeth snorted. "No. There was supposed to be, but then he found love on the second floor of our apartment building."

"Bastard," Rachel said. "I hope you torched his clothes and smashed his Xbox."

Elizabeth laughed. That sounded like something Sophie would say. Elizabeth had no doubt Sophie would love these book club women as much as Elizabeth already did. "No, but I considered it."

"Well, I think the best cure for a broken heart is a Southern charmer." Charlotte grinned. "And we have some sexy ones here."

Katie Ann scoffed. "If you see one, let me know. I haven't found a guy worth shaving my legs for in a month."

The other women laughed at that, then settled back in their chairs and picked up Susie's romance novel for the next discussion. While they were debating the amazing attributes of the six-packed man on the cover, Amberlee glanced at Elizabeth, then back at the others. "I could be wrong, but I think my brother is interested in you, Elizabeth."

Conversation ground to a complete halt. "Wait . . . Hunter? Interested in Elizabeth?" Rachel leaned forward, elbows on her knees. "Do tell."

Elizabeth's face heated. Hunter wasn't interested in her. Well, maybe a little, but not in anything more than just a passing glance. "There's nothing to tell. Besides, I'm only here for a few days—"

"Long enough to have one heck of a hot fling," Charlotte said.

"Southern belles do not have flings," Noralee said. Then

she winked and grinned at Elizabeth. "We have scandalous dalliances."

"And the more scandalous the better," Susie said, "so that we can all live vicariously through you at the next book club meeting."

"Trust me," Elizabeth said, reaching for another cookie before she said anything stupid like, *I would love to do something scandalous with that hottie Hunter McCoy,* "I'm not planning on doing anything like that in the few days I'm here."

"Pity," Rachel said, giving Elizabeth a wink, "because if there's one thing we all love more than books—"

"It's hot nights with hot men that we can all brag about the next day," Charlotte finished. "All of us except Rachel here."

"Hey, just because I'm married doesn't mean I'm dead. Besides, I'm lucky enough to spend every night with a hot man now." She grinned the smile of a woman deeply in love.

Elizabeth realized she had never smiled like that about any man in her life. Never had that swept-off-her-feet-into-a-crazy-whirlwind feeling of love before. What would it be like to think of the man in her life and smile the kind of smile that reached all the way into her bones?

"And we are all jealous as hell," Charlotte said, as if voicing Elizabeth's thoughts, "but we still love you."

"For now, all we have is this," Susie said, holding up her romance novel. "So let's get intimate with Storm Jackson here, and dream of meeting a man like him in real life."

"I think that's a great idea," Elizabeth said. Because the sooner the women focused on the fictional novel, the sooner they would stop asking her about a fictional romance with Hunter McCoy. But that didn't stop her from picturing

Hunter on the cover of the novel or thinking of Hunter as the women talked about the book.

Okay, so maybe they were right. Maybe she needed a scandalous dalliance. Not to forget her ex-fiancé, who seemed twelve million miles away, but to once and for all get that frustrating, tempting cowboy out of her mind.

∽

Hunter should have gone to bed an hour ago. But the words he'd exchanged with Johnny Ray still churned in his gut, and every time he thought about quitting for the day, his mind would replay the tape of their conversation. So he worked hard, stacking hay bales that didn't need stacking, scrubbing down tack that didn't need scrubbing, and sweeping the barn floor until it was clean enough for a five-course meal.

His arms ached, his back twinged, and sweat beaded on his brow. But still the nightmares that haunted his nights danced at the back of his mind, waiting for him to cave to sleep. Foster had given up on his master ever heading back into the warm and cozy house and was curled into a ball in the corner of the barn, asleep.

Thunder rumbled outside, then the skies opened up, and rain began thudding hard and fast against the stable roof. Foster roused enough to decide the rain wasn't worth his attention, then went back to sleep. Hunter opened the stable door, letting in a gust of wind loaded with fat rain drops that whisked across the threshold like anxious new brides.

Barbara Jean had read him the riot act about skipping dinner. He knew his aunt meant well, but she didn't understand how hard it was for him to talk about the Silver Spur— and with a woman who made him face all the things he'd been running from for two years. Just by being here, asking questions, with that interested look in her eyes. Elizabeth had made him open doors he'd left shut. Best to avoid her and this interview all together. Maybe have her interview Barbara Jean instead.

He swept up the pile of debris and dumped it into the trash, and admitted to himself that none of that was the truth about why he kept avoiding Elizabeth.

Deep down inside, he didn't want to do this interview because he didn't want to answer for what had happened two years ago. To try to explain how those mistakes had damned near broken him. To tell another soul that if it hadn't been for this place, these horses, and this family, he wouldn't be here today.

The storm began to escalate. Hunter stood, stretching his back, and crossed to the open doors, watching the wild wind ripple through the trees, while the rain battered the buildings and fields. In the stable, one of the horses whinnied, and a second answered the sound. Every inch of this place held a memory, some so sweet they made his heart ache and some so painful he could hardly breathe. Some days he thought he was a masochist for staying here, for thinking that if he turned things around or saved one more horse or grew some goddamned flowers that he'd change a thing.

Because he hadn't. And he wasn't going to. He either needed to accept that or move on, but considering how many people were counting on him to stay right where he was, moving on wasn't an option.

That made him think of Elizabeth Palmer. How she'd just quit her job and driven down here to interview him. For a girl who said she didn't like taking risks, that sure as shooting sounded like a risk to him. He envied that about her, more than he wanted to admit.

His gaze went to the house, ablaze with lights, beckoning like a warm friend. But he knew when he went in that house that he wouldn't find comfort or peace. He'd be plagued by regrets, haunted by mistakes. Best to stay here and work until his body reached the point of total exhaustion, as he had every night for close to two years. Work, work, and more work, the only sleeping pill he knew. He started to turn away when he noticed a figure dashing across the lawn. Barefoot, long pale hair streaming behind her like a flag.

"What the hell are you doing?" he had to shout above the storm, which seemed to double in volume in the last few seconds.

"Checking on you." Elizabeth skidded to a halt inside the stable, and shook off the worst of the water. Her shirt was once again plastered to her chest, and her dress pants were snug against her hips. Her bare feet, with those tempting crimson toes, added a sexy, undone edge. "It's one in the morning. I saw the light on in the stable, and I worried that maybe you'd gotten hurt or mugged or—"

"Mugged?" That made him laugh. A good laugh, the kind that came so rarely, he sometimes wondered if he'd forgotten how. "Lizzie, this is a ranch, not gang territory."

She propped her fists on her hips. That only made her breasts rise under the thin, wet fabric. Hunter's hormones stood up and took notice. Hell, they'd been taking notice of her since the first time she'd stood in front of him, wet and bedraggled. And here she was, wet and bedraggled again, and he wanted her even more.

"I come from New Jersey," she said. "Muggings are about as common as sunrises there."

"If some random mugger from Jersey comes running in, I'm sure Foster would protect me." He gestured toward the dog, who didn't so much as flick his tail.

Lizzie scoffed. "He's about as much of a guard dog as a teddy bear."

"Well, that's because there isn't anything to guard me from right now. Except maybe tough Jersey girls." He took a step closer to her, his gaze dropping to her shirt, plastered against her body. He couldn't focus on anything but that, on the way her peach skin seemed dark, mysterious, beneath the flimsy wet fabric. How much he wanted to see what was under that shirt, to touch her, to finish what had been brewing between them ever since she showed up on his doorstep. "Seems you're always running around in wet clothes."

Her cheeks flushed. "It seems to rain . . . a lot here."

"It's fall. Storms happen. Whether you expect them or not."

"Those storms can come out of nowhere. Sweep you up into something . . . dangerous."

"And it's hard to be prepared for that," he said. They weren't talking about rain or clothing choices. They were talking about the undercurrent between them, a storm that could be as destructive as a hurricane if he wasn't careful.

She glanced down at her shirt, then back up at him, her eyes wide and dark in the dim stable. "Maybe I should have bought a jacket when I was in town tonight."

"Or maybe you should just . . ."

"Should what?"

"Just . . ." His brain had stopped working a while ago. All he could see, all he could think about, was the lacy outline of her breasts, the stiff peaks of her nipples. Desire pounded in his veins, and before he could think twice about what he was doing, he reached up, tangled a hand in her long, damp hair, and drew her to him. She let out a little mew of surprise, then tipped her head to meet his.

They came together like an explosion, his mouth tearing hungrily at hers. She surged into his chest, her arms going around him, gripping his back, pulling him closer, until his shirt was as wet as hers.

Hunter hoisted Elizabeth up, perching her on the bottom half of the open Dutch door. It banged into the wall with a thud of metal on wood, and Foster let out a surprised yip. But Hunter didn't care if the door punched through to next Tuesday. He had this amazing woman in his arms and all he wanted was more. He slid between her legs and gripped her ass, still devouring her mouth.

She was warm against him, soft where he was hard. He reached between them, yanked open her silky shirt, dragging back the lacy edge of her bra. She let out a gasp when the cool night air hit her skin, but he was there, his mouth on her breast, teasing her nipple with his tongue. She clawed at his back, her legs wrapping tight around him.

"Oh God, Hunter, oh, this"—she gasped, breathed, gasped again—"is wrong . . . we shouldn't."

Wrong. We shouldn't.

His common sense returned like a boomerang to his temporal lobe. God, what was he doing? He barely knew her, and worse, this kind of thing wasn't supposed to happen. Not with the woman who was profiling his ranch. And not with him. He wasn't fit for a relationship—or whatever this was between them.

We shouldn't.

No, they sure as hell shouldn't. He drew back, releasing the fabric of her shirt. It settled back in place over her breast. He took a couple steps back. "I'm sorry. I don't know what came over me."

"It wasn't just you." A half smile flickered on her face. "I didn't exactly say no."

"You're right." He drew in a ragged breath, another. "That shouldn't have happened. It was a mistake." Was he telling himself? Or her? "I'm not . . . interested in you like that."

"For someone who isn't interested, it sure felt otherwise."
She hopped off the Dutch door and brushed at her pants, as
if wiping away any trace of him. Her voice had gone harsh
and cold. "I'll head back into the house. And look for somewhere else to stay tomorrow, if we haven't finished the interview by then."

"We haven't even started the interview yet."

"No, Hunter, we haven't." She stopped at the open door
and turned back to him. The rain fell in sheets outside the
stable, with thunder crackling above them. "Because for
some reason, you are afraid to trust me. I have done everything you have asked of me. And yeah, I know I don't have
a ton of experience, but that doesn't mean I can't write a
good story, one that will help you save this place you say
you love so much."

"I do love this ranch. It's everything to me."

"Then prove it." Then she walked out into the rain, disappearing a moment later in the dark night.

∞

Two days in, and thus far, Elizabeth had exactly one page
of notes. Not enough to base a 1,500-word article on. Heck,
she didn't think she even had two hundred words of notes,
and unless she wrote the lyrics to "Stairway to Heaven" on
the page, there was no way she could stretch that into a full
article.

Of course, there were other things about Hunter McCoy
that she could write about. Like how every time her gaze
met his, something melted inside her. Like how he kissed
her, with the kind of heat that should have been rated on the
Richter scale. Like how he had touched her and she had
come undone and started fantasizing about having sex right
there, against the wall in the stable.

And like how it had taken every ounce of her common sense, and a whole lot of willpower, to tell him she thought going any further was a mistake. Because it was. Except a part of her thought it was one of those mistakes that seemed so delicious and wonderful and thrilling to make.

Yeah, that might not make the best article. At least for a horse magazine. Maybe if she ever started working at *Playgirl* . . .

That led to her imagining a photo spread of a very naked and very fit Hunter McCoy, lying across that white quilt on her bed, all muscles and man.

Okay, not getting anywhere. Elizabeth powered up her word processing program, and made a few starts at the article. Maybe by doing that, she could get back on track. If she had the start to the article, maybe it would make the interview go easier today. Because the faster she asked the questions, the faster she could leave.

Hunter McCoy is one of those unforgettable, intoxicating men.

Backspace, backspace, backspace.

Hunter McCoy makes horse breeding sexy.

Backspace, backspace, backspace.

Hunter McCoy is a frustrating enigma with a great butt.

Elizabeth closed the laptop, pushed back from the small desk in her bedroom and let out a sigh. Maybe she could just write about something else. Leave the profile of Hunter McCoy until after she was well into menopause and didn't turn into a giant raging hormone every time the guy was in the same room.

She lifted the lid on the laptop again and started composing an e-mail to her editor when one popped into her in-box, titled Another Assignment. For once, Elizabeth thought, serendipity was smiling on her.

> Since you're already in the area, I wanted to gauge your interest in possibly writing a story on a miniature pony breeder in Atlanta? Two thousand words, be sure to highlight the growing—ha ha—market for these smaller horses.

Elizabeth clicked on Reply, and started typing.

Sure. I could even start with that one and leave the profile of Hunter McCoy to a later issue. Like in the next century, she thought but didn't add.

A soft ping, and a reply popped up.

> You're still learning the ropes. Let's not get too far ahead of ourselves. Write the piece on Hunter, which we are counting on for our December issue, and then, if that turns out well, I'll send over the assignment sheet for the miniature pony story.

Elizabeth sighed. That meant she needed to finish everything with Hunter, and get that article written. Without being tempted by him. If the first article went well, she'd be moving on to assignment number two, which was one step closer to making this a career.

The thought of that both thrilled and panicked her. There were so many what-ifs—what if she failed and had to go back to bookkeeping? What if she was a terrible writer?

What if it took another three hundred and seven queries to get a third assignment?

Two days. That was how long she had been untied from a day job, from everything dependable and sane and predictable. Two days, and she needed a paper bag just to breathe. Elizabeth fiddled with her mother's ring. Maybe she wasn't as different from Winnie as she thought. Maybe they were two peas in the same pod, and Elizabeth had been fooling herself, thinking a few years as a bookkeeper made her any less of an irresponsible dreamer. She pulled out her phone and dialed the one person who understood.

"Talk me down, Sophie," Elizabeth said when her call was answered on the other end. "I'm five steps away from running back to Trenton and going back to my old job. This is not the kind of unpredictability I wanted."

"Then tell me again why you did it?"

Sophie's question brought everything back to center again. The moment of panic ebbed. A bit. Elizabeth sighed. "Because I was tired of spending every day under shitty fluorescent lights wishing I had a life."

"And . . . having a life comes with risk," Sophie said, repeating the same advice she'd given to Elizabeth months ago when she'd first started querying and testing the freelancing waters.

"But what if I end up like my mother? Working a job here, a job there, never having much more than change in my pockets, and never knowing where I'm going to live next month or the month after that?"

"Do you have life insurance?"

"Yes."

"An IRA and a 401(k)?"

"You know I do."

"And at least six months of savings, socked away in an

interest-bearing account, along with a ready-to-go résumé, a list of potential job prospects, and a one-year, five-year, and ten-year plan?"

Elizabeth laughed. "You know me well."

Sophie's voice quieted. "You are not your mother, Liz. You never were, never will be. She was . . . flighty and irresponsible and you are the exact opposite of that. Just because you jumped off a cliff like she used to do, doesn't mean you weren't smart enough to strap on a couple parachutes before you leaped."

Sophie was the best kind of best friend. She always knew the right words to say, the ones that drew Elizabeth back from the edge. "You're right. I know you are, but still . . . I worry and stress and make lists."

Sophie laughed. "And that's what makes you awesome. And smart. You'll be fine. And remember, when it comes to the actual article, I'll be right there to help you if you run into any trouble. You have this, Elizabeth."

"What I have is a blank page. And no interview."

"Are you telling me a girl from Jersey can't get a cowboy to sit down for five minutes and talk to her? Put your boots on, buttercup, and rassle that boy into submission."

"There are so many bad clichés in there, I can't even begin to start pointing them out. But you're right. And he did promise to talk to me today. I'm just"—Elizabeth smoothed a wrinkle out of the hand-made quilt on her bed—"scared."

"Scared? Of what?"

Of falling for Hunter. Of falling for this place. The wedding ring pattern on the quilt was filled with interlocking loops that seemed to just draw her in, make her want to stay. "Of . . . everything."

"You are strong and amazing and smart. And whatever

happens, you will be fine. Because you have me for a best friend."

That made Elizabeth laugh. "You always know just the right thing to say."

"Who do you think I learned that skill from? You've pulled me out of a funk a hundred times before. Now it's my turn to do the same for you." Sophie called out to someone behind her. "I have to go, Liz. My plane is getting ready to leave. I'll text you when I land. And remember, this whole thing with that hunky cowboy will be easy as pie—"

"And delicious as cake." That part was true, especially when it came to kissing Hunter McCoy. As long as she did no more of that, maybe she could actually get some work done.

Ha. Good luck with that, considering her every other thought—and even that was an understatement—revolved around kissing him, touching him, being with him.

Elizabeth pulled on the jeans, boots, and T-shirt she'd bought last night, then at the last second, exchanged them for the white dress. It was a dress kind of day, she thought, with the warm sun and the pretty skies. Not that she cared if Hunter noticed she was wearing a dress, not at all. She pulled on the boots, too, then headed downstairs. She could hear Hunter talking to Barbara Jean in the kitchen. "I've been worried about her," Hunter was saying.

"She's fine. A little tired but nothing out of the ordinary." Barbara Jean put a hand on Hunter's cheek. "You worry too much."

"I don't worry enough. If I had—" He cursed and turned away. "Just talk to her, will you?"

"I will. I promise." Barbara Jean saw Elizabeth, lingering at the kitchen entrance. "Come on in, have yourself a cup of coffee and some breakfast."

Hunter's gaze connected with Elizabeth's for one long, hot second, then he looked away. She wondered if he was thinking about that kiss last night, about plastering her to the wall and peeling open her shirt. Because she sure was. "Wow. That looks . . . beautiful."

"Thank you." She brushed at the waist of the dress. "Your sister talked me into it."

"Amberlee was right. Uh . . . anyway, I have something I have to take care of, but I'll be back for you in an hour," he said. "Can you be ready then?"

"Ready for what?" she asked, because her brain had kind of short-circuited when he'd complimented her.

Now his eyes met hers again, fast and hot like magnets. "The interview, of course."

Okay, so maybe delaying this interview until she could look at him without fantasizing about him would be a good idea. Uh-huh. And that was going to happen in the next sixty minutes. "Oh, yeah, sure. Great."

Hunter tipped his hat at her, and then he was gone, with Foster tagging along at his master's heels. Elizabeth leaned against the counter, watching him go. She tried to bite back the sigh in her throat but it escaped all the same.

"That's good that he's doing the interview today," Barbara Jean said, while she stirred a bowl of pancake batter.

"Yes, of course. Yup. Very good."

Barbara Jean turned on the stove, then set a long flat skillet atop two burners. She opened a package of bacon and began laying the pieces into a hot cast-iron pan. "You're falling for him, aren't you?"

"Me? No, of course not. I'm just . . . tired. Sleepless night last night." Yeah, tossing and turning because she'd been fantasizing about Hunter. And holding herself back from running down to the stables again and finishing what they'd started.

"I wouldn't blame you if you were. He's a good man, one of those who will give the shirt off his back to anyone in need but when it comes to opening up about himself . . ." Barbara Jean sighed, then crossed to the sink to wash her hands. "He's guarded, I guess you could say. He always has been."

"I don't need him to give me his life story. Just the ranch's story." Uh-huh. Then why had she been so curious about his personal life? And why was she constantly thinking about kissing him?

"So you aren't interested in him on a personal basis?" Barbara Jean turned to the refrigerator and drew out a pitcher of cream.

"I'm not here for that."

"That doesn't answer the question." Barbara Jean retrieved a white stoneware coffee mug from the cabinet and filled it with coffee.

Elizabeth plopped down at the kitchen table. "I just broke off an engagement and uprooted my entire life. A long-distance relationship is the last thing I need."

"It's not long-distance as long as you are here in Chatham Ridge." Barbara Jean smiled, then handed Elizabeth the mug, along with the cream and a bowl of sugar. "Stay awhile. You might just start to love this town and never want to leave."

Elizabeth sat in the morning sun at Hunter McCoy's kitchen table, watching the horses run across green, green fields, and knew she was already past that point.

Chapter 9

Amberlee put the inhaler to her mouth and drew in deep. She closed her eyes as the steroids traveled down to her lungs, imagining, as she always had, a million tiny little soldiers pushing back the walls that threatened her breaths, pushing, pushing, until the air began to flow again. Her heart slowed, and the panic that had clutched her earlier began to release.

She saw a car pull into the visitor's space outside her dorm. Damn. Amberlee yanked open the nearest drawer and shoved the inhaler inside. Then she rinsed her mouth, straightened her hair, and checked her reflection in the mirror. Her face was still a little flushed, but there wasn't much she could do about that. At the last second, she grabbed a rag and some Windex, then opened the door. "Auntie Barbara Jean, I didn't know you were coming over. I was just . . . cleaning."

"I brought muffins." Barbara Jean held up a basket. "A couple chocolate chip ones and some blueberry ones."

Even though she suspected her aunt was here because she

was worried about her health, and not necessarily her break-fast options, Amberlee's stomach rumbled. Aunt Barbara Jean made some awesome muffins, and Amberlee wasn't about to refuse them. "Come on in. I just put on a pot of coffee."

They headed into the kitchen, which was really just a corner of Amberlee's crowded dorm room, and sported only a hot plate, coffeepot, and a microwave smaller than a box of popcorn. Barbara Jean reached in the basket, retrieving a tub of butter, some knives, and paper plates. She set them on top of the microwave. Her aunt had come prepared. She had been here often enough to know Amberlee's "kitchen" was just a glorified ramen noodle cooking space.

"How's Elizabeth?" Amberlee asked. "I think she had a good time at book club."

"She's doing well. Should be talking to Hunter right about now." Barbara Jean grinned. "I'm glad she hung on and stayed around. I like that girl."

"I do, too." Amberlee hoped Elizabeth stayed in town for a good long while. Elizabeth was real, in a way that so few women around here were. And she didn't look at Amberlee like she might fall apart at any moment, like pretty much every-one in her family had for the past eighteen years. It was like starting a friendship with a clean slate, with no one worrying about how she was breathing or whether she was getting tired.

Aunt Barbara Jean put the muffin basket on the small table holding the hot plate, then turned to Amberlee. "How are you feeling, dear? You seemed a little tired when I saw you yesterday."

"I'm fine, I'm fine. I've been busy, that's all. Studying a lot."

"You should take a few days off. Come stay at the ranch. Let me spoil you."

The exhaustion that had plagued Amberlee for weeks

weighed on her shoulders. Maybe her aunt was right. Maybe a few days off would get her back on track. She thought of the inhaler in the drawer, of how many times she'd had to use it in the past month. Too many times.

And if she stayed at the ranch, she could work on convincing Hunter to let her start working with the horses again. Damn the doctors and all their caution. Amberlee wanted to live her life—and live it there, among the horses she loved so much. She'd bring her inhaler and she'd be just fine. Besides, it had been years since she'd had a bad attack. Surely she could handle being on the ranch, maybe even go back to helping with the training. "I'll come out this weekend. How's that sound?"

"Perfect." Barbara Jean smiled.

Amberlee put on a bright face. "Good. Now let's eat. I'm famished."

They took their muffins out to the common area and sat at a round table beside the window, with a view of the small garden at the back of the dorm. Every season, there was a new flower to see, another color to enjoy. The gardeners had planted some pansies in the planters yesterday and now the flowers waved their bright purple friendly faces to the sun. They were ever hopeful, and so, too, was Amberlee. Despite what that inhaler in the drawer had to say.

∞

After he tended to the foal who'd banged up his leg because the youngster had thought he could sneak out the gate when Carlos was bringing in a mare, Hunter headed out to the stable to set up his surprise for Lizzie. He had paperwork on his desk that needed filing, orders that needed to be placed, bills that needed to be paid, but Hunter ignored them all. He was going to spend the day with Lizzie, and that thought made him feel indescribably . . . light.

At the fourth stall, he found an old friend. Zephyros swung his large dark brown head over the stable gate and nickered softly when Hunter approached. Hunter dug in his pocket for a carrot and held it out to the old stallion. He was a good horse, the father of dozens of foals over the years. He'd always been Hunter's favorite horse, with a good temperament that made him perfect for riding.

In an instant, the carrot was gone, snarfled up between the horse's big lips and teeth. "How about a ride?" Hunter said. "I could use a few minutes in the sun, and I bet you could, too, old boy."

He slipped a bit into Zeph's mouth, then slid the bridle over the horse's head. Hunter draped a thick blanket over the horse's back, then hefted the saddle into place, cinching it beneath the horse's belly in quick, practiced movements. He added a pair of saddlebags, already filled with everything he'd need for today. Then he led Zeph out of the stable and into the sun. The horse's pace picked up and his ears twitched, excitement tensing in his muscles.

Hunter swung into the saddle and cradled the reins in one hand. He clicked his tongue and Zeph moseyed forward. They ambled past the main corral and down the path that led to the house.

Lizzie was waiting on the porch, a brown leather messenger bag draped over her shoulder, probably filled with those notepads and pens and that little tiny recorder. She was still wearing the white dress from this morning, which pleased him to no end. The dress tapered at her waist, belled a little over her hips, emphasizing every one of her curves. She'd paired the dress with a new pair of cowboy boots that hugged her calves and gave her another couple inches of height.

But it was the hat that drew his attention. An off-white cowboy hat, plopped on her head at a little bit of an angle, leaving long locks of her blond hair curling around her shoulders. She looked sexy and serious, all at the same time.

"Nice hat," he said.

"Thanks." She smiled and pressed a hand to the brim, as if she was a little embarrassed by the compliment. "Your sister talked me into it. I thought it would keep the sun off me."

"It'll do that and also make you fit in down here like a bluebird in a tree." He gestured toward the back of Zeph. "Hop on. I want to show you something."

Her eyes got wide and she shied back a little. "Hop on? That huge horse?"

Hunter chuckled. "Zephyros isn't huge. He's average. But he's strong, dependable, and gentle, so he won't mind a second rider."

"I've never ridden a horse."

"Well, what better time to start than now?" He doffed his hat and leaned down toward her. "This is my clumsy way of apologizing for yesterday. I'm not used to strangers, and especially not used to pretty strangers asking me a lot of questions."

She peered up at him from under the brim of the hat. "You think I'm pretty?"

He shifted in the saddle. Of course he thought she was pretty—not just pretty but stop-a-man-in-his-tracks beautiful, but he wasn't about to say that. She wasn't here to date him, she was here to interview him. Besides, he wasn't in a place where he should be dating anyone, much less a woman who was going to flit out of his life as quickly as she'd entered it.

Uh-huh. That was what he wanted. That's why he kept kissing her and fantasizing about her. Because he was so *unin*terested. "I said pretty *and* strange. That word was in there, too."

That made her laugh. "Boy, you sure know how to flatter a woman."

"Who says I'm trying to flatter you? I'm just trying to get you to go for a ride."

She gave the horse a wary glance. "Are you sure I won't fall off?"

"I'll hold tight to you. I promise." Just the thought of holding her tight made a part of him ache. For a second, his mind pictured her in his lap, legs wrapped around his hips, arms secure around his chest, her breasts sliding up and down his—

Okay, that wasn't going to get him anywhere but in an uncomfortable spot.

"Are you asking me to trust you?" She propped a hand on her hip, which made her chest jut out a little, and give her a sassy air. And only made him want her more.

"Are you saying you don't?"

"I hardly know you," she said, echoing his words from earlier.

He liked that about Lizzie. She gave back as good as she got. He imagined what she'd be like in bed. If she'd take the lead, be as adventurous as he was. He shifted in the saddle, and reminded himself—for the ten thousandth time—that thinking about sleeping with Lizzie wasn't getting him anywhere good. "Well, there's no better way to get to know a man than to ride his horse."

A deep laugh rolled out of her, and a blush filled her cheeks. He liked that. A lot. He wondered if the blush would extend down her chest, bloom just above those tempting breasts.

"We're talking about this horse here, right?" she said. "Not the one you keep in the bedroom?"

The innuendo made him think of last night, in the stables, and all the times they had come close—so close—to ending up in that very bedroom. And how much he wished he had just scooped her up and carried her upstairs. If only to end this tempting agony of wanting her.

Instead he gave her a grin and put out a hand. "Are you coming or not?"

She hesitated a moment longer.

"Trust me, Lizzie."

She met his gaze, held it for a long second, then put her palm in his. "How do we do this?"

"Get up on the step there, then when I move my foot out of the stirrup, put yours in to help you swing your leg over. Then slip in behind me and hold on."

She gave him a wary look, but did as he said and stepped up onto the top step, then took his hand. Her palm held tight to his, nearly turning his knuckles white. "Ready?"

"Yup. Zeph won't move. Don't worry. And I've got you."

Lizzie let out a breath, then stepped into the stirrup and pushed off at the same time he pulled her up and onto the saddle. She settled her weight behind his, and leaned back, putting a couple inches of space between them. Her bare legs skated against his, making him wish he'd worn shorts instead of jeans.

He craned his head to the back. "You're going to need to hold on to me, unless you want to end up on the ground."

She stayed where she was. "Are you sure this isn't just some ploy to get the hapless female to put her arms around you?"

He laughed and clicked to Zeph. "You, darlin', are far from hapless."

The horse lumbered forward, the movement causing Hunter and Lizzie to sway from side to side. Hunter clicked again and Zeph picked up the pace, which thrust Lizzie into Hunter's back. A second later, her arms went around his chest, and her head pressed to his shoulder. God, that felt good. Really good. He wanted to ride this horse from here to Mars and back, just to keep Lizzie right where she was.

"Riding a horse is easy," Hunter said to her, turning his face as he spoke, his cheek brushing against her lips. He held his position for a heartbeat, inhaling the sweet floral fragrance she wore, wanting to turn his face just that little bit more and kiss her. "Uh, you, uh, just settle into Zeph, move with the horse when he moves. The horse is smart and knows where to go. All you have to do is trust him with your body."

A devilish glint lit her eyes. "Just the horse, not you, right?"

"Both. Since I'm in charge, darlin'." He clicked to Zeph, and the stallion picked up the pace a little.

Lizzie did as he said, settling into him like she was made for that space, her lithe legs marrying against his, thigh to knee. Her breasts curved into his back, and as much as he told himself to concentrate on anything but the feel of her body on his, his mind disobeyed. He kept the reins in one hand, the other on the pommel, because some crazy part of him wanted to cover her hands with his own. Actually, he wanted to cover a lot more of her body than that, but if he did any of the things his mind was thinking about, they'd fall off the horse.

"Where are we going?" she asked, her mouth close to his ear, her breath warm on his neck.

"I want to show you the Silver Spur from the best vantage point there is." He tapped Zeph with his heels, and the horse broke into an easy canter. Lizzie held on tighter, pressed into him like they were one person. Nice. Very, very nice.

In a few minutes, the ranch was behind them, the stable and the barns mere blips on the landscape. The seventy-five acres he owned opened onto lush green rolling hills, sprawling before them like Mother Nature reclining in the sun. Zeph charged up the hill, his black mane flying out behind him, tickling against their hands and arms. Clods of dirt sprayed into the wake kicked up by Zeph's shoes, but the horse kept on, charging for the top of that hill as he had done a thousand times before.

Lizzie tightened her grip on Hunter's chest. She was practically glued to him now, but she'd lifted her head to watch the acres rushing by. "This is gorgeous!"

"You haven't seen anything yet." He tugged a little on the right rein, but Zeph was already halfway into the turn. The horse knew the route as well as Hunter did and picked up his pace, skirting the big oak tree at the top of the hill, then slowing as he began to descend into a valley on the other side of the hill. A small pond filled the space, shaded by a trio of oak trees older than Hunter himself. Zeph slowed to a trot and stopped at the edge of the pond, dropping his head to get a drink. Hunter slid off the horse, then reached a hand up for Lizzie. "My lady."

She laughed, then took his hand and dismounted. She slid into his hands, which sat as natural on her waist as a belt. He didn't want to let go, but knew if he stood there a moment longer, he'd be kissing her, and that wasn't the plan.

"This place is gorgeous." Lizzie turned to take in the view. "I had no idea it was part of your land."

"You can't see it from the main house because of the hill. So it's like a secret tucked away up here. Some springs, we get so much rain, the pond overflows. And some summers, the pond dries to a puddle. But most years, it's the perfect size. Big enough for a drink for Zeph, and a little cooling off when the day gets too hot."

She arched a brow. "Are you suggesting skinny-dipping?"

"Are you offering to go?" Half of him hoped she'd say yes. The other half wondered what the hell he'd do if she did say yes. Because seeing Lizzie naked and wet was more than a man could bear. His no-kissing-her-again rule was having trouble staying in his mind.

"I, uh, don't think that'd be the most professional thing I could do."

She hadn't said yes or no. He didn't know whether to be disappointed or relieved. But he was intrigued, mighty intrigued. It had been a long damned time since Hunter had thought about a woman in the way he was thinking about Elizabeth Palmer right now. "Might be better suited for an interview for a whole other kind of magazine."

"Well, should I land an assignment at the kind of magazine they put in a paper wrapper, you'll be the first person I call." She tossed him a grin, then wandered down to the water's edge. She brushed her bangs off her forehead. "It is warm out today, though. Is it always this hot here in the fall?"

"Pretty much. Welcome to the South."

"It's a whole other world for this Jersey girl." She turned her face up to the sun, closed her eyes, and smiled.

He had to take a breath, because right then, Lizzie looked like something in a painting. The sun dusted her hair with gold, and she had such a peaceful, happy expression on her face, that he wanted to steal a moment of that peace for himself. Just one moment, where he thought of nothing but the warmth of the sun and heard no other sound but the happy chirp of the birds above.

It was a moment of serenity, something so foreign to Hunter that for a second, he wondered if he was imagining all of it.

She turned her head and opened her eyes. "You're staring at me."

"Just enjoying the view."

"Stalker." She grinned, then scanned the acres surrounding the Silver Spur, for the most part untouched, as if this part of the world was on a different planet from the metropolises a short ride away. "That field of flowers over there is . . . stunning. I just love them. They're so beautiful, and look so . . . happy. I've been meaning to ask you, what kind of flowers are they?"

The flowers. No one had ever asked him about them because everyone at the ranch knew why he'd planted them. He'd been foolish enough to think if he planted a big enough field of the deep purple blooms, that it would prove something. In the end, the flowers hadn't changed anything. A thousand times, he'd been tempted to plow them into the ground and fill that field with hay, but he hadn't. "They're Georgia asters."

"They are? But they have white centers. I thought asters had yellow centers. My grandma had some in her garden, and I remember them being white and yellow."

"Georgia asters are much less common. Used to be, you'd see them round every corner of this state. But they've gone the way of anything else endangered."

"And so you planted them to help rebuild the population?"

"No. I planted these because . . ." He let out a long breath and tore his gaze away from the field. Instead of answering her right away, he stalked back up the hill to Zeph, grabbed the red plaid blanket he'd brought, and returned to Lizzie. Putting off the truth didn't make it go away, and maybe it was past damned time he started dealing with it all. He'd been living in the same place for too long, and he was ready to move forward, or at least move a couple inches in a forward direction. "I planted them because I thought it would make someone happy."

"And did it work?" Lizzie asked.

"No." He spread out the blanket, then dropped onto the ground, removing his hat and propping it on the corner of the plaid fabric. Lizzie sat down beside him, close enough to touch. "Jenna loved Georgia asters. And I thought if I planted them here, she'd love this place, too."

"I don't know how anyone couldn't love this place." She

drew in a deep breath, held it for a moment. "It's so beautiful. Tranquil."

"Jenna grew up here, but always hated Chatham Ridge. Hated the small town life. Every chance she got, she ran off to the city. She liked the excitement of it, the busyness, the pulse, as she called it. At heart, she was a city girl, like you."

Something he kept forgetting. Lizzie loved the Silver Spur now, but would she down the road? He'd been foolish enough to think Jenna would, too, and been wrong. But he'd never seen anyone look as happy and peaceful as Lizzie looked right now, with her face in the sun, and her boots pointed toward the pond.

He reminded himself that Lizzie lived in a place with a rapid heartbeat, and would return there soon, regardless of what insane fantasies he had late at night in the stable. He'd made that mistake once before. He wouldn't do it again.

"I thought if I planted her favorite flowers," he said, "it would make living here better for her. But it never did. Instead, she was mad that I did that, said I was trying to trap her in the very place she wanted to leave." And now it was too late to make up for that. He sighed. "Can we talk about something else?"

"Sure." Lizzie dug in the messenger bag for the notepad, pens, and recorder. "I promise, this will be far less painful than you expected."

He chuckled. "You promise to make me look smart?"

"I don't think I'll have to work very hard to do that." Then she dropped her head and looked away before he could decide if she was flirting or trying to get on his good side. She depressed the record button. "Okay, so let's start at the beginning. I know you gave me the basics of how your grandpa started the Silver Spur, but can you give me more specifics about the origins of the ranch?"

He leaned back on his elbows and looked at her. He loved the way her blond hair draped over her shoulders, and how her white cotton dress dipped a little in the front, giving him an all-too-short peek at the swell of her breasts. It all made concentrating damned hard. Especially when he was wondering if she'd worn the dress for him, or just because it was warm out. "How about we trade questions?" he said. "I'll answer one of yours if you answer one of mine."

Lizzie chuckled. "I don't think that's how an interview is supposed to work."

"Well, who said I played by the rules?" He got to his feet, retrieved something from the saddlebags, then came back to his spot on the grass beside her. "And speaking of breaking the rules, I managed to sneak out two pieces of my aunt's pecan pie."

"A horseback ride, a warm sunny day, a picnic by the pond . . ." She lay back on the blanket and turned toward him. "Are you trying to bribe me, Mr. McCoy? Or romance me?"

Bribe her or romance her? Either choice sent him down a dangerous path.

"Just trying to make you smile." And yes, convince her to open up to him as much as she wanted him to open up to her. Ever since she'd shown up on his doorstep looking like a drowned rat, he'd been curious about her. She'd intrigued him in ways he hadn't been intrigued in a very, very long time.

"With the purloined pie, you have succeeded." Another of those amazing smiles bloomed on her face. If that was all it took, he was going to bring her pie every single day.

"I'll have to learn how to bake if you keep smiling like that, Lizzie." Heck, he'd become a regular Betty Crocker if necessary.

"You are incorrigible." She shook her head, but the smile didn't dim. "Okay, we'll trade, one question per question. But only because there is pie involved."

Definitely, he was going to bring her pie every day. He settled back, and waited for Lizzie to ready her pen before he started speaking. "My great-great-great-grandpa bought this land in 1828. He married late in life, and believe it or not, he married one of those mail-order brides from England."

"Really?"

"Really and truly. He ran the Silver Spur as a farm, then passed it on to his son, who also ran it as a farm, as did his son. It wasn't until my grandpa inherited it that it became a horse ranch and was dubbed the Silver Spur. My grandpa was young, freshly home from ten years in the military, when he started raising quarter horses. Back then, the big thing was versatility competitions. But by the time I took over, the money was in reining competitions, which is why we shifted directions."

"What's the difference between versatility and reining?"

He put up a finger. "My turn to ask a question."

She laughed. "The interview is going to take twice as long this way."

"That's okay. It's a gorgeous day and I have a lot of pie." That made her laugh again, the sound warming him as much as the sun above did. "You know where I grew up. Tell me about where you grew up."

A shadow dropped over her features. She shrugged, as if it were a small matter, but he could tell it was anything but. "It's nothing like this place. I lived in a lot of apartments, surrounded by a lot of concrete."

"Why a lot of apartments?"

"That's two questions."

"I gave you a five-generation answer to your question. You gave me a dozen words."

"Has anyone ever told you that you're a pain in the butt?" But she smiled as she said it, softening her words. She adjusted the brim of her hat, and drew her knees to her chest. "We were always moving because my mom would get behind on rent. Three months here, nine months there. The longest I ever spent in one place was a year and a half. One crappy apartment after another, all pretty much interchangeable."

"I can't even imagine that. I've lived here all my life, in this exact same spot." He'd spent so much time at the Silver Spur, it felt like the ranch was part of his soul. He could take a rocket to Mars, but he would still feel tethered to this land.

"You're lucky," Lizzie said. "Not too many people have that kind of home."

"I was lucky, and I don't know if I've always appreciated this place like I should." He rolled onto his side and propped his head on one hand. Hunter wasn't a man who relaxed a lot, who took much time off, but with Lizzie, he was content to stay in this very spot for a few hours, a few days. "Next question."

Her gaze dropped to the notepad and he thought he detected a little relief in her actions, as they got back to business only. "What's the difference between versatility and reining?"

He explained how versatility was more about training a horse to be calm and quiet, a good workhorse. A reining horse was bred for performance, speed, reaction. To do the drills they were commanded and do them at a lightning pace. "It's like the difference between a pickup truck and a Porsche," he explained. "Versatility horses were good family horses, but the reining horses, those are the fancy divas on the field."

She took dutiful notes the whole time, even though he was sure her recorder was getting his every word. Lizzie, the diligent bookkeeper, making sure she had a redundant system. It was kinda cute, in a way.

"Right now, reining is more popular in competition," he

went on. "In ten years, it might be something else." Then, before she could slip in another question, he asked, "So, what's your secret skill?"

She laughed. "What? What kind of question is that?"

"A legitimate one. Everyone has a secret skill. Opening a champagne bottle with a knife, tying a cherry stem with your tongue."

"What's yours?"

He pressed a hand to his chest, and made a dramatic flourish with the other hand. "I can tie a cherry stem with my tongue."

"Your, uh, tongue must be very . . . flexible." She flushed, but recovered fast, and he wondered if she was thinking the same thoughts he was now having, about tongues and flexibility and the fact that they were quite alone out here. "Okay, my secret skill . . . promise you won't laugh?"

He crossed his heart. "Scout's honor."

"That's not the Boy Scout symbol."

"When did I say I was a Boy Scout?" He grinned. "Us incorrigible types aren't allowed."

"Probably a good thing." Then, when she saw he was still waiting for her answer, she let out an okay-I-cave sigh. "I can juggle. Not chainsaws or anything, but give me three balls or three bowling pins, and I'll entertain you."

"You're serious? How did you learn to do that?" If someone had asked him to name ten things Lizzie could do, juggling never would have made the list. He could have seen a herd of cats swimming across the pond and it wouldn't have surprised him as much as she did.

"I told you I was home alone a lot. For a while, I thought I might try out for the cheerleading squad—"

"You would have made a hot cheerleader." That was an image that was going to stay in his mind for a long time.

Lizzie in one of those short little white skirts . . . nice. Very nice.

"Maybe so, but my mother didn't have the money for the uniforms. Plus, I never really stayed in one school long enough to join anything. So I just taught myself to juggle instead. It's not a skill that has come in handy very often." She brushed a lock of hair off her forehead. "Not exactly a lot of call for that in bookkeeping school, although there are some times when you are making some creative financial moves that are a lot like juggling."

"You can really juggle? This, I have to see." He got to his feet and jogged down to the water's edge, grabbed three equal-sized stones, and jogged back up to the blanket.

"Oh, I can't—"

"Can't really juggle? I knew it." He tucked the rocks behind his back. "Just making up a skill. Tsk, tsk. The Girl Scouts would kick you out if they knew."

"Oh, give me those." She reached around, snagged the rocks out of his palm, then stepped back and planted her feet in the soft grass. "I haven't done this in a long time, so I'm a little rusty. And for the record, I was never a Girl Scout."

He leaned in close to her ear, "I think a woman who can juggle is sexy. Especially if she's wearing a big red nose while she does it."

Lizzie rolled her eyes. "You are weird. Now, be quiet and let me concentrate." She weighed the rocks, putting two in one hand, one in the other, drew in a deep breath, let it out slow, then started to toss the rocks. Concentration knitted her brows, thinned her lips, but within a few seconds, a whirling trio of rocks whipped from one hand to the next. The rocks moved so fast, he swore they were attached to each other. A minute later, she caught them in one hand, then gave him a triumphant grin. "Told you so."

"That was pretty impressive. What other skills do you have that I don't know about?"

She shook her head, playfulness filling her features. "I'm not going to say. And, you've not only asked about thirty questions—but also required a demonstration—to my two questions. So now it's my turn."

They settled back on the blanket, while the sun warmed their skin and Zeph dipped his head in the pond and flicked at flies with a lazy tail. Lizzie asked Hunter about how he chose which horses to breed, how one bloodline over another produced different desired qualities in a horse, how the reining competitions worked. The conversation flowed as easily as the rocks she'd been juggling, with him returning the volley with the questions that tumbled in his mind late at night. Things like what had been her favorite subject in school— English, no surprise there; what superpower do you wish you had—the ability to make time stand still; and what one food would you eat every day for the rest of your life—apple pie, which told Hunter that Lizzie was what his grandma used to call "good folk."

She was more than that, a lot more, but he was trying not to let himself think those thoughts. He had no business getting involved with her, even if every cell in his body disagreed.

"Are all your questions going to be silly?" she asked.

"I don't think a discussion of superpowers is silly at all." He laid back on the blanket and put his hat over his eyes to block the sun, but angled enough so he could still see her out of the corner. "I take those things very seriously. That and pie."

"I agree with you on the pie." She wagged a finger at him. "Dessert is nothing to be trifled with."

"Ha ha."

She picked up his hat and grinned down at him. "Are you going to do the entire interview like this?"

"The hat helps me multitask. I can nap while you talk."

She swatted at him, but he caught her hand and pulled her close. Her lips parted, and she drew in a quick breath. "This isn't answering my questions, Hunter."

"I know." And he didn't care. He wanted her, as much as he'd wanted her that night in the stables. He pushed back the brim of her hat, still sitting slightly askew on her head, then he closed the gap between them and kissed her. He cupped her face with one hand and she melted into him, like chocolate spreading across a cake. It was a sweet kiss, as slow as a sunrise, the kind that seemed to linger long after she drew back.

"You're making this interview very, very hard," she said.

"You're the one making it hard."

She glanced down between them. "Well, I wasn't doing that on purpose."

"Darlin', just being within a hundred yards of you makes that happen. You," he brushed back the stubborn lock of hair dancing across her forehead, "are an intoxicating woman who makes it very *hard* for a man to think about anything other than taking you to bed."

Her features turned serious. "That will . . . complicate things."

"And complicated can be messy."

"Very messy."

He tucked the lock of hair behind her ear and thought he'd never known a woman with eyes that green. It was like looking into a forest that stretched on forever. "Maybe messy is a good thing."

She shifted off him and sat up again, grabbing the pen and pad of paper like they were security blankets. "Messy doesn't get my interview done. Tell me about the last two years in the reining circuit. You've had some strong showings, which has really created a lot of buzz about the Silver Spur again."

The mood between them chilled. He told himself he was glad, that the family business should come first, now and always.

So he talked about the competitions, about the plans he had for Loaded Gun, but his mind was on that kiss, on how she'd retreated when he'd talked about complicating things with sex. Because she didn't want him? Or because she was as scared as he was of taking that leap into the unknown with someone else? And did he really want to ask those questions? Because doing so would mean dealing with the answers. And the one thing Hunter McCoy didn't have a lot of right now was answers.

"Wow, there is a lot to learn when it comes to horses. I had no idea. I think I need a *Horse Breeding for Dummies* book." She jotted several notes on her pad, "So, you said the horses had to—"

"What made you propose an article about a subject you knew nothing about?" When she started to protest, he held up a finger. "You've asked me tons of questions. It's my turn to ask one."

She stopped writing and thought a second. She was quiet for so long, he wasn't sure she was going to answer. "I guess I was . . . scared. Yeah, scared."

"Well, hell yes, anyone would be. Starting a new job, one that involves something you didn't know much about, or have much experience with."

"No, you misunderstood me. I was . . . scared of being scared." She let out a long breath. "Scared of playing it safe for one more day and . . ."

She could have been echoing his own thoughts. How many times had he stayed in the safety zone of work, sleep, work, sleep, rather than dealing with everything the last two years had brought? Maybe if he understood why she had made that change—leaving her job, her life, her comfort zone—he could find some answers for himself, too. "And what?"

Her gaze went to the field beyond the pond, to the flowers that waved happy purple faces in the sun. "And missing out."

"On what?"

"This is going to sound all sappy and silly."

"I love sappy and silly."

That made her laugh. "Yeah, right. Mr. Strong Cowboy is a sentimental fool?"

"Only in the privacy of my own room." He winked.

"Incorrigible," she muttered again, then leaned back on her elbows. She held on to the view for a while. When she spoke again, her voice was quiet, wistful. "As silly as it sounds, I didn't want to miss out on happiness. My mother was flighty and crazy and undependable and poor as a church mouse, but she was happy. She looked at clouds in the sky and celebrated the rain that was going to give the flowers a drink. She once handed away half her paycheck to a homeless woman at Christmas because the other woman had nothing and my mother wanted to give her a reason to smile. All my life, I have been trying to live the opposite life of my mother. I had a retirement plan and a savings account and I had a steady nine-to-five job, but I wasn't happy."

"And now?"

"Now I'm scared as hell that I'm going to screw this up, and have to go back to being a bookkeeper until the day I die." Lizzie hugged her knees tighter. A duck settled onto the pond, bobbing for minnows in the shallows.

"You are too smart and too stubborn to screw this up, Lizzie."

Every time he called her that, it made her smile. This

time, the smile wobbled a little. "I thought you said I wasn't stubborn."

"I was being nice."

She scoffed. "You're never nice."

He tugged her hands away from her knees and slid into the space before her. He tiptoed a finger along her lips, wanting that velvety touch all over again. "I'm always nice."

Her breath caught, and her eyes widened. Her hat tumbled off her head and onto the blanket. He could feel her heart racing, the warmth of her skin. Every time he said he wasn't going to get close to her, he ended up touching her, kissing her.

"This isn't getting the interview done," she said, then got to her feet and resettled the hat on her head. "I really need to focus on that. Because if I don't finish the interview, I won't get the article written and then—"

"I thought you were tired of being scared, Lizzie." He gestured toward the space on the blanket. "This . . . backing up, pushing me away, has scared written all over it."

"It's not about fear, Hunter. It's about being realistic. I'm on deadline. That means I can't spend time doing"—she waved between them, but with an air of dismissal—"doing this. Playing *Oklahoma* with the pie and the picnic and the kissing. That's a fantasy. This"—she pointed at the notebook, the pen—"this is real and it's my life. So do me a favor and respect that. Just as you asked me to do with yours."

Chapter 10

Elizabeth sat in the bright, cozy guest bedroom on the second floor while the sun went down, and typed faster than she'd ever typed before. The article poured out of her, like opening a vein. She let her words paint a picture of the Silver Spur, with its lush green acres and its spirited horses and most of all, its unforgettable owner.

She ate half her dinner at her desk, then let the rest grow cold while she wrote and refined, and wrote and refined some more. When she was done, she e-mailed a copy of the article to Sophie, then headed downstairs for a well-deserved slice of pie, considering they never got to the pie at the pond. They'd wrapped up the interview, all businesslike the rest of the day, then headed back to the ranch. A part of her had been disappointed, even though she'd asked for exactly that. It was that same crazy part that wished Hunter would see past the walls she kept throwing up. But he hadn't. He'd heeded her request and stayed distant and businesslike.

Elizabeth kept telling herself that was exactly what she wanted.

If that was so, then why did the disappointment sting so badly?

As Elizabeth headed down the stairs, she noticed the light on in the stables. Hunter, working late. Burying himself in his job, just as she kept doing. It had been too easy this morning to get caught up in the horseback ride and the flowers and the picnic blanket. She'd started falling for him, falling hard, and that meant forgetting why she was there.

To secure her future, not to make some stupid mistake, the kind of spontaneous infatuation that had made her mother move in with Joe this week, Larry the next week. Give her car to Jim, get another one from Bob. In the end, every one of those men had broken Winnie's heart. Elizabeth had watched it happen enough to know better than to let some smooth-talking cowboy distract her from her goals.

Except her gaze kept straying to that lone light burning in the stable. A yearning roared in her gut, to be with him again, to see his smile, to hear that drawl.

Elizabeth jerked away from the window and continued down the stairs. Maybe if she consumed enough sugar, she'd forget all about him.

Amberlee was just laying the leftover pecan pie on the counter when Elizabeth came into the kitchen. "Seems we both had the same idea," Elizabeth said.

Amberlee fished in the drawer and pulled out two forks. "Want to split the last piece?"

"I should probably be polite and let you have it, since you're part of the family and I'm just a guest, but"—Elizabeth grinned and sat down on one of the bar stools—"okay."

Amberlee handed Elizabeth a fork, then leaned across the counter and cut off a bite. "So, is my big brother being nice?"

That made Elizabeth think of that moment by the pond, and the way he'd teased her. And how very, very much she'd wanted him to do more than kiss her. But then she'd brushed him away, and in response, he'd gotten distant and cold, and just like that, the Hunter she was falling for had disappeared. Maybe that was a good thing, because the last thing she needed to do was fall in love with a brokenhearted cowboy living in Georgia.

Except a part of her suspected she was doing that very thing already. Every time he smiled at her, every time he spoke to her and his warm Southern drawl spread through her veins like wildfire, her heart tripped. Her thoughts wandered to Hunter every other second, and she realized, standing here in this warm, cozy kitchen, eating a pie that made her think of him, that now that the article was done, she had no reason to stay.

She was done here, and expected to move on.

Leave and go interview the miniature pony owner, whom she suspected wasn't even going to come close to being as interesting as Hunter McCoy. This place, this man, was one of a kind, and damned if the thought of leaving all this behind didn't leave her with a cavern in her heart.

"Earth to Elizabeth," Amberlee said. "Are you sleep-walking? Or sleep-eating, rather?"

Her face heated. "Sorry. My mind wandered. What did you ask me?"

"Rachel wanted me to ask you if you wanted to try to get together with the book club girls one more time before you go back to New Jersey. They were thinking of hitting the Thirsty Dog tomorrow night. I can't go because I'm too young, but I hear it's a blast. It's karaoke night and Rachel says if they bribe Charlotte with a couple of martinis, she'll sing. She's amazing, but so shy about it, you'd never know she could sing."

How Elizabeth wanted to stay, to be in that warm little circle. She liked those women, every single one of them, and wanted to be here next week to go to the book club and talk about the book Noralee had given her, and to enjoy those cookies, but most of all, enjoy the company of the Southern Belle Book Club.

"You all have been so welcoming to me. I guess I'm just not used to that." She ate a bite of pie, then turned to the fridge for a glass of milk. "I moved a lot when I was young, so I never really had that big posse of friends. My best friend Sophie is a travel writer, so she's always off to some country or another. But these women, they just seem to have been best friends forever."

"Oh, they have been. Grew up in each other's pockets, as Noralee would say. Even though I'm a lot younger than them, I've been friends with their younger sisters forever. This town is so small, all of us suffer through puberty and acne and bad boyfriends together, and just never grow apart. The book club girls even had one giant debutante ball together, with the white gloves and everything. Maybe it's because it's such a small town, and we've all just kind of stayed put so far. Like a giant family."

Elizabeth had never had that. She'd switched apartments and neighborhoods so many times, it was a wonder she'd been able to stay connected with Sophie. The only saving grace was that Sophie had moved nearly as much as Elizabeth, so they were often both the new girls in a new school. Sophie had formed a career out of her wanderlust, but Elizabeth was craving roots and permanence, in that same sweet way that Amberlee talked about this town. "That's really nice. Not something you see all the time."

"Then why don't you stay through the weekend? Since I'll be here, it'll be like a girls' night every day. We'll invite the book club girls over and drive Hunter crazy with an overload of estrogen." Amberlee grinned. "There's nothing I like more than driving my big brother crazy."

"I think I could make it my part-time job." Elizabeth sipped her milk. Did Hunter know he drove her just as crazy?

"You don't drive him crazy." Amberlee popped a bite in her mouth, chewed, and swallowed. "I think he likes you a lot. In fact, when he's around you, he's the happiest I've ever seen him. And I mean that. He loved Jenna, but he was always . . . trying so hard to make her happy. I've known Jenna all my life, and she was a really nice person, but just not the right one for Hunter."

Elizabeth wanted to ask what Amberlee meant by that, but doing it would show that she was interested. And she wasn't. Not even a little. "Thanks for the pie. I better get some sleep."

"Don't let Hunter scare you away," Amberlee said as Elizabeth started to walk away. "He means well, even if he's a bit overprotective."

Elizabeth turned back. "Isn't that the job of a big brother?"

"Yes, but Hunter takes it a little more seriously than most. I love him, I really do, but between him and my aunt, it's a wonder they let me breathe the air around here." She rolled her eyes. "Every time I talk about wanting to go out on the horses or help out with the training, they all have a dying duck fit."

"Why?" Surely a ranch this big could use all the extra hands it could get. And Hunter's sister clearly loved this place as much as he did. Wouldn't it make sense to let her help?

"They just worry." Amberlee picked at the pie, her gaze averted. "Maybe they forgot I grew up a long time ago."

"Then maybe you should just show them all. I haven't known Hunter long, but one thing I've realized is that he respects actions more than words."

"You're right about that." Amberlee thought on that for a second, then nodded. "Thanks, Elizabeth." She got to her feet, and drew Elizabeth into a hug. "You're a good friend."

The hug surprised Elizabeth. She had never expected to be welcomed into this world so warmly and so quickly. She wondered how in the world she was ever going to leave Chatham Ridge and all the people that filled the Silver Spur. Already, it felt like home. It was the stoneware and the lace curtains and the hugs.

And Hunter.

His face lingered at the edge of her every thought, her every word. She wondered what he was doing right now, if he was thinking of her while he worked, or if he put her from his mind the second he walked away. He drove her crazy and at the same time intrigued her to no end.

She headed upstairs, got ready for bed, and climbed under the handmade quilt, but sleep didn't come. Her mind tossed and turned, filled with a million questions she didn't have answers to. She got up, checked her e-mail, replied to Sophie's enthusiastic response after reading the draft of the article, then gave up on sleep altogether.

Elizabeth turned on her light and opened the book Noralee had given her. *Sometimes, you need a book that shows you the way,* Noralee had said as she pressed the hardcover into Elizabeth's hands. *Like a moonbeam in the forest.*

Elizabeth settled in against the down pillows and started to read. Outside, thunder rumbled in the distance and rain began to fall, but Elizabeth barely noticed. Within minutes, the story had captivated her. A woman whose life had been upended, with a sudden divorce and a job loss, embarking on a cross-country journey with nothing more than a backpack and a credit card. As the chapters whizzed by, Elizabeth became engrossed in the towns the woman visited, the people she met, each of them touching her life and changing her a little bit.

Maybe that was the message Noralee was trying to get across. That these days in Chatham Ridge, in this town as foreign to Elizabeth as another planet, would change her. Help her grow.

Maybe they already had. And with any luck, she'd leave here smarter, wiser, and with her heart intact.

Chapter 11

After he ran out of work to do in the stables, Hunter had come back in the house. He'd stood in the hall, debating between his bedroom at the opposite end of the hall from Elizabeth's, and paperwork in the office. The paperwork won. Maybe he'd do enough facts and figures to make him forget the intoxicating woman upstairs.

Two hours later, Hunter sat back in the chair in the small office, really a converted closet that had been repurposed years ago, and rubbed a hand over his eyes. All that work, and still the numbers were down, but not as bad as he'd expected. The Silver Spur was a long way from its former glory days, but for the first time in a long time, he could see hope on the horizon.

He made a mental note to thank Barbara Jean and Lizzie in the morning. With the ranch on an upward trajectory, the positive publicity in a nationwide magazine would be exactly the shot in the arm the Silver Spur needed to remind people that the ranch was back to turning out quality quarter horses.

But having the article finished meant Lizzie would leave, go back to New Jersey. Maybe as early as tomorrow morning.

Which was the best thing, really. His heart wasn't ready, he told himself, to take a risk like that again. Plus he knew where a relationship with a girl like her led—to a stormy breakup, or worse. Much, much worse.

He shut off the banker's light that shone over the mess of paperwork before him, then headed out of the office. The house was quiet, the lights off, everyone on the ranch tucked in for the night.

He thought of the bedroom upstairs, the one where Lizzie slept. He wondered if she slept in an old concert T-shirt or some silky nightgown. If she slept on the right side of the bed or the left. If she would curl into a man in her sleep, or hug the edge alone.

Not productive. He reached into the fridge, pulled out a beer, and flicked the top toward the trash. It bounced off the rim and landed on the kitchen floor with a soft ping. Hunter bent down to retrieve the runaway cap when his gaze lit on some very familiar red toenails and a pair of long, creamy legs. "Lizzie."

"Sorry. I couldn't sleep." She pushed her hair out of her eyes, which only made the tumble of curls resettle around her shoulders in one of those sexy Brigitte Bardot–poster kind of ways.

She had on a short white robe, knotted loosely at the waist. It peeked open at the top, revealing the pink satin scalloped edge of a short, silky nightgown. Way better than a concert T-shirt. His pulse quickened and he took a long pull of the beer, before the rest of his body reacted to that too-brief glimpse of satin. "Uh, want a beer?"

She smiled. "I'd love one."

He grabbed a second beer, flipped off the cap, and dropped it in the trash. He handed the bottle to Lizzie, then tapped their bottles together. "Cheers."

"Cheers." She leaned against the counter, then took a long sip.

The moonlight streamed through the kitchen window, glinting off her hair, her skin, giving her an almost ethereal quality. Last night, she'd been soaking wet and yelling at him, and he'd found her just as sexy as he did right now, a little sleepy and at total ease in the kitchen.

He leaned against the island across from her, his bare feet pairing alongside hers. It was such an easy, intimate moment. Lizzie's face bare of makeup, her hair a riot of waves, the two of them doing nothing more involved than sipping some beers. He liked this, more than he wanted to admit. A part of him almost felt guilty, as if he was dishonoring Jenna's memory by enjoying the time with another woman in the house where Jenna once lived.

"Tomorrow," he said, "I'll be all yours."

She arched a brow. "All mine? In some kind of sacrificial rite or something?"

He laughed. "No, no. I'll be all yours, if you need me to finish this interview so you can write your story."

Relief flooded her features. "Oh, thank you, but I already wrote the article this afternoon. I got pretty much everything I needed."

She was done? That meant she'd definitely be moving on. Leaving. It was what he wanted, but still the thought left him with a stone in his gut. "Are you sure? I mean, I know I delayed a lot of this whole process and I'm sorry for that. I just . . ."

"Didn't trust me." She shrugged, like the sentence didn't hurt. "I get it. I'm new and—"

"I didn't want you to leave." Well, that just kind of blurted out. And once he said the words, he realized they were true. For all his arguments against Lizzie staying, he truly didn't want her to leave.

She scoffed. "All you have done since I got here is try to get me to leave."

"Okay, so maybe I didn't go about this the best possible way. Putting off the interview, making your life miserable."

"Well, I wouldn't say you made it *miserable*. . . ." Another of those amazing smiles filled her face, and brightened the dim space. How could one woman do that so easily with something as simple as a smile?

Hunter put the beer on the counter beside him and closed the distance between them. He looked into her eyes, into those deep green forests, that seemed so much deeper and more mysterious in the dark. A man could get lost in those eyes. "Good. Because I don't want to make you miserable."

"You don't, Hunter. You make me feel"—she let out a breath—"reckless. And that scares me and excites me all at the same time."

"I know all about being scared and excited at the same time." He let out a long breath, and thought it was about damned time he moved forward, and got honest with himself, with someone else. "Jenna died two years ago, and I have spent two years in a hell of my own making. I never thought I'd care about someone else as much as I did her. Or that I'd ever want someone else like that. I kept thinking if I worked hard enough and long enough, that it would fill those holes in my life. And then you showed up on my doorstep, soaking wet and dressed like a lawyer, and I wanted you gone."

"I sensed that when the Welcome Wagon didn't show up."

He laughed. "Like that—you make me laugh, Lizzie, and

I didn't think I could do that again. I've been an ass, and I'm sorry."

"Apology accepted." She tipped her beer in his direction. "Should we start over again?"

"I can think of a better way to start over than by toasting." He planted his hands on either side of her hips, watching her breath quicken, her eyes light with anticipation. Her lips parted, still curved in a half smile, and his heart skipped a beat. "I want to kiss you. But I don't want it to influence your story."

"Well, I was seriously considered going with the Hunter-McCoy-is-a-hottie angle, but figured my editor might not like that." She grinned. "And since I already wrote the story, as long as I don't add an addendum saying Hunter McCoy is the most amazing kisser in Chatham Ridge, I think we're good."

"You think I'm an amazing kisser?" He leaned in, pressed a light kiss to the corner of her mouth, a flutter of a touch, nothing more. And still fire erupted in his veins.

She closed her eyes, as if savoring that small morsel, then opened them again. "You know you are an amazing kisser."

"Hmm . . . I don't know. Maybe I need" —he kissed the other corner, to be fair— "more practice."

"And maybe I . . .," she murmured against his lips, the words becoming mingled between their mouths, their breaths, ". . . need more kisses to make an accurate determination."

"How many kisses would you need for that?" Being this close, this intimate, was the sexiest damned thing he'd done in a long time. And he hadn't done anything more than kiss the edges of her mouth.

"Hmmm . . . I don't know." A tease lit her face. "The bigger the sample pool, the more accurate the results."

"True. Very true. Let's see if I can help you with that . . . research." Hunter trailed light kisses down her jaw, into the valley of her neck. Another kiss, then a third, meandering into the tempting hollow of her throat, inches above that slip of pink satin. Already every one of his senses was in overdrive. And this was just kissing. "If you publish these research results it, uh, might, uh, sell more issues."

"That's . . . um . . . true." She gasped when he pushed the shoulder of her robe to the side and kissed the cool skin there. One cotton sleeve slid down to her elbow, and he followed the path with his mouth, the back of his fingers. "But I would much . . . much . . . much rather keep that information to myself."

"I think that's a . . ." He slipped a finger under the spaghetti strap of the satin nightgown and drew it down the side of her arm. The swell of her breast peeked above the scalloped edge, drawing his mouth down another lazy, tantalizing road that began at her shoulder and ended above that sweet curve. "A very good idea."

"Yes," she whispered, and he wasn't sure if she meant the article or the kissing. Then she arched into him, hands sliding along the bare skin of his back, igniting his skin wherever she touched, and he gave up caring. The nightgown dropped, and his mouth covered her breast, drawing the sensitive tip of her nipple in, toying with that soft-hard bud with his tongue. His hands settled at her waist, thumbs splaying along her belly, the satin fabric sliding beneath his grip.

"Hunter . . . what are we doing here?"

He didn't know. He didn't care. All he wanted was her. This minute. "Finishing what we started."

"And after that? What then?"

He raised his gaze to hers. In the dark, her eyes were bottomless pools. "I don't know, Lizzie," he said, because he truly didn't have an answer for anything beyond right now. "I don't know."

Her face clouded. "I've never been the kind of girl who jumps off a cliff without knowing where I'm going to land. And that seems to be the only thing I've done since I met you."

He knew all about jumping off cliffs and not knowing what would be below you. It came with owning a business, and taking risks based on his gut. But with his heart, he hadn't done that in a long, long time. And even now, he could feel a part of him holding back, afraid of being wrong again. She was leaving in a day, maybe two. This wasn't a permanent arrangement, and probably ninety-nine out of a hundred men would love that.

But Hunter wasn't so sure. Did he want more? Or did he just want tonight?

"I'm not making any promises," he said, because it was the only fair thing to say. "And I'm not asking any in return."

"The last thing I need is a promise someone won't keep," she whispered, "so let's not make any of those."

He brushed that errant lock of hair off her forehead again, tucked it behind her ear. "That sounds like a good plan."

"Then we shouldn't do this," she said, but when she spoke, she moved until her lips were just below his chin, her words whispering across his jaw.

"Definitely not," he said, leaning down, catching her mouth with his own. How the hell did one woman make kissing seem like the most intimate thing a man could do? "It would be a very . . ."

"Very . . ." She licked her lips, which made her tongue slide against his.

Good God. He was going to explode right here. "Bad . . ."

"Idea," she finished. Their gazes connected, and if it was possible for two people to start a furnace with a look, they would have been heating half of Georgia in that moment. A heartbeat passed, another, then she rose on her toes and opened her mouth to his.

That was all it took to tip Hunter from the *maybe I should make love to her* into the *oh hell, yes* column. When she pressed into him, fitting against his chest like she was a part of him, he stopped thinking about whether this was a good idea or not, and instead scooped her up against his chest, then headed out of the kitchen and up the stairs.

∽

It was the way he touched her waist that had swayed Elizabeth into the *yes, oh, yes* column. Hunter's touch had been strong, secure, but almost . . . reverential, as if he was inordinately blessed just to be with her. She had never felt that honored, that wanted.

It was risky, heady. She knew, as well as she knew the beat of her own heart, that making love to Hunter McCoy wouldn't be something she would forget anytime soon. That it would open a door and break down a wall that she had always thought was impenetrable. Because he was a man who loved with his whole heart, who invested that heart into everything he did, and would expect nothing less in return.

He laid her on the soft cotton quilt of her queen-sized bed, and then stepped back. The only light came from the moon outside her window, washing the room with pale soft fingers. "You are damned beautiful, darlin'."

She *felt* beautiful when he looked at her like that, like deep-down-to-her-core beautiful. As if Hunter could see past all the bravado she'd worn all her life. "I'm just a girl from Jersey, Hunter."

"You," he said, crawling onto the bed beside her, his tall frame making the queen mattress Lilliputian, "are so much more than that."

Then she kissed him because her throat was tight and her heart was full and she was sure that if she spoke, she would tell him all the things that scared her and worried her, and all the things she had kept locked in her chest for years. His hand went between them, and he undid the knot on her robe, and spread one panel to the side, then the other.

He took a moment to look down at her, to trail his strong hand along the silky fabric under the robe. She pressed her hands to the soft cotton of his T-shirt, feeling the strength, the man beneath. "I want to see you," she whispered.

He rose, tugged off the T-shirt and tossed it on the floor. He undid the button on his shorts, the zipper, and let them drop to his feet, followed by a dark pair of boxer briefs. Then he stood there, looking for all the world like a Greek god in that shaft of moonlight, and Elizabeth had to remind herself to breathe.

"Your turn, darlin'," he said with a grin.

She reached for the hem of the nightgown and drew it over her head, tossing it atop his clothes. His hands were there a second later, big and strong and sure, on her hips, one finger hooked in the satin edge of her white panties.

"I want to savor you," he said. "One inch at a time."

Oh, my. That sounded . . . amazing. A thrill ran through her.

"I don't think I've ever been savored." Just the word made her want to melt into Hunter, the anticipation for his touch now a palpable thing.

His blue eyes held hers for a long, long time. "Then let me be the first, Lizzie."

He cupped her jaw, and traced along her bottom lip with his thumb, then leaned in and kissed her, soft at first, as soft as a cloud. Just when she wanted to beg him to kiss her hard, kiss her fast, he moved down, along her shoulder, her neck, her breasts, just as he had in the kitchen. She curved into his kisses, everything inside her already on fire, but his hands and his mouth kept up their downward journey, one agonizing inch at a time.

He tugged on her panties, and she raised her hips. A second later, they were off, gone the way of the T-shirt and the night-gown, and she was naked under the moonlight. "Damned beautiful," he whispered again, then his mouth went to the most intimate part of her, and in that instant, she knew what it was like to brush against the underside of heaven.

If she'd thought he was an amazing kisser, he was even more amazing with his tongue and what he did to her with it. He circled the outside of her, then drew her clit into his mouth and within seconds, she went from dying of anticipation to standing at the edge of a precipice. His hands covered her breasts, thumbs skating across her nipples, and she was on fire and dying, and then his tongue did something delicious and she was rising and falling, all at the same time.

He reversed direction, kissing the inside of her thigh, the divot of her bellybutton, and then her breasts, her neck, and her mouth again. She liked the taste of herself on him, the intimacy of that.

She skated her hands along his back, over the hard curve of his buttocks, the backs of his thighs. He was hard where she was soft, strong where she was weak, and he felt like the kind of man a woman could lean against and never fall down. Then she brought her hand between them and slid it along the shaft of his erection.

He let out a sharp breath, and went even harder against her touch. "You keep touching me like that, and I won't be able to wait much longer."

"Then don't, Hunter. Don't wait."

He got up long enough to fumble on the floor for his shorts and a bit of common sense from his wallet. As he slid on the condom, she chased his hand with her own, wanting again to feel the weight of him, the hardness of him, in her palm.

He brushed the hair back from her eyes, and looped the lock behind her ear. His eyes were so dark, so deep, and it felt like she was drowning, just looking into those depths and getting carried away by the storm that had been brewing from the day she arrived. "This isn't just sex for me, Lizzie. It's . . . more. So much more."

"For me, too." There were a lot of words the two of them left unsaid, two broken people who were still afraid to trust, to lean into one another.

Then the smile she had begun to know as well as her own curved across his face, and he settled between her legs. When he entered her, it was hot and sweet and amazing, all at the same time. She wrapped her legs around his hips and tangled her hands in his dark hair. They kissed as he slid in, out, deep into her core, then tantalizingly back again. Then the kisses sped up and the strokes sped up and she was clutching at him, caught in that mindless cavity between want and need. She lost track of where he ended and where she began. The tide began to rush over her, faster, harder, like a tsunami barreling toward the sand, and when she came, she cried out against him, just as he gasped her name and pulsed into her.

Her heart was still hammering when Hunter rolled to the side, drawing her against his chest. She laid her cheek on his heart, listening to it beat as fast as her own.

And in that moment, Elizabeth realized that she hadn't just made love to Hunter McCoy. She'd fallen in love with him, too.

Chapter 12

The Silver Spur was full and brimming with life again, just the way Barbara Jean liked it. Amberlee was here for the weekend, Elizabeth was still in the guest bedroom upstairs—becoming almost a part of the family already—and Hunter was out in the paddock, working with the new foals. She swore she'd seen a smile on his face this morning, too.

Barbara Jean whipped up some blueberry muffins, and while they baked, she whisked some local honey into a container of butter to top the warm muffins. The door opened and Carlos came in, already here on a Saturday morning. He looked good, with his dark skin, dark hair, and dark eyes. He was wearing a chambray shirt and faded jeans that hugged his muscular frame. "Good morning," he said.

"Good morning." She handed him a cup of coffee, with two hands so her shaky grip didn't betray the sudden desire brewing inside her. "You're working today? Don't you ever take a day off?"

"There's nowhere I'd rather be than right here," he said, but his eyes met hers when he said it and she wondered if he was talking about the Silver Spur or her kitchen.

"Uh . . . do you want butter on that muffin?" she said, because now she was as nervous as a teenager, and wasn't sure what to do except keep offering the man some food.

"It's perfect the way it is." He broke off a piece and just when she thought he was going to eat the bite, he held it out to her. In his big, strong hands, the morsel looked tempting and sweet. "You should try some."

"Oh, I shouldn't . . ." But her protest died on her lips, and when she stopped talking, Carlos brought the piece of muffin to her mouth. She opened against his touch, against his fingers, thinking this had to be the sexiest damned thing she had ever done in her life. When the bite hit her palate, she barely tasted the muffin. All she could think of was how Carlos looked and smelled, all man and soap. "That was . . . delicious."

"Everything you make is delicious," he said. "You're an amazing woman, Barbara Jean."

She loved the way her name slid off his tongue, with a tiny roll across the *r*. "Thank you."

His gaze held hers for a long time. "You know, I've worked here for as long as I can remember. And ever since my divorce, I've noticed you. Noticed the way you smile. The way you talk. The way you walk."

Her face heated. Was she blushing? Good Lord, she was. "I . . . I don't know what to say." And she didn't. It had been so long since she'd been around a man like this, a man interested in her, a man who complimented her, that Barbara Jean's brain could only sputter.

"Say you'll have dinner with me. Tonight. Tomorrow night. Soon."

Dinner with him? As in a date? Half of her wanted to say yes, go right now, but the other half, the half that had spent too many years telling herself she didn't need a man to be happy, exercised caution. "Oh, I shouldn't. I mean, I have the ranch and the kids and . . ."

"This ranch can run for a few hours by itself," Carlos said, in that quiet, confident way he had. "And those 'kids' are grown adults now. Time for you to live your life, too."

Wasn't that what Amberlee had been saying to her earlier? That it was past time for Barbara Jean to put herself first?

He broke off another bite of muffin, and pressed it to her lips, letting his touch linger there. She opened her mouth against his fingers, almost kissing them as she ate the piece of muffin.

"Think about it. I'll come back for your answer." Then he gave her a grin, and headed out the door.

Barbara Jean leaned against the counter, fanning herself with the dish towel. Was that what she thought it was? And what was she going to do about it? If she did date Carlos—and that was a big *if*—it could get complicated quickly. He was an employee, and she was . . . sort of a boss, sort of just an employee, too. Maybe better to steer clear of anything like that. Except she kept watching his retreating figure until he disappeared inside the barn.

Just then, Elizabeth came into the kitchen, looking sleep-rumpled and happy. She slid onto a bar stool and smiled at Barbara Jean. "Good morning."

Barbara Jean popped to attention, put on a bright smile and pushed Carlos from her mind. "Good morning, sweetie. There's fresh coffee and warm muffins this morning. Oh, and Noralee is coming by to visit this afternoon. She keeps trying to wheedle my raspberry thumbprint recipe out of me."

"That's nice," Elizabeth said. Her gaze went to the back of the property, lingering on the long white stable. Apparently Barbara Jean wasn't the only woman pining after a man on this ranch.

Barbara Jean sipped at her coffee, trying not to be obvious about pushing for information. "You seem a little tired this morning. Late night?"

"I was, uh, writing." She slid off the stood and crossed to the coffeepot, her back to Barbara Jean. "I finished my article. I wanted to show it to you and Hunter before I sent it off to my editor. I know that's not normally the way it's done, but you all have become . . ."

"Like family," Barbara Jean finished.

A warm smile filled Elizabeth's face. "Exactly. I don't know how I'm going to go back to New Jersey."

"Then don't. Stay here." Barbara Jean covered Elizabeth's hand with her own. She liked this girl, liked her a lot. "Writers can live 'bout anywhere. And you already fit into this place like a fence post in the ground."

"It's not as simple as that." Elizabeth leaned against the counter and toed a circle on the tile floor. "I wish it was."

"Sweetie, life is as simple as bees making honey." Barbara Jean poured a second cup of coffee for herself. "You find what makes you happy and you build your hive right there. You nestle in and make a home."

"Is that what you did here? Hunter said you moved here after his mother died."

"I did." She cupped her hands around the mug. Her mind reached back, and her heart filled with warm memories and cool regrets. So many years, so many decisions. Not all were the right choices, except for one. "I never thought I'd settle here, either. I was traveling the world, living my own life. I had given up on ever having the kids-and-dog kind of life."

"Given up? Why?"

"The Lord blessed me with broken parts down there. And I say that it's a blessing, because if I could have had my own kids, I would have been married to the wrong man, and I wouldn't have moved in here and finished raising Hunter and Amberlee." There were many days Barbara Jean was grateful for the call that brought her back to the Silver Spur, back to center again. She'd been going down a bad path with Joey Dylan, the boy who'd convinced her to ditch everything and travel all over. He'd been wild and unpredictable, a whirling dervish in the wind, her mother had said. Far as Barbara Jean knew, Joey was still sailing the seas and traveling the mountains, living off whatever he could make at odd jobs here and there.

For years, she'd used the experience with Joey to shield her from heartbreak. But maybe it was just her own fears, the same ones she saw in Elizabeth, that made her worry she'd pick the wrong man again and be sad and lonely in the end. Was that what Carlos was? The wrong man? Or was the dependable, strong, affable horse trainer someone she could lean on, build something with?

"The wrong man." Elizabeth shook her head and let out a gust. "I seem to have picked a lot of those even though I saw my mother do it a hundred times and vowed I'd be smarter about the whole thing."

Barbara Jean gave Elizabeth a half smile. She heard so much of herself in Elizabeth's voice, in the internal debate she was having between giving her heart to a place, a man, and just being on her own. "The way I look at it, you get the wrong men out of your system, so that when the right one comes along, you are smart enough to hold on tight."

Elizabeth's gaze went to the window. "And what if you're not sure if he's the right one?"

"The only way to be sure is to get quiet with yourself." It was how Barbara Jean had made the decision to change everything and come here. She'd never looked back, never regretted it for an instant. And maybe now, with Hunter and Amberlee grown and on their own, it was time, as Amberlee had said, for Barbara Jean to find a man who wanted a slightly set-in-her-ways woman with great baking skills. A man who really liked her quesadillas and muffins. "In the end, you listen to what your heart is saying."

Elizabeth scoffed. "Mine doesn't talk much."

"Oh, sweetie, our hearts are always talking. We just let the rest of the world get too noisy to hear it."

"That's good advice," Elizabeth said. "But awfully hard advice to follow."

As Elizabeth headed out of the kitchen, Barbara Jean whispered a little prayer that Elizabeth's heart would keep her here, on the Silver Spur. And that Hunter's heart was smart enough to recognize the one woman in the world who could fill those aching spaces deep in his soul.

Bill Winters, DMV, was a short, stout man with an owly face and wire-rimmed glasses. He'd been the vet in Chatham Ridge for as long as anyone could remember, and was as good as a family member to most of the ranchers in the area. He tucked his supplies back in his medical bag, then nodded toward Hunter. "See you soon, Hunter."

"Thanks, Bill." The two men shook. "Appreciate you coming out." Even though Hunter was the one to make the appointment with Doc Winters, when the time had come to meet the vet, Hunter hadn't wanted to leave Lizzie's side. He could have stayed in that bed with her for a week, and even that might not have been enough time. The way she had curled into him in her sleep had awakened this bone-deep protective instinct in him. It had been sweet and wonderful and the best way he had started a morning in a long, long time.

"Not a problem." Doc Winters stowed the bag in the back of his SUV. He'd checked on the injured foal, pronounced Hunter's bandage job good enough, then spent some time assessing Dakota. Even though the accident had been two years ago, Hunter had wanted the doc to make sure there wasn't any residual damage that Billy Ray might not have mentioned. "You've come a long way with that mare. Honestly, I never thought she'd be the same after that accident."

"Me, too." Dakota still had a ways to go, but Lizzie and her apple slices had made progress Hunter had thought would never come.

"It's gonna take time and patience, but she'll be a good horse." Doc Winters pushed his glasses higher on his nose. "She'll never be a showstopper again, though."

"I don't want a showstopper. I just want . . ." Hunter's gaze went to Dakota, standing against the far end of the small paddock, her tail flicking at the flies, her head averted from the humans who had been invading her space.

"Patience and time will heal more than the horse. She was in a bad place at Billy Ray's, and I suspect things were a lot worse for her than he let on." Doc Winters's face hardened. "I don't like to speak ill of others, but Billy Ray is one of those men who doesn't deserve the horses he has. I'm glad you rescued Dakota before it was too late, and I'm sure she's glad, too."

"She's got a funny way of showing it," Hunter said.

"Give her time." Doc Winters clapped a hand on Hunter's shoulder. "Give her time."

Then the old vet was gone, hiking across the field to a

battered, muddy SUV that had enough miles on it to have gone around the world twice. Dakota kept her back to the humans, not at all happy to have been disturbed with a prodding from the vet.

Hunter gestured to Foster. "You stay here." Foster whined, but lowered his body to the ground and let out a doggy sigh.

Hunter unlatched the gate and slipped into the corral. Dakota eyed him with a wary glance. "Shhh, girl, it's okay. I come bearing gifts this time." He reached in his pocket and pulled out a carrot. "See?"

Dakota's tail swished, but she didn't move.

"Listen, I know you aren't at all happy with Dr. Bill coming over and touching you, but this is all going to be better soon."

The horse ignored him. She stood tall and still, her eyes wide. Her nostrils flared, and she shuffled back. He thought back to what Doc Winters had said. He'd heard rumors about Billy Ray, and the vet's words only confirmed Hunter's worst fears. Billy Ray wasn't a man known for being patient with his horses, and more than one had turned out skittish, mean. For the hundredth time, Hunter cursed his father for selling Dakota to a man known to treat his horses badly. Based on how Dakota reacted every time a man came within ten feet of her, there was more than an accident at the root of her fears.

Hunter understood that. Hell, hadn't he pushed away every human being in his life in the last two years? He'd gotten along a lot better with the four-legged creatures on this ranch than the two-legged ones.

Except for Lizzie. Just as she had with Dakota and the apple slices, Lizzie had a way of pushing at those walls he had built around his heart, forcing him back out into the sunshine.

Maybe that wasn't such a bad thing. And maybe if there was hope for Dakota, there was hope for him, too. After that amazing night with Lizzie, hope was definitely taking root in Hunter's chest.

"Can I try?"

He turned at the sound of his little sister's voice. "You think you have the magic touch?"

"You know I do." Amberlee grinned. "The horses always liked me best. Because I'm not grumpy like you."

"I'm not grumpy."

"Yes, you are. Grumpiness practically emanates from your veins." Before he could protest, she'd plucked the carrot out of his grip. "Hence, the nickname Grumpyface."

"Wait, do you have your inhaler?"

Amberlee let out a dramatic sigh. "I'm fine, Hunter. I haven't had an incident in years. Stop acting like I'm ready to die or something. I'm eighteen, not eighty."

"Amberlee—"

"Hunter, please." She raised her chin in a pleading smile. "Please? I'm fine. I swear."

He never had been able to resist his little sister when she gave him those big eyes and guilt-inducing *please*s. Maybe it came from being so much older than her, but he'd always been indulgent when it came to Amberlee. "Okay, but be careful. At the slightest hint of—"

"Yeah, yeah, I know. Now watch how the expert does it." His sister loped forward, swinging the carrot and talking softly to the horse. Unlike with him, the vet, and Carlos, Dakota didn't back up or tense at his sister's approach. Once again, he suspected Billy Ray had hurt this horse. Maybe even ruined her for male handlers for the rest of her life. The thought made his blood boil.

"Heard you need a little exercise, Dakota," Amberlee said, inching forward with the carrot. "I do, too. Maybe we could exercise together sometime. What do you think?"

Dakota's ears perked at the new person in her corral. She eyed the carrot.

"Yup, we'll take it easy. Because you've got an injury and I'm out of shape." Amberlee closed the distance between herself and the horse. Dakota's tail flicked, but she didn't move. She kept her attention on the carrot. Amberlee held the carrot toward the horse at the same time she reached for the lead.

Dakota's gaze flicked to the leather strap now in Amberlee's hand, then away. The mare munched on the carrot, calm as could be.

Hunter climbed onto the wooden fence and propped a heel on the lower rung. He watched his sister, cautious, worried. It had been years since Amberlee had had an asthma attack, but that didn't mean she couldn't have another. He watched for any sign of tension, any hitch in her breathing.

"So, Hunter, since I'm here for a few days . . . I was thinking I could help you train again," Amberlee said, her back to him, her attention still on Dakota as she petted the mare. Her tone was as casual as a spring breeze, but Hunter knew there was a much bigger question in there.

"Absolutely not. There's a big difference between you giving a horse a carrot and riding them. You know what the doctor said—"

"That was six years ago. I'm all grown up now, Hunter, in case you haven't noticed. And you don't have to go around keeping me in this little cocoon." She turned and crossed to him. "Just because one bad thing happened doesn't mean another's going to happen anytime soon."

"You're my responsibility—"

"I stopped being your responsibility the day Aunt Barbara Jean moved in. And I stopped being hers the day I turned eighteen. You are not responsible for every person in the world, you know."

"No, I'm not. But I am responsible for every living, breathing thing on this ranch. Including you." He shook his head and cursed. His sister didn't understand, didn't see the weight on his shoulders. Ever since Jenna had died, that responsibility had multiplied in Hunter, feeling ten times heavier than before. No way was he going to let his little sister take a risk like that. "You are not helping me train the horses. And that's final."

"Dictator," she muttered.

There were days when his sister pushed every last button, and other days when they were the best of friends. Today was not one of those days. He could tell, by the set of her lips and the tension in her shoulders that she wasn't happy with him. At all. She didn't understand that it was his job to protect her, to watch out for her. She didn't remember all those days she'd been scared and crying after their mother had died, when she'd begged him to make it all go back to the way it used to be. It had been easier after Barbara Jean arrived, but for a long while, it had seemed like the world had consisted of just Hunter and Amberlee, pairing up to withstand the changing tides. Now she wanted her freedom, wanted him to turn off that older brother protective gene. Amberlee didn't understand the overwhelming need Hunter felt every single day to shield the people he loved, the animals he loved, and make sure every living creature on the Silver Spur was far from harm.

The one time he'd let down his guard, taken his eyes off what was important, Jenna had died. He'd vowed that day to never, ever, let anyone or anything he loved get hurt.

"You'll thank me some day," he said. "Now head on up to the house and see if Barbara Jean needs any help."

Amberlee propped her fists on her hips. "I am not a child, Hunter. Quit treating me like one."

He just ruffled the top of her head and headed off to do some work. She might be mad at him now, but eventually his sister would come around, and go back to calling him Grumpyface or whatever the jab *du jour* was. That was when he knew he and Amberlee were okay.

He spent an hour or so checking on the foals, brushing down the horses, cleaning up the stalls. When he was done, he rounded the corner of the stable with the wheelbarrow and saw Amberlee, her thin back pressed against the side of the stable. She was bent forward, hands on her knees, drawing in a deep breath. He dropped the wheelbarrow and ran for her, his heart in his throat. "You okay?"

Her cheeks were red, her eyes wide. She looked thin to him, too thin, and he wondered if she was taking care of herself. "I'm fine. Just leave me alone."

"Are you having an attack? If you are, we should get you to the doctor—"

"I'm fine, Hunter. For God's sake, quit acting like I'm a china doll. I was a little out of breath, nothing more. I'm just fine. You're not my mother, so quit acting like you are." She pushed off from the wall and stalked across the lawn toward her car.

He headed toward the house, because if he followed after his sister, she'd read him the riot act. Maybe she was right and he was being overprotective. Okay, yes, he was overprotective. Maybe it came from their mother dying when Amberlee was a little girl. From the years of being responsible for every life on this ranch. From losing Jenna, and seeing how one instant could change everything.

He paused on the porch step and watched his sister sit in her car, probably sulking about him confronting her. Her radio was up so loud, the car thumped like a drum. Later, he'd smooth the waters with Amberlee. Right now, he was in too good of a mood to let anything bother him.

Because inside the doors of that house was Lizzie. All morning, everything he did, the thought of her lingered at the fringes. He'd had to force himself out of bed this morning, when all he wanted to do was stay with her and repeat what they had done last night. She was becoming part of his life, and he was starting to think that might not be such a bad thing. Seeing Lizzie's smile every day, hearing her call his name, bringing her to his chest at night.

"Good morning, Auntie," he said to Barbara Jean, drawing her into a one-armed hug. "I smell muffins."

"Is that an honest-to-God smile on your face?"

"What? I smile."

Barbara Jean rolled her eyes. "You know what I mean."

"I do, indeed, Auntie." He pressed a kiss to her cheek, then reached behind her to steal another muffin. Damn, he was in a good mood. Best mood he'd been in for as long as he could remember. Even after the little disagreement with Amberlee, the smile Hunter had woken with still lingered.

"I saw that."

"I know you did." He grinned, and thought he hadn't felt this . . . light in years, maybe ever. The sun was shining, the horses were running, and the day was as beautiful as it got. "Where's Lizzie?"

"Lizzie?"

"Suits her better, don't you think? Elizabeth is too stuffy."

His aunt rolled her eyes. "You are smitten, positively smitten."

"For one, I am a hardened cowboy from the hills of Georgia. That's not an adjective you can use for me."

"Smitten," she said again, tapping a finger against his chest.

He wasn't admitting to anything. If he did, his aunt would drag him off to the First Presbyterian Church before he finished his breakfast. "For another, Lizzie and I are just . . . friends. Good friends."

"The kind of good friends that hold hands and kiss and do Lord only knows what late at night?" Barbara Jean smiled and shrugged. "I have two people running around this house with big goofy smiles on their faces. It doesn't take a mechanical engineer to figure out what that means."

"A gentleman does not kiss and tell," Hunter said, then he took a big bite of muffin, and washed it down with some coffee. The last thing he was going to tell his aunt was what had happened last night between himself and Lizzie. And not just because it had been earth-shatteringly amazing and a part of him didn't want to share that with anyone else in the world but Lizzie.

Just thinking her name brought a smile to his face. Maybe Barbara Jean was right and he was smitten.

Might not be such a bad thing. A man could get used to having a woman like her around all the time. She lingered in his head and heart like honey, sweet and tempting.

"A gentleman would marry that girl before she runs back to Jersey," Barbara Jean said, as if reading his thoughts. And taking them up a hundred notches.

Marriage? Who said anything about marriage? That was taking twenty steps further than Hunter had pictured in his head. Though the thought of Lizzie running back to Jersey, of not waking up every morning and seeing her smiling face, damned near tore his heart in two.

Smitten.

Nah, never. Not him.

"You are a hopeless romantic, Aunt Barbara Jean. And I"—he glanced around the kitchen, down the hall—"should get back to work."

A knowing smile crossed his aunt's lips. "She went upstairs to change. If you wait five minutes, she'll be back down for breakfast."

"Well, you know, those muffins are mighty good. Wouldn't hurt to eat another one. Or three. Guess I might as well settle myself here, so I don't track crumbs all over the house." He grabbed a plateful of muffins, then sat down at the table.

"Good Lord. I'm leaving so I don't have to watch you moon over her." His aunt kissed his forehead, like he was a kid again. "Even if seeing that smile on your face makes my heart so full, I think it might burst."

Barbara Jean headed out of the kitchen. For a moment, Hunter ate his muffin and drank his coffee, watching the horses through the window. Loaded Gun was prancing around the corral, his head high, his tail proud. The mares and foals roamed happily in their paddock, occasionally raising their heads to listen to a sound or catch a scent on the wind. In the distance, the Georgia asters waved, happy and sunny and beautiful.

Then a sound drew his attention and he turned to see Elizabeth standing in the doorway of the kitchen, wearing a lemon yellow dress that skimmed along her knees. His heart stuttered.

"Good morning," he said. Frankly, he was surprised he managed to string two words together at all. The woman was positively stunning.

"Good morning." A smile flitted across her face, then a flush filled her cheeks and he wondered if she was thinking about last night. He had left her bed early this morning, before the crack of dawn. She'd looked like an angel, long blond hair splayed across the pillow, the sheet dipped low enough to expose the ridges of her back. He'd come so close to staying there, in that bed with her, waiting for her to wake up.

But then he'd realized that she wasn't staying. That in the light of day, she was still a city girl who was going to blow out of his life as fast as she blew in.

"I brought you a copy of my article," Lizzie said. "I wanted you to read it before I sent it off to my editor. See if there's anything I got wrong."

He took the sheaf of papers she handed him. He tried not to be disappointed that she didn't want to talk about last night. That it all circled back to that article. The damned article. He should have been glad—that article was part of securing the future at the Silver Spur—but a part of him was disappointed. "You want me to read it now?"

"Sure. I need to e-mail it as soon as possible." She thumbed toward the sink and gave him an embarrassed smile. "And . . . I'm just going to do the dishes so I don't hover over you like the panicked first-time writer I am."

She started the water, and he settled in against the banquette to read. From the first word, he was captivated. Lizzie had begun the article by painting a picture of the ranch with her words and it was as if he were watching a movie about the Silver Spur.

The quarter horses stand in the breeze, tails and manes flowing behind them like flags. Their nostrils quiver, their ears prick. They sense the change that is coming, the change that is on the horizon for the Silver Spur.

He read straight through, forgetting his breakfast, his coffee going cold. When he looked up, she was leaning against the sink, her face anxious, a dishtowel clenched in her fist. "Well?"

"That was . . . incredible."

Her face brightened, and amazement filled her features. "You liked it?"

"I didn't just like it." He laid the papers on the table, then got to his feet and crossed to her, standing in the same spot they had last night, feet paired on the tile, their bodies a few inches apart. "I loved it."

"I wasn't sure if I described the reining competitions correctly or the—"

"It's perfect. Damned perfect. It's like a song." He shook his head. "Now I sound like some mushy greeting card."

"You? No one would ever consider you mushy."

"You saying I'm all strong and hard and tough?"

She ran a hand down his chest and his pulse ratcheted up a few notches. He wondered if he had enough time to take her back upstairs before he finished up the tasks on his list today. "Definitely. Strong, tough, and . . . hard."

He chuckled. "Darlin', you keep saying things like that and I am not going to get a lick of work done today."

"And would that be a bad thing?"

"The horses might not like it. They like to get fed on time. Have clean stalls. But there is some work I could probably skip." He trailed a finger along her lips. "And since it's such a nice day, maybe we could ride up to the pond again. Get a little swimming in."

"I don't have a bathing suit with me."

"You aren't going to need one." Just the thought of seeing her naked again made his pulse race.

She cocked a smile at him. "What if I get sunburned?"

"Oh, I'll make sure you don't." He kissed her lips, shifted his hips against hers. He'd just left her bed a couple hours ago and already he wanted to be back there and stay there for a week. "I'll make damned sure you don't."

Elizabeth started to say something in return when the back door opened and Carlos charged into the kitchen. His face was white, his breath coming in fast gasps. Carlos, who never panicked, was always as steady as a rock, looked like he'd just seen a ghost. "Boss, it's your sister. She saddled up Loaded Gun before I could stop her. I thought she'd be okay, but then I saw her bag on the floor of the stable. And I saw this beside it." He held up the inhaler.

Hunter's blood ran cold. Why would his sister do something so foolish? What was she trying to prove?

And in that instant, he was there again with Jenna, with that fight, with Jenna running out to the truck, squealing out of the drive, angry and not thinking straight, and all because of him. Because he'd been too stubborn, too hard-headed, too everything. Just like he had been with Amberlee earlier today. She'd kept telling him she wanted to train with him and instead of soothing her, he'd laid down the law and made her mad. Made her do something foolish.

He was out the door and on a horse of his own a minute later. Hunter rode harder and faster than he'd ever ridden before in his life. He pushed his horse, nudging at Zeph to hurry up, just hurry the hell up. Zeph was no match for the younger, faster Loaded Gun, which put Hunter at least five minutes too far behind. Five minutes could mean the difference between life and death.

All he could think of as he rode was the last asthma attack Amberlee had had, six years ago. He'd found her on the ground, slumped beside her horse, her lips blue, her breath so strangled, he was so afraid that she wasn't going to make it until the paramedics arrived. Two days in intensive care, two agonizing days, and Hunter had vowed he would never let his sister near the horses again.

Until today. Until he'd convinced himself that she was okay, all these years later. That she was eighteen, old enough to know if she had her asthma under control. He never should have agreed. Never should have let her out of his sight.

He pounded across the ranch, then up the hill, rounding past the pond. He didn't see her anywhere, didn't see the horse. Then a nicker, and Hunter finally spied Loaded Gun, standing riderless in the middle of the field of Georgia asters. He spurred Zeph, and they thundered up the embankment and then down into the wide field of purple, the flowers parting like a wake as they plowed through the field.

Hunter slowed the stallion's pace as they neared Loaded Gun. "Whoa, whoa, boy." He leapt off the horse, and dropped to the ground beside his sister. "Amberlee!"

Her face was red, her eyes wide with panic. But her lips were still cherry pink, and her breathing was bad, but not horrible. It wasn't as bad this time, not as bad. He kept repeating that in his head, as he raised her head, shook the inhaler, then held it to her mouth. "Calm down," he whispered against her ear, holding her to his chest, trying to breathe with her, to ease the fear in her big blue eyes. "It's okay. Breathe in. Out. In. Out. You've got this."

She was stiff in his arms, but she did as he said, drawing in deep of the medicine. Hunter held his own breath, waiting, counting out interminable seconds. And then, inch by inch, Amberlee relaxed, each breath coming easier than the one before.

Her color returned to normal, and the panic drained from her face. She sat up, and brushed the hair out of her face. "Thank you."

He helped her to her feet, but she was already brushing him off, shoving the inhaler into her back pocket and turning toward her horse. Was she crazy? Stubborn? Or a little of both?

"You're not going anywhere," he said. "You can't ride him again, after what just happened."

"I'm fine, Hunter."

He grabbed her arm, stopping her from taking another

step. "You had an asthma attack. If I hadn't found you and had your inhaler—"

"Stop playing what if. You did find me, now I'm fine." She yanked her arm out of his grasp. "I'm going for a ride."

"You are not taking that horse anywhere." He let out a gust of frustration. "What were you thinking? If you're still having trouble with your asthma—"

"I'm fine."

"That inhaler in your back pocket would disagree. You should have told me. If you had, I would have—"

"Forbidden me from doing what I love." She parked her fists on her hips and glared up at him. "I'm eighteen, Hunter, and that means I can take care of myself—"

"I just rescued your ass, so try another tack."

She shrugged, like it was no big deal. "I forgot my inhaler. That's all."

"You can't just do that." He plucked the inhaler out of her pocket and held it in front of her. This tiny little thing, which had saved his sister's life more than once, and that she treated as a weight around her neck. "You can't just forget this, because when you do, you can die, Amberlee." His voice cracked and he wanted to both hug his sister and send her to her room at the same time. In his eyes, she was still the little girl he had protected and sheltered when their mother died, the little sister who'd sat on the end of his bed a hundred times and asked him why their mother was no longer there. "Don't you realize that?"

"It's you who needs to realize I'm not some kid you have to baby anymore. Even Elizabeth said you are too strict, and I should just live my life." She poked a finger into his chest. "I'm fine, and I can handle myself and I can handle the horses and I don't have to be cooped up like some . . . invalid."

Elizabeth had said that? "If you could handle it, you wouldn't have been on the ground gasping for air."

"I just forgot my inhaler. Quit making it into a big deal." She yanked the plastic container out of his hand and tucked it in her pocket again. "I'm fine. You can go back to work."

"And what are you going to do?"

"Get on the horse and ride." She said it like it was no big deal, like he hadn't just found her on the ground five seconds ago.

Why was she so stubborn? Why didn't she see what a risk she was taking? "Amberlee—"

Before he could stop her, she charged off, grabbed Loaded Gun's rein and lifted her foot into the stirrup. "I'm going whether you want me to or not, Hunter. I'm eighteen, and this ranch is part mine."

She was right, and he hated that. She was old enough to make her own decisions, even if he thought they were foolish ones. "You're playing that card now? What happened to common sense? To the fact that it's not smart to go riding a horse after what just happened?"

"Yeah, maybe it's not." She swung her other leg over and settled into the saddle. "But that's not going to stop me, either." Then she kicked at Loaded Gun's flanks and a second later, horse and girl were gone.

Hunter climbed into Zeph's saddle, and aimed his horse in the direction Amberlee had gone, then reined him back. His sister was headstrong and determined, and going after her would only make her dig her heels in further. So he watched her go, his heart in his throat, then turned Zeph toward home.

Chapter 13

Elizabeth took a deep breath, then hit send. Sophie had read the article and pronounced it a masterpiece. Barbara Jean had loved it, as had Hunter. All that mattered now was whether her editor thought the same. While nerves churned in her gut, Elizabeth ran a preliminary Internet search on the miniature horse breeder in Atlanta, and started a list of questions.

But each word she jotted down put her further away from Chatham Ridge. That was the reality. Her job wasn't here, her home wasn't here. By the end of the day, she needed to get in her car and leave.

Barbara Jean had told her to stay, and oh, how Elizabeth wanted to. But then she glanced back at her bed, the sheets still rumpled and scented with Hunter's cologne, and she realized he hadn't asked her to stay. They'd made incredible, amazing, holy-hell-unforgettable love, but in the end, there'd been no promises asked or made.

It was what she'd told him she wanted. Only, she'd sorta lied.

Elizabeth slid the ruby ring on her finger. It settled against her right ring finger like it was made for that spot. The faux stone glinted in the light. How many times had she seen this ring on her mother's finger and thought her mother was crazy for wearing it, knowing it was fake? Always believing in pipe dreams and illusions. And here Elizabeth had gone and done the same thing.

She'd gotten swept up in this ranch, in these people, and dreamed of forever. Like a fool, like her mother. Elizabeth took off the ring and shoved it into her pocket. No more of that nonsense. From here on out, reality only.

There was a knock on her door and Noralee poked her head in. "Hey there! Barbara Jean said you were still in town, working away at that article. Thought I'd pop my head in and say howdy."

"I just finished the article. Hit send. It's done." A little sense of pride filled Elizabeth's chest. She'd done it—and on time.

"Well, good for you. I bet it will be amazing. Can't wait to read it in print." Noralee came into the room and nodded toward Elizabeth's packed bag, sitting on the end of the bed. "So now you're leaving?"

"I have to go to Atlanta." Elizabeth tore her gaze away from the bag because the bag was by the bed, and just a few hours ago in the bed had been Hunter and. . .

Elizabeth sighed. "There's a miniature horse breeder there my editor wants me to talk to. And then . . ."

"Home?"

"Yes." Wherever that was, because right now, that empty apartment in Trenton sure didn't feel like home.

Noralee sat on the edge of the bed. Her face was kind and

warm, her smile big enough to welcome an entire town. Elizabeth was sure going to miss Noralee and her bookstore.

"Thank you for the book," Elizabeth said. "I've really been enjoying it. I'm almost done with it, too."

"What'd you think about that woman in the book?" Noralee asked. "And how she left everything she knew to head off into the unknown?"

"I think she was really brave. Just leaving like that, going off on a long adventure."

"Which is what you did, coming here."

Elizabeth shook her head. "Oh, I wouldn't call this an adventure. Besides, I'm going back. This was a temporary destination. Sort of like a vacation."

"Perhaps so," Noralee said. "But the more important question, the one that woman asks herself over and over at each place she visits, has being here changed you?"

"Yes," Elizabeth said softly, thinking of the day by the pond, the night in her bed, "it has."

"Then that's all that matters. I think every person we meet, every experience we have, every book we read"— Noralee waved at the hardcover on Elizabeth's nightstand— "should touch our lives, shift our direction a little bit."

Elizabeth didn't want to think about all the changes coming to Chatham Ridge had brought to her life because it hurt too much. Soon enough, she would leave here and it would all become a distant memory with time. Lesson learned: never trust your heart to a cowboy whose own heart was already broken.

Noralee propped one leg on the bedframe and wrapped her hands around her knee. "You know, when I was young, I had a terrible wanderlust. My momma always said the only way she could keep me home was to tie me to the porch railing. I'd wander here, there, everywhere. Always going on

adventures. Climbing trees, swimming in creeks, doing whatever the boys did. I told my momma there was no way I
wanted to be tied to anything more permanent than the leaves
on a tree."

"I'm the complete opposite. I'm not the kind to go here,
there." Elizabeth shrugged. "Maybe it's because my childhood was so crazy. Dozens of moves and changes. I wanted
a place I could depend upon. Stay in for a really long time."

"Yet you gave all that up to come here."

"It was only for a few days. I'm not staying." Every time
she said those words, they hurt. She thought maybe if she said
it enough, the reality would sink in. But it only made her ache
in a place buried so deep, she wondered if she would ever
forget the few days she had spent at the Silver Spur. And the
cowboy with intoxicating blue eyes.

"That's what I always said. I wasn't staying. I was moving
on, to bigger, better things. Then I met this boy." Noralee
smiled. "It's always about a boy, isn't it? Oh, and he was
quite the boy. Tommy Lee Rouson. He was one of those tall,
dark types. Had a smile that reached for miles." Noralee's
features turned wistful. "He was in love with me. He was
bad as a newborn puppy, following me everywhere I went,
with that big old goofy smile. Right after senior prom, he
asked me to marry him. Wanted to take a job at the factory
where his daddy worked, set us up in a little house at the
back of his granddaddy's land."

Elizabeth glanced at Noralee's bare left hand. "And you
said no?"

"I heard those words, *settle down*, and I panicked. I'd seen
where settling down got my momma. Dirt poor and living
in a glorified cardboard box. When I was a little girl, Momma
worked in a laundry, and every time she came home, her
hands were red and raw from the water and the soap. My

daddy, well, he was never much use after four o'clock. The whistle would go off at the plant and he'd hit the bar with his buddies. Come stumbling home sometime after dark, eat his dinner and go to bed, then get up and do it all over again. The last thing I wanted was to live a repeat of that life, with me and Tommy Lee as the stars." She smoothed the blanket and shrugged. "Who knows if we would have ended up that way. Tommy Lee was a dreamer, always talking about how one day he'd run the plant and make his old man proud. I thought he was just all bluster and bluff, like my daddy after a couple of Buds. But wouldn't you know, ten years ago, Tommy Lee became the plant manager. He's still there, far as I know."

"Did he ever get married?"

"Yup. Met a really nice girl who lived in Alabama. She moved here, they set up in a little house on the end of a quiet street, had three kids." Noralee shrugged. "It ended happy for my momma, too. She kicked my daddy out, scraped together her pennies and bought the shop, carved out a space for her dream of a dress shop, before I turned it into a book-store. Now I'm there, sitting in the same place every day, and happy as a pig in mud to be doing it."

"But you didn't marry your true love."

Noralee waved a hand. "Tommy Lee was too much of a momma's boy for me. I like a man who can brush his own teeth and wash his own socks. I got enough to do, taking care of me and that little corner of my world. That bookstore, it . . . fills my soul." A peaceful smile stole across Noralee's face, the kind of smile that said she'd found where she wanted to be and had no desire to ever leave. "Anyway, I told you this, not to fill your ear with my nonsense, but because I want you to know that sometimes we get pushed in a direction we don't expect. That's part of the message in the book I gave

you, which is why I picked it out. If we're smart, we'll take
the chance offered to us by this new direction. Because sometimes it doesn't come around a second time."

"I haven't been offered any chances like that," Elizabeth
said. Her gaze went to the window, then back to the suitcase
by the bed. There really was no reason to stay, to delay her
departure. "No promises, no future."

"Then that Hunter is a fool. Barbara Jean says he has
fallen for you like falling over a cliff, hard and fast."

Elizabeth thought of last night, of the exquisite care and
attention Hunter had paid to every single inch of her body. If
it was true that actions spoke louder than words, then she
believed Barbara Jean. But in the end, Hunter hadn't said any
of this, and she'd be a fool—a fool just like her mother had
been a hundred times—if she put stock in a man like that.

∾

Hunter rode back to the Silver Spur, pushing his horse the
entire way. A hundred times, he glanced over his shoulder,
hoping to see Amberlee, but neither she nor Loaded Gun
had returned. Zeph had worked up a lather by the time
Hunter unsaddled him and brushed him down, then led him
back to the corral.

Every few seconds, Hunter's gaze went to the land at the
back of the Silver Spur, hundreds and hundreds of acres of
riding space. But Amberlee didn't appear, and the sun began
ticking its way from its zenith. Maybe he should go back out
after her.

He paced the yard for a while, realized that wasn't getting
him anywhere, and instead headed up the walkway toward
the house. Amberlee wanted him to see her as grown up, to
let her make her own decisions, good or bad. Maybe it was
time he did that. Didn't stop him from worrying and berating

himself for letting her get back on the horse. Damn it. Why couldn't his sister listen to reason?

Just before he pulled open the door, he saw Lizzie sitting on the porch, her feet perched on the railing, a book in her lap. She looked so damned beautiful there, wearing a pale yellow dress that skimmed her curves. Her bare feet, with that peek of crimson toenail polish, reminded him of last night, their feet paired together on the tiled kitchen floor. The cowboy hat was tipped over her brow, shadowing her gorgeous green eyes.

But then he thought of what Amberlee had said, about how Lizzie had told her to ignore his warnings and just do what she wanted. She'd encouraged his sister to take a chance she shouldn't have taken. This was what he got for letting a stranger into his life, into his home. Especially this woman, who had done nothing but drive him crazy ever since he met her.

Lizzie looked up at the sound of his footsteps. "Hunter. You're back. How's your sister?"

"Bull-headed and riding alone. She refused to listen to me." He cursed and shook his head.

"Gee, and who does that remind you of?" She smiled at him, but he didn't echo the gesture.

"Are you saying I'm stubborn?"

"I'm saying your sister is a lot like you. And maybe she set out to prove something to you and herself."

"Prove what? That she can take a risk she shouldn't be taking?" He waved toward the corral, his voice rising with each syllable. The worry chased up his throat. What if Amberlee had another attack? What if it was so bad, she couldn't ride back? His sister was an experienced rider, a real natural in the saddle, but he'd also seen her down on the ground, immobilized by her ravaged lungs. "That she can refuse to listen to the people who love her? To the doctors? To common sense?"

Lizzie shifted a few inches back. "Why are you yelling at me? I'm not the one that took off on the horse."

"No, but you encouraged it. With all that talk about going after your dreams, and taking risks. My sister, for whatever reason, thinks you are the voice of wisdom when it comes to her future, and so she got on that horse, and damned near died today." This was why he didn't need this woman in his life. She muddied the waters, disrupted the predictable calm. Made him, and everyone around him, take risks they shouldn't. Like fall for her. Trust her. Open his heart to someone who was just going to leave.

"Amberlee will be fine," Lizzie said. "She's a smart kid and—"

"You don't know that Amberlee will be fine. She's out there on that horse, going God knows where, with about as much sense as a headless fly. Because you encouraged her to live her life, or whatever other New Age bull you gave her."

"New Age bull?" Lizzie's eyes flashed, her cheeks flared. "She's eighteen, Hunter. She's supposed to be branching out on her own, and yes, taking risks. She's been around horses all her life. I'm sure—"

"You don't live here, Elizabeth. You barely know a thing about horses. You don't get to tell me how it's going to be. Nor do you have a right to tell my sister it's okay for her to do something that foolish."

Lizzie got to her feet and tucked the book under her arm. "You really think that's what I did? On purpose? That I'm marching in here and taking over?"

"I'm saying that since you got here, nothing has been the same and if there is one damned thing I wanted in my life, it was for everything to be the same, every damned day."

"All I did was come here to help you out. I didn't come to Chatham Ridge to do anything other than interview you and leave." She shook her head and bit her lip. "You're the one who changed everything, the one who made me—"

She didn't finish. He knew he could push her, could ask her what she wanted to say, but if he did, he knew he'd be opening a vein that he didn't want to open. Right now, he was barely holding what he had together. "You've written your article. I assume you have another one to write. Someone else to interview. Somewhere else to be."

Her face crumpled and he felt like an ass of the highest order. Then she recovered a second later and raised her chin. "I do have somewhere else to be. So I guess that's my cue to leave. I already loaded my car up earlier. I was just waiting to say good-bye. This seems like a damned good time to do that." Lizzie slipped her feet into her shoes, then headed down the stairs and toward her car.

He wanted to stop her, to take it all back. But he didn't.

She got halfway there, then turned around and came back up the steps. "Do you know what your problem is, Hunter McCoy? You're so damned busy being protective that you're using it as a shield, a wall. Yes, a bad thing happened two years ago, and yes, I'm sure you have a lot of regrets. No one would blame you for that. But you can't spend the rest of your life paying a penance at the cost of relationships with the people who care about you."

"I have relationships with the people who care about me."

Her eyes filled, and she shook her head. "No, Hunter, you don't. You're like a porcupine, anytime anyone gets too close, you push them back. Well, don't worry, I'm leaving before you drive me away." He wanted to stop her, and almost did when her step hesitated on the walk. But in the end, Lizzie got inside her car, started the engine and pulled away.

He stood on the porch, watching her go, and told himself it was for the best. A woman like her, a woman who over-turned the predictable, steady days he had followed for two years, would only distract him from getting right back to the comfortable rut he'd been in.

∽

Elizabeth made it all the way to downtown Chatham Ridge before the tears started to fall. She thought she'd at least make it out of the area, but as she neared the bookstore and the sign for the Three Buck Bundle and the place where it had all started, her heart began to break.

The light was on outside the bookstore, just like it had been that first time, a bright, welcoming beacon. Elizabeth paused at a stop sign, but when she saw the door to the Happy Endings Bookstore open and the book club women enter, in a balloon of laughter and smiles, Elizabeth swung her car left, parked out front, then grabbed her book from the seat and dashed inside. She knew she should keep going, head up to Atlanta, or back to Trenton, or somewhere other than staying in this town, but she just couldn't leave that warm light behind just yet.

"Elizabeth!" Charlotte drew her into a tight hug, like a long-lost friend. Elizabeth hugged her back and knew she'd miss these women a great deal when she went back home. "I'm so glad to see you again!"

"And look, she got the memo." Rachel grinned, then pointed at the dress Elizabeth was wearing, a match for the dresses all the other women wore. They were like a sea of pastels. "We always dress up on girls' night, because if there's one thing other women can appreciate—"

"It's awesome shoes on a friend. Especially a friend

who's the same shoe size." Katie Ann drew Rachel into a one-armed hug. "Right, Rach?"

"You can suck up all you want, but I'm keeping these Manolos." She kicked one foot forward, displaying a strappy pair of blue heels. "J.W. bought them for me for a wedding present, and I swear, I am going to wear them to my funeral. Open the bottom of the casket, baby, cuz momma's got some shoes to show off."

Laughter filled the bookstore with affection and light. Elizabeth liked that feeling, the way it wrapped around her like a cloak. For a second, she allowed herself to imagine living here, seeing these girls every week, going to book club and girls' night and shopping trips. But no, she was leaving. Going to Atlanta, maybe, then definitely back to New Jersey. Where she had friends, but none like these women. They were like Sophie multiplied, and Elizabeth knew it would hurt to leave them. Hurt a lot.

It wasn't just the women or the store that it would hurt to leave. But she refused to think about Hunter, because if she did, she'd crumple, and a Jersey girl didn't crumple. Didn't fall apart. Didn't let one man break her heart and soul.

"Are you all here for book club again?" Elizabeth asked Rachel. To change the subject, to think about something else.

"Nope. That's not till Tuesday. Tonight is ladies' night. We're just stopping in at Noralee's for some dinner—"

"Cookies," Charlotte corrected. "Which encompasses several food groups, so we call it a meal."

"Exactly. Dinner, before we hit the Thirsty Dog. That's the local watering hole," Rachel explained.

"Chatham Ridge's version of a dating website," Katie Ann added. "If your standards are low—"

"And your vision is poor," the others chimed in, then burst into gales of laughter.

"Oh, well, I'm glad I got to say good-bye then," Elizabeth said. Though she was sorely tempted by the cookies and the friendship. Not to mention the thought of hanging around with all these women who already felt like lifelong friends.

"Why don't you come with us?" Charlotte asked. "There's always room for one more. And the guys at the Thirsty Dog will practically break an ankle trying to meet the new girl in town."

New girl in town. A reminder that she was only a visitor, and not one for much longer at that. Besides, was there really a single man at the Thirsty Dog or any other bar that she wanted to meet and talk to? The only man she wanted to see lived on the Silver Spur, and that man had broken her heart. Even if she went out with the girls, Elizabeth knew her mind would be on Hunter, on that night they'd shared, of how she'd given him her heart and had gotten nothing in return. "I'd love to, but I have to go to Atlanta tonight." Get out, leave, before it hurt any more. "I already reserved a room and everything."

"That's too bad." Katie Ann accepted a cookie from the platter in Noralee's hands. "You're going to miss out on a lot of really bad beer and even worse pickup lines."

Noralee brought the platter around to Elizabeth. "Here, hon. Have a cookie. It makes everything better."

Elizabeth took a giant chocolate chip cookie from the platter and tried to work a smile to her face, but it wobbled, then fell, and before she knew it, tears were welling in her eyes and her chest was tight. Damn these stupid tears. Damn this town. Damn Hunter McCoy.

Noralee immediately handed the platter off to someone else and enveloped Elizabeth in a warm, vanilla-scented hug. So accepting, so caring, so . . . perfect. Elizabeth felt like she'd come in from the cold. Before she knew it, she was hugging Noralee back and tears were leaking from her eyes.

"There, there. Don't cry. I swear, the cookies don't have that many calories," Noralee said.

That made Elizabeth laugh. She stepped back, and swiped at her eyes. Someone handed her a tissue which only made her eyes water again. "I'm sorry. I just got . . . emotional. I don't know why."

A soft, understanding smile filled Rachel's face. "Because it's hard to leave something you love."

"I . . . I don't . . ." But the protest died on Elizabeth's lips. What was the point in fighting it any longer? A handful of days and wham, she'd gone and fallen for the one man who hadn't fallen for her. "Oh God, I do."

Noralee beamed. "Nothing wrong with a little love."

"I don't love him. I couldn't possibly. I barely know him and I don't do this kind of thing." *And he doesn't love me back. And I have a life in New Jersey. And I'm not at all sure what I want or what I'm going to do next.*

"Hon, all of us say that." Charlotte laid a hand on Elizabeth's arm. "Then next thing you know, you're running down the aisle and tying empty Miller Lites to the bumper."

Rachel laughed. "In case you haven't noticed, Charlotte is our resident romantic."

"Well, there's nothing to get romantic about here," Elizabeth said. The last thing she wanted these women to think was that there was something to her relationship with Hunter. Okay, so maybe they had shared some kisses—not just kisses but lift-you-off-your-feet-and-leave-you-breathless kisses—and yes, had one unforgettable, amazing, nothing-compared-to-it-night together, but that didn't make it a relationship. Especially not after what had happened today, with him lashing out at her because of his sister. He was a man still stuck in neutral, and the last thing she needed was another relationship that was going nowhere. She'd been there already with Roger—who was already a distant memory, which told her that her engagement had been nothing more than biding time.

Until she met the one man who turned her inside out and upside down and invaded her every thought. She'd checked her phone a thousand times, wishing for a text, a call, anything that said *come back, I'm a moron.*

Best for her to leave. Put Chatham Ridge in her rearview mirror. Okay, so she hadn't left yet, but she *would* leave. Soon. Very soon. And she would forget all about Hunter McCoy as soon as she did. At least that's what she told herself. Maybe if she repeated it enough in her head, it would come true.

"He doesn't love me," Elizabeth said, to the women and herself, "and besides, it's too fast. And it's a crazy thing to even think that we could fall in love over a few days."

Her heart was racing, her pulse pounding. Good Lord, was she having a panic attack at the thought of being in love with Hunter McCoy? Because she wasn't in love. Not at all.

Rachel put a hand on Elizabeth's back. "Oh, sweetie, just breathe."

"I can't. I don't do this. I don't make rash decisions or fall for men overnight." Or uproot her entire life plan because some quirky little town and one cantankerous cowboy had grown on her. The sooner she got on the road to Atlanta, the better.

But she stayed where she was, among the women and the cookies and the hugs. Because some tiny part of her didn't want to leave, not them, not the town, and especially not him.

A wry smile crossed Noralee's face. "Seems to me you did both those things, honey. And there ain't nothing wrong with that at all."

"But I'm going back to New Jersey." Saying it enough might make it happen. Like get in the car and get on the road real.

"Why?" Rachel asked.

"Because . . ." And the sentence trailed off. Why would she go back to New Jersey? To an apartment that she'd never really liked, an apartment as sterile as the rest of her life? To a job she had quit? To a life she'd never really settled into, not like she had here, with the bookstore and the ranch and the horses and—

Hunter.

Just the thought of him made a chasm open in her heart. She missed him already, missed him like she'd lost a limb. And she'd only been gone for thirty minutes.

How was she supposed to move on, move forward, and forget those days at the ranch?

"I should go," Elizabeth said. "It's getting late and—"

"And hotel reservations can be changed." Rachel looped her arm through Elizabeth's. "Come with us, honey. We have all been where you are, and if there's one thing us girls are good at, it's finding ways to forget men who have broken our hearts."

"Oh, he didn't break my heart. He just . . ." Elizabeth sighed. She thought of the night they'd spent together, the day by the pond, the way he called her Lizzie and touched her hair, and left her wanting more. "He just pretended it didn't exist."

"Well, the man is a fool," Charlotte said. "So let's head over to the Thirsty Dog and drink until you forget you ever met Hunter McCoy."

Elizabeth let out a small laugh. "You think the bar has enough alcohol for that?"

"Honey, the Thirsty Dog is well stocked, with liquor *and* men," Rachel said. "One way or another, you'll be leaving there with a smile on your face."

∞

Hunter stood outside Dakota's stall, watching the horse nibble at the apple he'd brought. She still wouldn't eat it from his hands, but she had come close enough to take it from the top of the gate. He'd been out here every day, sometimes several times a day, working on getting close to the horse, and now, finally, he could see a ray of hope. Foster lay at Hunter's feet, his tail swishing against the wooden floor, waiting for his master to finish working and go back inside the house.

Except Hunter didn't want to go back inside. Lizzie had left, and even as he told himself it was exactly what he wanted, his heart ached. He kept expecting to see her come running into the stable, or see her striding across the lawn, or hear her say his name the way she had in her bed. Like one long syllable of a sigh.

Damn, he missed her. But it was for the best. He wasn't the kind of man who should settle down with anyone. Relationships just distracted a man. Like it had today, when he'd missed the signs that Amberlee was still dancing on the edge of a medical cliff.

His sister had been gone all afternoon. He'd seen her and Loaded Gun cresting the hill in the distance a couple of times, so he'd known she was okay. The urge to send out a search party and find her still rose in his chest every few minutes. Instead, he'd done what he always did—he'd worked until his thoughts blurred from exhaustion. Then he'd come here, to Dakota's stall, partly to work with the horse, and partly because Dakota reminded him of Lizzie, of that amazing smile on her face the day the mare had eaten an apple from her palm.

God, he was desperate. Like he thought an apple and a horse would make him forget Lizzie's incredible smile or the way her eyes darkened with desire, or the way her touch had awakened a part of him he'd thought had gone dead.

You're like a porcupine, anytime anyone gets too close, you push them away. Well, don't worry, I'm leaving before you drive me away.

Hunter let out a gust and dropped his head into his hands. Regrets piled on his shoulders, a heavy burden that never seemed to ease. No matter which way he turned, what he did, he seemed to be hurting the people he loved.

Or worse, driving them away, as Lizzie had said. He rubbed at his temples, wishing he could do over the last week, the last year, the last two years. The last afternoon, most of all. "Goddamit," he whispered, to the heavens above, to himself, to everything. "Goddamit."

Something nudged at his head, something heavy and strong, leaving a streak of wet along his forehead. Hunter lifted his gaze to big brown eyes filled with patient interest.

Dakota.

Very slowly, Hunter raised a hand, and trailed a gentle touch along the horse's velvety muzzle. "Hey, girl."

Dakota stilled. Her breathing grew heavier, faster, but she didn't move. He kept his light touch on her, and kept talking, his voice low and quiet, even. "Guess I'm not the only one having a tough night, huh?"

The horse snarfled, but didn't back away. Her tail flicked from left to right, then back again. Her eyes remained wary, waiting, he was sure, for the dynamic to shift, for him to give her a reason to fear him. He wanted to tell Dakota not to worry, that he would never hurt her. That she should trust him.

Trust me.

He'd told Lizzie that, then he'd gone and lashed out at her. Blamed her for Amberlee's impetuousness.

And driven Lizzie away. Lashed out at her like everything was her fault, when really, the fault resided in his chest. In this wall of regret he couldn't seem to get past.

"You're making good progress with that horse."

Hunter turned, and saw his aunt standing a few feet away. She looked pretty, with her hair down, and without the apron that seemed to be a part of her daily outfit. He wondered vaguely if Barbara Jean was dressed up to go somewhere. "Dakota is getting there," he said. "She's come a long way since the day I brought her home from Billie Ray's."

Barbara Jean nodded at Dakota. "A horse like that, one that's been scarred and hurt, needs patience and time," she said, unwittingly repeating Doc Winters's advice from earlier. "Seems you've been giving her plenty of both." She took a couple steps closer, and leaned on the stable wall beside him. She gave Dakota a light rub, then turned to Hunter. "Almost anything that's been hurt and scarred needs patience and time. For a while."

He scoffed and shook his head. He'd had enough of these kinds of conversations with Barbara Jean over the years to know what she was driving at. "You're not talking about the horse."

"Nope."

"I'm not a horse, Aunt Barbara Jean. It's not the same thing."

"Nope. I suppose it isn't." She put a hand on his shoulder, a light, knowing touch. The kind that said she'd been there through his worst days and was going to love him through whatever else came down the road. "But, like Dakota, you've been scarred and hurt, and you keep standing in your own little stall, shut off from the world. Then someone comes along that gets you to open up, and instead of ambling toward that new life, like Dakota here just did, you just shut the stable door and keep everybody away. 'Cept, unlike Dakota, you do that by growling and lashing out, and hurting the very people you don't mean to hurt."

People like his sister. Like Lizzie.

Which was exactly what he'd done on the porch this afternoon. Like an idiot. *Porcupine.* Yeah, that was the right word for him. "It's better that she left," he said. "She'd never be happy here."

"Did you ask her that? Or are you just telling yourself that?"

He pushed away from the stall and crossed to a wall of tack. He straightened the harnesses and bridles, even though they were already neat and ordered. "Either way, she's gone. So I'm just going to go back to work."

"And bury yourself in guilt for another two years?" Barbara Jean came up and put a hand on Hunter's back. "Don't you think it's about time you found a way to forgive yourself and move on? You were not the one behind the wheel that night, Hunter. You were not the one who caused that storm. You were not the one who—"

He wheeled around. "I'm the one who brought Jenna here. I'm the one who tried to convince her that she would be happy with me." His voice cracked and he drew in a deep breath. "And I'm the one who let her leave that night when she was upset and angry."

"You had a fight. She left, and she got in an accident." Barbara Jean's gaze softened. "That's all it was. Stop blaming yourself."

"Who the hell else am I going to blame?" He ran a hand through his hair, then cursed and stepped away. He thought of Johnny Ray's face, of the funeral, of the pain that had hung over Chatham Ridge ever since, like a heavy fog. "It was my fault, Barbara Jean. Mine and mine alone."

Barbara Jean's face scrunched and her eyes grew hard. It was a look he knew well, the look that said she was about to show him where he'd gone wrong.

"Come here." She grabbed his shirtsleeve and hauled him over to Dakota's stall again. "I want you to look at that horse."

"I was just here—"

"Look at her." Barbara Jean waited a beat, until Hunter's gaze rested on Dakota. On the deep scars running along her legs, the wariness in her eyes, the nervous flicker of her tail. "Do you blame yourself for what happened to Dakota? What Billie Ray did to her?"

"Yes. No." He threw up his hands. "I don't know. I should have bought her back sooner." But the ranch had been struggling financially, and for a long time it was all Hunter could do to keep them from going under. He'd been too busy trying to save the whole ship to stop and rescue the one treading water.

"Your *father* sold her, not you. When he did that, he knew full well what kind of man Billie Ray was, and he sold that horse to him anyway." Barbara Jean rested an arm on the gate and looked at Dakota. The horse watched the two humans with wary interest. She stood stock-still, a few feet away. "I heard a little something from Noralee about why Billie Ray beat her," Barbara Jean said. "You know she's friends with Art, who's lived next door to Billie Ray for years. Art told her he sees a lot of what happens over there, maybe too much."

"What did she tell you?"

Barbara Jean let out a sigh, then looked up at Hunter with sympathy in her eyes. "The night this happened, Billie Ray had been drinking, like he did most days, and I don't know if Dakota sensed something was wrong, or what she felt when he tried to load her in the trailer. He said she was being difficult, blamed it all on the horse, not his idiot self. He loaded her, along with a foal that he was going to bring to an auction. Sell them both, probably to get more money for whiskey, knowing his irresponsible drunken priorities." She cursed, something Barbara Jean did so rarely, the words seemed to shock the air. "So he starts the truck, and Billie Ray, he's weaving before he even gets down the ranch drive-way. The truck tips a little, because he takes that turn, you know that one onto Alderman, it's a little hairpin and it's nasty in the dark, even worse when you ain't thinking with your whole head. The trailer starts to tip, and Billie Ray overcorrects and lands his truck in a ditch, hits it hard, totals the whole front end. Billie Ray got a nasty cut on his fore-head, and a hell of a black eye.

"In the trailer, Dakota panics. She kicks at the back gate, kicks it hard, but it doesn't open all the way. She goes out anyway, cuts the hell out of her legs, but she doesn't run. She comes back, beats on the other side and gets that foal out. The foal took off, gone who knows where. Last I heard, Billie Ray never found it." Barbara Jean's gaze rested on Dakota, and her features softened for a moment at the horse who had hurt herself just to help another. "Billie Ray got out of his truck, mad as a wet hornet at the horses for getting out. Takes off his belt and . . ."

Hunter closed his eyes. He couldn't imagine ever doing such a thing to any living creature, much less a horse who had done nothing wrong. A horse who trusted, loved, worked for the humans who cared for her.

"Noralee said she heard that Dakota was lucky she could still walk after Billy Ray got done with her. He didn't call a vet for two days, and even then called one in from another county, probably so no one would know half the damage on that horse was from his belt and not the trailer."

Hunter's hands curled around the hard wooden ledge until his knuckles whitened. "I'll kill him. Take him outside and whip him like he did her."

"As much as I would love for you to do that, and line up for a chance to beat him myself, that isn't going to heal this horse. It isn't going to make up for what happened to her. All you can do is love her and give her a place where she can thrive and be happy."

"I'm doing that." For the rest of her life, Dakota would be well cared for, if it was the last thing he did. He would never sell her, never let her go. She meant too much, not just to the ranch, but to him. Having her here was like holding on to the roots of the Silver Spur, to all that it had once stood for—and would once again.

"For her, yeah." She covered his hand until his grip on the gate eased. "For you, no."

"Aunt Barbara Jean, I'm eating and sleeping," he said. "Thriving."

"Thriving isn't being happy, Hunter."

He shook his head. "Happiness is overrated."

Her features softened. "You can't go back and undo what happened in the past, Hunter. You can't take those truck keys out of Jenna's hands. You can't stop the rain from falling. You can't stop her from driving too fast. But what you can do is honor her memory, help those who loved her heal, and stop locking the stable doors on your own self."

Hadn't he been trying to do those very things? Or was

his aunt right, and he wasn't really doing anything more than locking himself away with work?

He shook his head. "It's not that simple."

"It is." She raised up on her toes and cupped his face, her wise blue eyes full of love. "You brought Dakota around, made her trust again. Now it's your turn."

Chapter 14

As the sun set, Amberlee finally turned toward home, hot, sweaty, and hungry. Her inhaler wasn't the only thing she'd forgotten when she'd hopped on the horse today. She should have packed some snacks, some water. But all she'd wanted was to get on the horse, feel the wind in her hair, the power under her legs, and watch the world rush by at a gallop.

It had been so long, far too long, since she'd gone out for a ride. All those years of Hunter and Aunt Barbara Jean worrying about her like she was as fragile as a newborn chick.

So what if she'd had to use the inhaler three times today? So what if her chest felt tight, her lungs like bricks? She was happy, and free.

But also a little scared. She'd come too close to ending up in the hospital, or worse, and all because she'd been too stubborn to admit the truth to her family. She'd been so tired of being the one they hovered over, worried about, but in the end, if Hunter hadn't done both those things, she likely wouldn't have made it out of that field on her own. She'd ridden for hours after that, thinking she could put enough distance between the things she didn't want to face and the realities that had hit her hard, but as the sun began to wane, she realized running away was far from growing up.

So she urged Loaded Gun toward home. The horse was still young, given to his own notions about pace and direction, and by the time she reached the stables at the Silver Spur, her body ached. All she wanted was a bed and a giant dinner. She'd stayed out too long, far longer than she'd intended, and now she was paying the price for overdoing it.

She slid off the horse, then paused a moment, drawing in a deep breath, letting the air settle in her chest. As she straightened again, she saw her brother waiting for her. His face was a scowl, but the look eased the closer she drew. "I'm back, so you can call off the bloodhounds."

He rolled his eyes. "Can we have a civil conversation?"

"I don't know." She raised her chin, even though every inch of her ached to collapse on the ground. But she pretended she wasn't tired, because if Hunter had any idea how she was feeling, he'd be on her back in a second. "Are you going to lecture me?"

"Nope." He reached forward and took the horse's reins from her hands. "But I am going to take care of your horse while you eat that sandwich I left on the shelf." He nodded toward a small plate on a wooden ledge in the stable.

While Hunter led Loaded Gun away, Amberlee stumbled on her way toward the sandwich. She grabbed the plate, the glass of sweet tea beside it, and sank onto the floor to eat and drink. She wolfed the turkey and cheese sandwich down, drank a little tea, then laid her head back against the wall and waited for the food to settle.

A few minutes later, Hunter returned. He took one look at her, and dropped onto the floor beside her. He was so much taller than her, broader, but he was like a comforting wall. She'd never admit it, but just having him sit beside her made Amberlee feel a hundred times better.

"You look like hell," he said.

"Thanks. I can always count on you for the big compliments."

He gestured toward the empty plate. "Need another sandwich? I can run up to the house—"

"I'm fine." The food and few minutes of sitting had done her a world of good. She felt almost human again. "Just let me rest here a bit."

He stopped staring at her like she was sitting at death's door, and leaned back against the wall, resting his hat on his knees. "You done?"

"Yeah. I ate the whole sandwich and drank most of your tea. Sorry."

"I didn't mean are you done eating," he said. "I meant are you done running off and acting like a brat?"

She bristled. Great. Here came the lecture. Just what she needed after today. "I'm not a brat."

"Way I see it, a brat is someone who doesn't listen to the people who love her." He shrugged. "Does her own thing."

Amberlee sighed and started to get to her feet. Maybe it had been a mistake staying here this weekend and having this conversation with Hunter. No turkey sandwich was worth him reading her the riot act. "I'm not having this discussion again, Hunter."

"And," he continued, putting a hand on her knee, stopping her from leaving. "Someone who sticks to her guns. Until everyone else realizes she's near all grown up."

Amberlee had a ready argument on her lips, then stopped

when she finally heard what he'd said. Amberlee sank back onto the floor, settled against the brother who irritated her and protected her and loved her. "'Near all grown up'?"

"Well, you *are* eighteen. Living in a dorm. Making most of your own decisions. But even when you're eighty, you'll still be my little sister and I'm still going to worry about you and boss you around." He ruffled her hair. Nine times out of ten, that annoyed her. Not this time.

"You're not so bad." She laid her head on Hunter's shoulder. As always, it was steady and strong, like a rock, just waiting for her to need his strength. "And sometimes I need to be bossed around. A little."

"Is that your way of saying I was a tiny bit right today?"

She nodded. Lord, she was tired. All the way to the tips of her toes tired. "I guess I just wanted to prove I was okay. Even if . . . even if I'm not."

Hunter's arm went around her. He drew Amberlee tight against his side and pressed a tender kiss on the top of her head. "I know you're not. You have to take better care of yourself. Talk to us when you're tired or worried or need a break. And most of all, listen to the doctor."

"But if I listen to the doctor, I won't be able to ride," she said. How many times had she sat on the cold vinyl table and heard the doctor tell her to stay far, far from the horses? And there's nothing I love more than being here, Hunter. Please don't take that away from me."

"Maybe it's time we found another doctor. One who will help you find a way to manage your asthma so you can go back to training again."

"*Another* doctor? *More* tests? I am so sick of being—" She stopped then looked up at him. "Wait. Did you say go back to training the horses?"

"Yes, I did. But on one condition." He put up a finger.

"You listen to the medical advice and don't push it too hard. And you still get a degree in something, because Lord knows I'm sick of being the only smart one in the family." He grinned, teasing her.

Tears welled in her eyes. Amberlee pushed at them with the back of her hand, but they were chased by new tears, and so she let them fall because she was only eighteen, after all. And sometimes it was nice to only be near grown up. "I will, Hunter. I promise. And you really are the smart one. You're doing great with the ranch."

"I'm doing my best, and hoping that's enough. I love you, kid, and you're the only sister I got. So maybe I do get a little overprotective, but I do it because I don't know how I'd get through the day without you around here to annoy me."

She slugged him, not hard, just enough to tease him and thank him, without getting all mushy. "Have I ever told you that you're a good big brother?"

"Nope."

"Good. And I'm not about to start." But she grinned as she said it, and gave him a quick kiss on his cheek. Hunter pretended to wipe off her germs, but really, he was grinning like the moron he was. Amberlee said good night, then headed back inside the house, her belly and her heart full.

∞

In the end, Elizabeth turned down the drinks with the girls, and got in her car. The longer she stayed in Chatham Ridge, the worse it hurt. A light rain started up as she headed out of town, like a faint echo of the night she had arrived. It made her want to turn around and run back to the Silver Spur, to start all over again at the beginning. Except doing that would mean reliving the painful end, and there was no way she could do that twice.

She drove through the night, keeping Sophie on speakerphone beside her, like a virtual passenger. "Tell me I'm doing the right thing," Elizabeth said.

"You're not. But that's okay. You're doing something, which is better than just sitting around, pining for him."

Elizabeth laughed. "I thought you were supposed to support me."

"I do. In everything. You know that." In the background, some kind of calypso music played, at whatever beach destination Sophie had traveled to this week. "But if you want my unvarnished, straight-up opinion . . ."

"You know I do. That's why I called."

"You fell in love with this guy. Fell hard. For him, his town, even his horses. And even though he is going through a whole lot of hell in his own head, he sounds like a keeper."

A sign for the next exit appeared above Elizabeth's car, like a beacon. She knew that exit would loop her back around to Chatham Ridge. To the Silver Spur. To Hunter. She shifted to the right lane, debating. "Do you think I should turn around?"

"No. I think you should go to Atlanta, do that interview, and let him sweat it out. Then go back to that little no-mall town and tell Hunter McCoy to either get his act together or lose the best thing to ever come along in his life."

If Hunter had seen her as the best thing ever to come along in his life, he wouldn't have let her leave. He would have made it about more than a single night in bed.

"I'm not going back there, Sophie. I can't." She eased back into the middle lane, ignoring the exit. A second later, a green sign that said ATLANTA, 30 MILES appeared on Elizabeth's right. Another ranch, another horse, another cowboy, but it wouldn't be the same, not one bit. "I don't even think I can go to Atlanta. It's too close to Chatham Ridge. Too close to Hunter."

"So you're just going to run back to New Jersey?"

"My life is there. My stuff. My job, if I can get it back." Though just the thought of sitting under those fluorescent lights for one more minute made Elizabeth want to run for the hills. Still, it was a steady paycheck and a mindless way to help her forget the last few days. It would be enough, she told herself. It would have to be.

"Whoa, whoa. Wait just a minute," Sophie said. "You're really going back to all that?"

"It's what I know, Sophie. It's what's comfortable."

Sophie scoffed. "First sign of trouble and you go running for the security blanket."

"I am not. I'm doing what makes sense." She rested her hand on top of the steering wheel and looked at that faux ruby ring. The streetlights caught it from time to time and made it sparkle, almost as if it were real. Almost. "I'm doing what makes sense," she said again.

The phone was silent for a moment. The miles ticked by, the road nearly empty at this time of night. "Do you remember that Christmas your mother took us to the park?"

Elizabeth thought back. "We were, what, eight, maybe? Nine?"

"Yup. All geeky and gawky, with long legs and no sense of style."

"Hey, speak for yourself. I rocked those striped pants."

Sophie laughed. "Only you could rock neon striped pants. And they did make you kind of glow in the dark."

"I remember that. My mother kept shining a light on me so I'd 'pop,'" Elizabeth shook her head. Her mother and her crazy ideas. Life had been an adventure, that was sure. Just not always one with a nice destination. "I loved that park. It had that little treehouse and the swinging bridge connecting it to the castle. I used to go there and imagine it was my house, and I would live there forever."

"With a knight on a white horse and a happily ever after."

"That's what I get for reading too many fairy tales. No knight ever came by, and three weeks after Christmas, we were evicted and had to go move to that one-bedroom disaster on Jenkins Street." That was the reality. There was no man on a horse who would ride in and save the day, no Santa coming down the chimney and leaving back rent on the kitchen table. There was only the next place, the next upheaval, the next broken dream.

"But that Christmas, it was special," Sophie said, her voice soft with memories, "and wonderful, and perfect. It snowed that night, too. Just a sprinkling, but enough to look pretty in the lights. And do you remember, you and me, sitting on the top of the slide, trying to catch the snowflakes with our tongues and promising to always come back to that place?"

"We never did get back there." Elizabeth cruised along the highway in the middle lane, the only car as far as her eyes could see. But in her head, she was back in that perfect little neighborhood, the best one she'd ever lived in, with her best friend living just a couple blocks away. It had been one of the few Christmases that she remembered feeling like maybe things would stay the same a while. That maybe she could have the kind of childhood her friends had, with annual traditions and predictable days ending around a family dinner table. What had Noralee said? *I figure the Lord planted me here so I could bloom.* That's what Elizabeth craved more than anything, a place to plant herself, so her life could bloom into more than just this empty shell.

"No, maybe we haven't been back there in real life," Sophie said, "but we are doing it in our hearts. I travel the

world, visiting real castles and treehouses and magical
places. And you did it when you went to Chatham Ridge."

"There are no snowflakes there." No castles. No fairy
tales. Especially no knights on a white horse, wanting to
whisk her away to a treehouse castle. There was only the
reality of a man she loved who didn't love her back.

Sophie chuckled. "Always the realist, Liz. There doesn't
have to be snow. Remember what your mom said?"

Elizabeth's mind reached back into the past, to those days
before she realized how her mother's dreaming had cost
them places to live, the father of the week, the dependable,
stable life that Elizabeth craved. That night, two or three
days before Christmas, had been one of the best memories
in Elizabeth's chaotic childhood. A magical night, when it
seemed anything was possible, as if Santa himself would
sail on by in his sleigh. The whole adventure had been
another of her mother's whims, when she'd woken the girls
in the middle of the night from their sleepover and bundled
them up, then taken them to the empty park to watch the
first snowfall of the year.

"She said that no matter how old we got, that we should
always remember to take time to soak up the magic." Elizabeth scoffed. "That doesn't help when you're out of money
and food and the landlord is banging on the door."

Sophie ignored the sarcasm in Elizabeth's words. "Did
you find magic in Chatham Ridge?"

Elizabeth thought of the sunrises she'd caught every
morning, like the world was being draped in gold. The field
of rare purple flowers, waving steady, happy faces at the
ranch. The moment with Dakota, when the injured horse
took a step toward her and plucked one slice of apple off her
palm, then another. That night with Hunter with the moonlight sneaking through the windows, when he'd made her

feel treasured, desired, special. That had been magic, the best kind, because it had flowed so naturally from her dreams into her reality. "Yes, I did."

"Your mother believed in magic because she knew it was such a hard thing to find, and an even harder thing to hold on to," Sophie said. "It's that feeling in your belly when you think about Hunter, that heady, intoxicating rush that terrifies you and excites you and makes you want to jump his bones, all at the same time. That's the magic. And that's worth holding on to."

Elizabeth shook her head. "How'd you know that's how I feel every time I think about him?"

"Liz, I hear it in your voice." Sophie's tone softened, her words dropping into a soft, concerned whisper. The kind that said she knew her best friend well, and wanted her to do the right thing. "You're head over heels for that guy, and instead of grabbing hold of something so rare some people spend their whole lives looking for it, you're running away."

"I'm not running away. I'm moving on. There's a difference. And besides, he doesn't feel the same way."

"How do you know? Did you ask him?"

The car covered another mile or so. Elizabeth glanced in her rearview mirror, as if she expected Hunter McCoy to appear behind her, chasing after her, begging her to stay. But he didn't, so she stepped on the gas pedal and added more space between herself and the man who had broken her heart and didn't even know it. "I don't have to. I already know the answer."

∞

Barbara Jean hadn't been this nervous since she was in ninth grade and asking some boy in her algebra class to the Sadie Hawkins dance. She couldn't even remember his name, or if they'd shared more than one awkward dance, but she remembered the feeling, that anxious knot in the pit of her stomach that told her she was either taking an incredible risk or about to make an incredible fool of herself.

She straightened her hair for the tenth time, then brushed invisible lint off her dress, and applied a quick swipe of a lipstick she wore so rarely, she was sure it had expired a year ago. Then she headed back out of the house and over to the small cabin to the west of the stables. A single light glowed on the porch of the cabin, another lit the rooms from within. She glanced toward the stables, but didn't see Hunter. Just as well. The last thing she needed to explain to her nephew was why she was going out to Carlos's room late at night.

She hesitated outside the door, then blew out a breath and berated herself for being nervous at her age. For goodness sake, the worst the man could say was that she had read him wrong. Then they'd go back to just being coworkers, and he'd go back to getting his coffee in the morning and she would forget this whole thing ever happened. Before she could chicken out, she raised her hand and knocked.

Carlos opened the door a second later, and Barbara Jean drew in a sharp breath. He was wearing jeans, slung low on his hips, but he'd taken off his shirt, and what she saw before her was nice. Very nice, indeed. A strong, muscular chest, with a trim waist that tapered down to those jeans and made heat curl in her belly. She'd never seen him without his shirt before, and had to drag her gaze up to his face before she caved to the desire to reach out and run a hand along those hard, smooth planes.

"Barbara Jean."

He so rarely used her name that it almost caught her off guard. Instead, she held up the small plate in her hands. Her excuse, to save herself a whole lot of humiliation if she wasn't right. "I . . . uh, brought you some pie."

"Thank you." He took it from her with a smile, then glanced down at the plate. "Apple? My favorite."

"I know." The admission slipped from her lips before she could haul it back. "I meant, you always remarked on how much you like my apple pie, and I just thought, there was a piece left over and I didn't want it to go to waste, and I wondered if you might want it . . ."

Her voice trailed off. When had she turned into this nervous, babbling person? And why couldn't she stop staring at his chest?

"I don't want to eat it." He paused a beat, and her breath caught. "Alone."

"Oh, well, I mean, if you have company—"

Another of those smiles crossed his face. Good Lord, the man practically made her dissolve into a puddle of honey when he looked at her like that.

"I'm trying to invite you in to share it with me, Barbara Jean. I admit I'm a little rusty at this. Haven't dated much since my divorce, and I'm a hell of a lot more comfortable around fillies than women, but"—he lifted his gaze to hers, those chocolate-brown eyes making her melt a little—"I'd sure like it if you would come in and share this amazing piece of pie with me."

"I'm a little rusty, too, Carlos," she admitted. It felt good, really good, to know she wasn't alone in feeling this way. "I haven't been on a date in a really long time and I don't even know if that's what this is or what you're asking. Half the time, I'm pretty sure I'm reading your signals wrong."

His gaze locked on hers, steady and hot this time. Then he laid the pie on the bench outside his door, and took two steps forward, never breaking eye contact. Barbara Jean's breath caught, held, and she waited, nervous, excited, and scared for what was coming. He cupped her face in his hands, a touch as gentle as the one he'd use with a newborn foal, then he leaned in and kissed her. Just a light, sweet kiss, that seemed filled with the promise of more. Of something special and unforgettable.

When he drew back, his gaze filled with questions. "That's the signal I've been trying to get across. Don't think I've been doing it right."

"That . . . that was as close to right as it gets," she said. The nervous flutter in her stomach shifted into one filled with breathless anticipation. Carlos's kiss was as delicious and tempting as the rest of him.

"Dessert?" he said.

"Oh, yes. Please."

He smiled one more time, then he put out his hand, and she took it, loving the way their palms fit together, like two pieces of one puzzle. Then he gathered up the pie and they went inside.

Chapter 15

The new morning dawned, and Hunter did the same thing he had done for the last seven hundred-plus mornings. He put his feet on the floor, pulled on some jeans and a shirt, grabbed his hat, and headed down to the back porch with his coffee and his dog.

He looked out over the land that had been loved and tended by countless generations of McCoys, watching the world come to life, one inch at a time. Hunter drew in deep gulps of the sweet Georgia air. The horses nickered in their stalls, already anticipating breakfast and another warm, beautiful day.

Hunter's gaze went to the fields at the back of his acreage. The hundreds and hundreds of purple flowers. He could just barely make them out in the dim early morning light, but he knew they were there. For two years, those flowers had served as a painful reminder of the mistakes he had made, the losses he had suffered.

But as the sun began to rise and wash over the field in degrees of gold, he saw the flowers in a different light. Saw their resilience, their strength. They kept on blooming, kept on bending to the wind, kept on greeting the sun every day, no matter what came their way. He could no longer see the path trodden by the horses yesterday. The Georgia Asters had lifted their petals and stems to fill in the gaps, as if they'd never been trampled.

Maybe it was time. Time to move forward, do something different, make amends. Finally heal these scars of his past, right the wrongs of the last two years, as best he could. He finished his coffee, left the mug on the railing, then trundled down the stairs and across the yard to the stable. Foster padded along at Hunter's side. Every few seconds, the dog's tail *thwap*ped against Hunter's leg.

"It's time," Hunter said to the dog, but mostly to himself, to keep his steps moving forward. He stopped in and talked to Carlos for a minute, then told the trainer he'd be back later that morning. With Foster in tow, Hunter headed toward the truck.

When Hunter pulled open the pickup door, Foster hopped up and settled into the passenger seat, where Lizzie had sat just a few days ago. He'd forgotten to repair the hole in the seat, and the torn vinyl had peeled back, exposing the old foam underneath. For a second, Hunter pictured Lizzie there, with her bright smile, her wide, deep eyes, that long blond hair that ran like a waterfall down her back. Damn, he missed her. He wondered where she was. If she'd gone to Atlanta or driven all the way back to New Jersey. If she was thinking of him or cursing his name.

Either way, he had fences to mend before he could be the man she needed. *You're so damned busy being protective that you're using it as a shield. . . . You can't spend the rest*

of your life paying a penance at the cost of relationships
with the people who care about you.

She was right, as was his aunt. The women in his life
knew him better than he knew himself.

He'd paid for his sins, a hundred times over, and it had
never been enough. Maybe, if he tried opening his heart,
letting others know the pain he suffered, he could begin to
heal. To ease the burdens on his shoulders.

He started the ancient truck, put it in gear, then headed
away from the ranch. He patted the papers in his pocket,
just to make sure they were still there. A few minutes later,
he pulled into an empty parking lot. It was early yet, the
feed store just now opening, and soon, the other ranchers
would be driving up to get their orders. Hunter should have
waited till later in the day, when business died down and
the store was quiet, but if he had, he might not have come
at all. His grandfather always said the best time to get anything done is when you're thinking about it, and that's what
Hunter intended to do.

He rolled the windows down halfway, then got out of the
truck. "Stay," he told Foster. The dog whined a little, but settled
down, his ears still perked, hoping for a change of mind.

Hunter drew in a deep breath, then headed inside. It took
a second for his eyes to adjust to the dim interior. There was
no one behind the counter, so he turned toward the ware-
house. Johnny Ray was hefting bags of feed into a pile at
the end of the second aisle. Before Johnny Ray could yell
at him or kick him out of the store, Hunter reached down
and picked up the opposite end of the next bag.

Johnny Ray glared at him. Sweat beaded on his brow and
his face was red with exertion. He was not a young man, but
he was a stubborn one who would rather collapse than accept
Hunter's aid. "I don't need your help."

"Probably not." Hunter kept holding on to the corners of the bag.

Johnny Ray muttered a curse, then took the other side, and together they hefted the bags into place. He didn't say a word, just kept working at a furious pace. When they'd stacked the last bag, Johnny Ray dusted off his hands and stepped back. "What the hell are you doing here?"

"Apologizing."

"I don't want to hear it." Johnny Ray spun on his heel and headed down the aisle.

Hunter followed after him, doubling his pace so he could swing around in front of Johnny Ray at the corner. Above them, a dying fluorescent light flickered like a strobe. "I never wanted anything to happen to Jenna. I loved her, Johnny Ray. I wanted to marry her."

"And I wanted to walk my little girl down the aisle. But that's never going to happen now. Because of you." Johnny Ray's words were tinged with two years of venom. His eyes were steel cold, fists clenched at his sides. "You took her away from me. You took my baby girl away."

God, how he hated hearing the pain in the voice of a man he loved like a father. Hunter would have done anything right then to rewind the last two years. He hung his head. "You're right. You're absolutely right. I'm sorry."

"I don't need your goddamned apologies. I need my daughter back."

The agony in Johnny Ray's voice nearly ripped Hunter apart. Johnny Ray had suffered so much. Jenna's death, then his wife leaving him, moving to Arizona or California or something, far from the memories. He was alone now, as he'd said, with just the feed store to fill the empty holes.

"I can't bring her back," Hunter said. "I wish to God I could. I would do anything to take that night back. To stop her from going out in the rain. She was so mad at me, and I never should have let her drive."

"Why was she mad at you?" Johnny Ray's gaze narrowed. "What did you do?"

What hadn't he done? He'd tried to convince a city girl to live in the country. Tried to get her to bend her nature to fit what he wanted, instead of realizing early on that she wanted another life, another world, outside his own. "That night, we had a big fight. I guess we finally realized that it wasn't going to work and we would never be truly happy together. She wanted to live in the city, wanted me to sell the ranch, move with her. But I couldn't do it. This place is my life, Johnny Ray, and I can't imagine being anywhere but on the Silver Spur."

"She never wanted to be here in Chatham Ridge, even when she was small," Johnny Ray said after a while, his tone resigned. "Five generations of my family have lived here, born and died on this very soil, and my little girl wanted to be everywhere else in the world except for here."

A melancholy smile crossed Hunter's face. "She was made for bigger things than this place. She would have been amazing, wherever she went."

Johnny Ray sank onto a stack of fifty-pound bags and drew in a long, deep breath. "My little girl was fiery and headstrong right from the second she was born. She came out crying and fighting, and never stopped. You'd tell her to go left and she'd go right and argue about why it was better the entire time she was doing it."

Hunter chuckled. "Half the time, going right was the better choice. Jenna was smart as hell."

Johnny Ray raised his head. Tears shone in his eyes. "She loved you, Hunter."

"And I loved her." Hunter heaved a sigh. "We just weren't

made to be with each other. I took a long time coming around to that realization. I couldn't make her stay any more than she could make me leave."

A long moment ticked by. Johnny Ray sat there, emotions flickering across his face like a movie. "God, I miss her."

Hunter dropped onto the stack beside Johnny Ray. The grain shifted under his weight. "I do, too, Johnny Ray. Every day, I wish I could go back and undo it all. I never wanted anything bad to happen to her."

Johnny Ray's gaze met Hunter's. Slowly, very slowly, he nodded. "I know that, Hunter. I just kept blaming you because . . ." He sighed. "Because I had nobody else to blame."

"It's okay." Hunter meant the words. If he could take more of the burden of Johnny Ray's grief, he would do it. Because he understood those regrets, that need to blame someone, something. "I would have done the same in your shoes."

"I just wish I had some part of her, you know?" Johnny Ray's face crumpled and his voice broke. "Something I could hold on to that would bring her back, in some little way."

Hunter rested his elbows on his knees and drew in a deep breath. "That's why I came here today. I wanted to give you something." He took the papers out of his pocket and handed them to Johnny Ray.

Johnny Ray glanced down at the folded sheaf. "What is this?"

"Jenna may have hated living on my ranch, but she loved those horses," Hunter said. "She was there the night Loaded Gun was born. Helped me deliver that colt."

"She told me about that. It was a tough delivery. He was breech and you had to turn him around and get him out. She said he wasn't breathing, and she watched you blow into the colt's muzzle and he came back to life. She said it was the most amazing thing she ever saw."

He remembered that night. Jenna, on her knees beside him in the stall, both disgusted and amazed by the beauty of a new life. She'd cried when Loaded Gun had come out, still as a statue, then laughed through her tears when the colt stumbled to his feet. "She loved that horse. I'd have to get on her about feeding him too many sugar cubes. But he had her wrapped around his little finger, and she would have done about anything for that horse. It was like he was her child, you know?"

Johnny Ray nodded, and his eyes welled again. Probably thinking of all the grandchildren that would never be born, the empty, lonely years stretching ahead.

"That's why I'm giving Loaded Gun to you."

Johnny Ray's brows rose. He glanced again at the papers, then back at Hunter. "What? Why? That horse is a champion. I've seen the reports on him and heard the talk about town. He's turning your ranch around."

Hunter took off his hat and spun it slowly in his hands, turning the brim again and again. He'd thought about this long and hard last night, and knew it was the right thing to do. The only thing he could do. "Yeah, he's quite the horse, I'll give you that, but he was part of Jenna, and I want you to have him. It won't bring her back, I know that, but maybe you'll look at him and see her feeding him sugar cubes and brushing his coat until it shined. And maybe that'll help. A little."

A single tear slipped out of Johnny Ray's eye and slid down his cheek. "I can't take your horse, Hunter. Not that horse. It'll ruin your ranch, just when it's getting on its feet."

"I'll be fine, Johnny Ray."

Johnny Ray sat there a long time, thinking. Pain flickered in his features, and tears welled in his eyes again. "I can't take your horse," he said again. "But I will take a foal next spring. You breed Loaded Gun, and if it's a filly, bring her to me."

Hunter thought of Dakota, of all that horse had been through. Of how she had been hurt and injured, and how she was coming back from the other side of hell. How pairing her with Loaded Gun would bring a little of their shared pasts together. The two families had shared so much over the years, and maybe Johnny Ray's request would begin to reforge that bond. "I'll breed him with Dakota."

Johnny Ray smiled. The first smile Hunter had seen on his face in two years. "Jenna would have liked that."

"She would have. She would have liked that a lot." Hunter leaned against the metal shelving, and so did Johnny Ray. The two men sat there a long time, while dust motes floated in the air and a wayward bird flitted among the rafters, each remembering the woman who had left a long and lasting mark on their lives.

∞

Elizabeth sat in her apartment in Trenton, and wondered how she had survived for so many years in such a sea of gray. Even her furniture was gray, the walls a pale slate. Outside, the concrete and asphalt world of the city stood defiant in the harsh light of a fall day.

For all her talk about craving roots and a place to call her own, there was very little in the nine-hundred-square-foot space that she cared about. The furniture held no special meaning, the trinkets here and there mostly just things she'd picked up to blend with the color scheme. The entire space was about as personal as a blank greeting card.

Roger had moved out in her absence, leaving little empty dents here and there. A space on the bookshelf that once held his favorite DVDs, a pocket in the closet that was now nothing but empty hangers, a blank shelf in the medicine chest that used to contain shaving cream and razors. She'd thought maybe it might be hard to come back and see him gone, but all she really felt was relief.

She thought of the kitchen at the Silver Spur, with its stoneware plates and white lace curtains. Every inch of that house held a memory. Hunter's mother's china, the hutch his grandmother had once owned, the boots by the door that he'd worn every day for years. Elizabeth had nothing like that here, nothing that spoke of who she was or where she'd been.

She ached for those plates and that hutch and the muffins, and most of all, for the warm comfort she'd tasted at the Silver Spur. The voices of the men working outside, the hum of Barbara Jean singing along with the radio, the deep drawl of Hunter's voice, teasing her.

Had she done the right thing? Coming back to this . . . grayness?

The doorbell rang, and a moment later, Elizabeth was welcoming Sophie in with a flurry of hugs and excited words. "When did you get back?" she asked.

"Just this minute," Sophie said. "I haven't even gone to my place. I had the cab driver drop me on your doorstep."

"I'm so glad to see you." She drew her friend into another tight hug. It wasn't just the month that Sophie had been gone, traveling here, there, and everywhere, but the whole last few days and then coming home to the emptiness of her apartment. Elizabeth had missed Sophie's laughter and the way she filled a room just by being in it.

Sophie tugged the ponytail out of her long brown hair. She shrugged out of a camel-colored jacket, dropped it on the chair by the door, then set her suitcase beside the chair. "Tell me you have wine."

"Two bottles."

Sophie grinned. "Perfect."

As Elizabeth poured them each a glass of chardonnay,

then unearthed a box of crackers and a block of cheese from the paltry space she called her kitchen, the two women caught up on Sophie's latest travels. They settled on Elizabeth's sofa—also gray and about as exciting as a piece of paper—and propped their feet on the glass-and-chrome coffee table.

"Okay, so tell me everything I missed," Sophie said.

Elizabeth laughed. "I just talked to you on the phone last night."

"And a lot could have happened in the meantime. Like, your knight could have shown up, riding his white horse and begging for your hand in marriage."

"No knight, no horse." She held up her glass. "Which is why we have wine."

"We'd have wine either way." Sophie laughed and clinked her glass against Elizabeth's. "So, tell me what the editor said. Did you do the interview in Atlanta?"

"My editor e-mailed me back a little while ago and"— Elizabeth let out a deep breath, then felt a smile burst across her face—"she loved the article. She can't wait to see what I write about the miniature horse breeder. And, even better, their publishing company owns several sister magazines and she wants me to start writing for those, too."

"Sounds like this is quickly turning into a real job." Sophie clinked her glass again with Elizabeth's. "Congratulations. I knew you'd be amazing."

"For a while there, you were the only one who thought so." Elizabeth drew her friend into a tight hug. "Thank you for everything. For showing me the ropes, for giving me the nudge, and for the rah-rah pep talks when I needed them most."

"That's what best friends are for." Sophie grinned, and plucked up a piece of cheese to eat. "So when are you going back to Georgia?"

"The interview with the miniature horse breeder was

rescheduled. He had a family emergency and wanted to wait until—"

"I didn't mean to go back and talk about pint-sized ponies. I meant to go round up that cowboy. Lasso his heart, and all that."

"For a writer, you sure use a lot of terrible clichés."

Sophie sat back against the sofa. "It's my special skill."

Special skill. That made her think of that day by the pond with Hunter. How he'd challenged her to juggle, how impressed he had been, how they had laughed. How much she'd wanted to go back to that pond with him on a hot summer day, strip off their clothes, and dive into that cool, deep water.

A second later, she was crying. She'd thought she'd left all her tears back on the long trip home, but they sprang anew to her eyes, and streamed down her cheeks. "How could I be so stupid?"

Sophie took her hands and held them tight. "We're all stupid when it comes to men. It's the hormones, I think. Muddles the brain."

"No, I meant, how could I be so stupid to think that I was living my life any differently than the way I grew up?" Elizabeth tugged one hand out of Sophie's and waved at the apartment. "Nothing in this room is permanent or meaningful. Yeah, I signed a lease for a year, but I didn't put down roots. I just bought furniture and filled up my savings account and told myself I wasn't anything like my mother."

"And what is so bad about being like your mother?" Sophie squeezed Elizabeth's fingers. "I know she had trouble paying her bills and showing up on time and being there for you. But she was a dreamer, and she did love you more than anything in the world. And there were times when she was fun, so fun. Who else is going to drag you out of bed in the middle of the night just to see the first snowfall?"

Hunter would, Elizabeth realized. Hunter would saddle up one of the horses, pull her onto the saddle behind him and take her to the top of the ridge to watch the sun rise, or a rain shower dust over the fields. Hunter was the kind of man who dreamed, and did what it took to make those dreams come true. Holding on to that ranch and breathing life back into it when the rest of the quarter horse world had written off the Silver Spur. Seeing the last hints of spirit in a broken horse, and giving her the room and understanding she needed to find her footing again.

Elizabeth hopped to her feet and grabbed her cell phone. "Let's order Chinese."

Sophie's brows knitted. "I'm always up for some moo shu pork, but why now?"

"Because I don't want to pack on an empty stomach. And I've got somewhere to go in the morning."

Sophie grinned, then raised her glass to Elizabeth's. "I'll drink to that."

Chapter 16

Barbara Jean stretched like a lazy cat, her skin warmed by the sun streaming through the window. Her clothes lay in a tangled heap on the floor, but she didn't care. She lay there, in the comfortable double bed, thinking that she was damned glad she hadn't waited one more minute to begin living her own life.

"Good morning, beautiful," Carlos said. He rolled on top of her and traced the outline of her face with a tender touch that nearly made her sigh. "I'm glad you're still here."

When he'd asked her to stay the night, whispering those very words along her neck after they'd made love, she'd thought there wasn't any other place in the world she'd rather be than right there, in Carlos's arms. "It's past breakfast time. I can't believe I slept so late."

Carlos chuckled. "Well, we were up pretty late."

"Very late, for two old people like us." Considering they had made love three times, it was a wonder the two of them hadn't slept until noon. She'd never expected that a piece of pie could leave her so sated, so happy, so . . . everything.

"Ah, *mi amor,* old is only in your mind." Then he started kissing her lips, her cheeks, her neck, his sinewy body moving against hers and awakening a renewed heat all over again. Good Lord, she was going to have to start taking a multivitamin to keep up with him.

"Who's . . . going . . . to . . . make . . . the . . . coffee?" she asked, peppering the words between his kisses.

"We will. Later." Then he ran his tongue along her lips and she arched into him. "Much later."

Then Carlos started kissing her again, each touch more tender than the last, and Barbara Jean sank into the small bed in the tiny cabin and fell in love.

When she finally made her way across the lawn and into the kitchen, her hair was a mess, her clothes barely fastened. She found Hunter standing in the kitchen, a knowing smile on his face. "Seems I'm not the only smitten one in this house, running around with a big goofy grin."

Heat rushed to her cheeks. She reached for her apron and fastened it around her waist, so Hunter couldn't read the truth in her face. "I'm not smitten with anyone. I was just visiting a friend."

"A *good* friend?" he asked, turning her own words back on her.

Barbara Jean raised her nose. "A lady does not kiss and tell."

"And a gentleman would marry that lady before too much time passed." Hunter raised his cup of coffee in her direction. "And before he leaves the rest of the ranch to its own devices at breakfast."

"I'm sorry, I meant to be back earlier—"

He put a hand on her arm, cutting off her sentence. "Aunt Barbara Jean, you have done more than enough for everyone in this family. Put your own life on hold to raise us kids, then worked here for years as the right-hand woman on the Silver Spur, while also helping me through my own grief and giving me a much-needed kick in the pants every once in a while. It's about time you lived for yourself. The coffee can wait, the work can keep. There is nothing I want more than to see you happy."

Tears welled in her eyes and she drew her nephew, who outweighed her by eighty pounds and stood a full head taller, into a tight hug. "I am happy, right here."

"I'm glad." He kissed the top of her head, then stepped back. "Though the next time you sneak off to see Carlos, could you at least show me how you make the coffee? I don't know what I did wrong, but this stuff is terrible."

Barbara Jean laughed, then dumped out the bitter brew and started a new pot. She moved around the kitchen, humming as she did, fixing breakfast for Hunter, Carlos, and the rest of the men. And when they all tromped in a little after eight thirty for eggs and bacon, she met Carlos's gaze across the crowded kitchen and thought Hunter was right.

She was smitten. Utterly, totally smitten.

Then she noticed her nephew, sitting at the kitchen table, his gaze going to some place far beyond the confines of the ranch and realized he was smitten, too. She could only pray he was smart enough to do something about it before everything he desired was gone for good.

∞

The women showed up on Hunter's doorstep shortly after breakfast, like a gaggle of geese. The day was just starting to ramp up, with the ranch hands bustling about the grounds, while Barbara Jean worked in the office. The entire Silver Spur held an air of hope, something Hunter hadn't felt here in a long, long time. He was glad to see his aunt happy with Carlos. Hunter had known the trainer all his life and knew Carlos would treat Barbara Jean like a princess. Given all the flirty glances they'd exchanged through breakfast, it was clear Carlos was just as head over heels for Barbara Jean as she was for him.

Seeing them had only made Hunter miss Lizzie even more. He'd debated calling her, then thought better of it. What he needed to say needed to be said in person, not over a phone connection hundreds of miles long.

But still he delayed on acting. What if he had read her wrong? What if she didn't want the life he had here?

Could he give it up to be with her? He hadn't done it for Jenna, and in the end, it had cost him dearly. He glanced out the window at the rolling green acres, the horses dotting the landscape, the bright sun washing everything he loved with gold, and wondered if staying here would be worth anything if he was staying here alone.

He was just about to head out to the stables when the doorbell rang. He opened the door to find a sea of pastel, and a quartet of irritated women. Noralee's book club. He'd known the women most of his life. That was the plus and minus of small town life. Near everyone in Chatham Ridge was kin or friend to someone else. And that often gave them license to show up unannounced and offer their opinion, which he had no doubt Rachel, Katie Ann, Susannah, and Charlotte were here to do. "Howdy, ladies. What can I do for you?"

"You can start by not being such a moron," Rachel said. She was the most vocal of the group, married to his friend

J.W. just a few months ago. A true spitfire, Barbara Jean would say.

"And start immediately. Before she gets too far away," Charlotte said. She had on a pair of oversized dark sunglasses, but even those didn't hide her scowl for him.

"By she, I assume you mean Lizzie?" he said. Even saying her name made something deep inside him ache with longing. She'd only been in town for a few days, but clearly, she had made some friends—and left a lasting impression on more than just the Silver Spur. He wasn't surprised. Lizzie was the kind of woman who lingered in anyone's mind long after she was gone.

Rachel propped a fist on her hip. "Do you know any other amazing women who will put up with you?"

"Put up with me? Hey, I'm not so—"

"You are horrible, Hunter McCoy. Easy on the eyes, but hard on the heart." Katie Ann took a step forward and pointed at his chest with a long red fingernail that might have been classified as a lethal weapon. "You broke Elizabeth's heart. And either you make it better or we will be here every single day until you do."

He glanced at their faces, each of them set in stone. "Who says I broke her heart?"

"She did," Susannah said. "Well, not in so many words, but we saw it on her face. I don't know what you said to her, but you better make it right."

"She's gone, you know." He could still see her car pulling out of the drive, the hurt on her face, the way her leaving had caused this aching, empty need deep in his gut. "Probably back in New Jersey as we speak."

Rachel narrowed her gaze. "You never heard of those inventions called telephones and airplanes?"

The other three stared him down, waiting for an answer.

Hunter chuckled. "Calm down, ladies. Put the pitchforks back in the shed."

"Well, are you going to do something about Elizabeth?" Charlotte asked. "Because if there's one thing this book club believes in, it's a happy ending."

"Are you sure she *wants* me to do something about all this?" For God's sake, it was like he was in ninth grade again and pumping his best friend for information about the cute girl in algebra. But Hunter had seen the hurt on Lizzie's face, heard the anger in her voice. The last thing he wanted to do was repeat the mistakes of his past.

And convince a woman who didn't love this place to live here, with him. Far better to let Lizzie go, than trap the city girl in a country world.

"That's something you're going to have to ask her yourself," Rachel said. "What's that old saying? If you love something, set it free, and if it doesn't come back, go get it with a really big net?"

"I'm not going to do that," Hunter said quietly. "If she's happier in New Jersey, that's where she should be."

"Well, you're never gonna know that answer if you don't ask the question," Katie Ann said. She fished in her purse and came up with a piece of paper that she pressed into Hunter's palm. "That's her address."

He glanced down at the piece of paper and recognized Lizzie's long, loopy handwriting. It made him think of her notebook and her questions and that day by the pond. Of seeing her on his porch. Of waking up to her in the morning. Of how she'd inscribed herself on his heart in a few short days. That kind of fast, all-encompassing emotion was crazy. Impractical. Most likely about as real as a unicorn.

He curled his hand around the paper and tucked it in his pocket. "Thank you, ladies, but I have to get to work."

· "That's it?" Rachel asked. "You're just going to go to work?"

"It's all I know," he said. Then he plopped his hat on his head and walked past the women, down the stairs and out to the stable. The tiny piece of paper seemed to weigh down his hip with unspoken expectations and questions.

Chapter 17

In the end, it was Carlos who made up Hunter's mind. He was standing beside the corral, one foot propped on the bottom railing, watching his sister's face as she put Loaded Gun through his paces. Carlos stood to the side, shouting instructions, watching her closely, as worried as a mother hen, even though Amberlee had taken precautions this time. Hunter could see the bulge of her inhaler in her pocket.

But it was the happiness on her face that sealed the deal for him. Anyone else would have been terrified by the near-death experiences Amberlee had suffered. Another girl might have moved far from the ranch, the horses, the danger. But Amberlee wasn't any other girl. She was a McCoy, and a McCoy didn't back down from a challenge or let a few setbacks change her course.

He called Carlos over. "You're doing great with the horse and with Amberlee. Thank you."

"Your sister's real good with him," Carlos said. "I think he even likes her better than me."

Hunter chuckled. "I think all the horses like my sister better. She's got a way with them."

"It's the women in your family. They're all pretty special." A slow smile spread across Carlos's face.

Amberlee thundered past them, then took Loaded Gun into a spin. The horse barely missed a step, almost perfecting the difficult movements. "Did you see that?" she yelled to Hunter.

"I did. You're turning him into a champ."

"Told you I could." Amberlee grinned, then urged Loaded Gun back into a gallop.

"As the oldest male McCoy," Hunter said, turning back to Carlos, and trying to look serious and not glad as hell that Carlos and Barbara Jean were so damned happy together, "it's my duty to inform you that if you break my aunt's heart, I'll have to shoot you."

Carlos chuckled. "I wouldn't do that. In fact, I was thinking it'd be mighty nice to maybe settle down with her someday."

Hunter leaned back, surprised. "Moving awful fast, aren't you?"

Carlos dipped his head, a shy grin peeking beneath his hat's shadow. "I ain't getting any younger, Hunter, and I've known Barbara Jean for a long, long time. The way I see it, the less time you waste thinking about being happy is the more time you can have being happy."

Hunter clapped Carlos on the shoulder. "That is damned good advice. Remind me in a few days to give you a raise for that."

"A few days?" Carlos asked.

But Hunter was already gone, charging into the house

and up the stairs. He grabbed a bag from his closet, and shoved a change of clothes inside. Just as he was leaving his room, he saw the ruined picture of Jenna, still on the floor.

Hunter picked it up, fished out the broken pieces of glass from inside the frame and dumped them into the trash. He studied her face for a moment, and realized that the guilt in his heart had begun to ease. The grief now only a faint echo.

"I'm moving on," he whispered to Jenna's image. "And hopefully doing it right this time." He turned the picture face down on his dresser, and felt a whisper of closure. He'd always remember Jenna, of course, and see her in the horse she had loved, but it was time to move on, to move past that night. His gaze went to the flowers beyond his window, those rare Georgia asters that had been planted for one woman, but loved by another.

He grabbed the bag, headed downstairs, stopping to give his aunt a quick kiss on the cheek. "I'm running out, Aunt Barbara Jean. I might be gone a few days."

"A few days? Why?" Barbara Jean's eyes widened. "Where are you going?"

"To get something I almost lost." He gave her another kiss, then headed out to his truck before he wasted another second. Hunter tossed the bag in the back, then opened the driver's side door, just as the dog came bounding up and hopped inside. Instead of lying down on the opposite seat, Foster sat up on the passenger's side, ears perked, tail *thwap*-ping against the seat, as if he knew this wasn't an ordinary trip to get feed or check on the horses.

Hunter never had been a man who cared much about what kind of vehicle he drove, how old it was, how many miles the engine had wearing it down, but this time, he wished he had a brand-new truck with a fancy, fast engine. Because no matter how hard he pressed the gas pedal, it seemed like the old Chevy was still moving at a snail's pace. Hell, he could have been in the Concorde and it would have been going too slow. He wound his way down the long driveway of the Silver Spur, kicking up small stones in the wake of the big tires.

He was just turning onto the winding road when he noticed a familiar dark blue sedan coming from the opposite direction. He slid to a stop, flinging out an arm to keep Foster from sliding off the vinyl seat and onto the floor. Foster barked, then started wagging his tail so fast and hard, it looked ready to fly off his backside.

Hunter grabbed his hat, plopped it on his head, then got out of the truck, his heart in his throat. A second later, the sedan came to a stop beside him. Lizzie stepped out of the driver's seat, wearing that yellow dress and her boots and looking more beautiful than anything he'd seen in a long damned time. He saw her cowboy hat sitting on the passenger's seat, still as pristine as the day she'd bought it. His heart leapt in his throat.

"I was just coming to you," he said.

"You were?" She smiled, then nodded toward the truck. "All those miles? In that thing?"

"Well, I didn't think the horse could make it all the way to New Jersey, darlin'." Though chances were pretty good that even poor old Zeph could move faster than that ancient truck.

She laughed. "Planning on riding into Trenton to capture my heart like a knight on a shiny steed?"

"That was the plan. Though I wouldn't call me any kind of knight, or call Old Faithful here shiny or a steed." He gave the truck a pat, and swore he saw some rust hit the ground. Okay, so maybe he should have rented a car or hired a taxi or something more dependable. He hadn't been thinking about anything more than getting to Lizzie as fast as possible. He pushed off from the Chevy and closed the distance between them. "What are you doing here?"

"I had a little more research to do."

His heart fell. He'd been hoping she'd come back for him, but it all circled back to the article. He should have been glad, because that exposure would help secure the future of the ranch, but right now, that seemed like the last priority on his list. "Whatever you need to know, I'd be glad to tell you."

"I wasn't researching you. Or the Silver Spur." She shifted one hip in his direction. "I was here to find out more about me."

"About you?"

"I thought I had myself all figured out until I met you. But I realized when I got back to New Jersey that I didn't have any of the answers I thought I did. And that everything I thought I knew, I was wrong about."

That little fissure of hope opened again in his chest. "Wrong about what?"

"Can we walk a little bit? I've been driving for hours and I need to stretch my legs."

"Sure." He let Foster out of the cab, then took her hand, and they set off across the field, toward the hill beyond the stable. The dog followed along, peeling off from time to time to harass a squirrel or flush out a bird. Lizzie's hand felt good in his, right. They fit together well, moving in an unspoken natural sync.

She bent down, plucked a long piece of grass and twirled it between her fingers. In the distance, the horses nickered, and someone started a tractor. "I told you that when I was a little girl, I moved a hundred times, it seemed like. I never stayed in one place for very long, and the only thing I wanted when I grew up was a place to call my own." She brushed the bangs out of her face, then paused to turn toward the sun and soak up its warmth for a moment. "Then I came here and found a place with roots that ran so deep, you couldn't even see where they began. Those roots are in the dishes in your mother's cabinet and the horses that are running in the fields. And the love you have for every person on this ranch."

He liked that she loved the same things he did. That she noticed the history, the intertwined lives that made up the Silver Spur. "All that is part of what I love about this place. That there's not a single square inch that doesn't have a story behind it. And my grandpa, he was the one who told the stories. He'd talk your ear off, but in the end, you'd be glad you listened."

"That's exactly the kind of life I always wanted and dreamed of, the kind of place where things were passed down from one generation to the next, where you would wake up in the morning and your shoes would still be exactly where you left them the last five hundred days in a row." Lizzie sighed, but kept on walking, her long legs making fast strides across the property, even though their pace was slow. "My mother would talk about us living in the country or moving to the beach or whatever her dream of the day was, but we never did. All we did was go from one crappy apartment to another even crappier apartment. I used to hate her for that because my life had no roots. No traditions. Nothing I could fasten myself to and, as Noralee has said, bloom from." She tossed the sprig of grass onto the ground. "But my mother did give me one thing. This ring."

He glanced down at the ruby ring that had been on her finger from the day he met her. It glistened in the sun, sent sparkles of red across the back of her hand. "Is it a family heirloom?"

She scoffed. "No. It's one of those fifty-cent rings you get out of a bubblegum machine. When I was little, my mother

convinced me it was rare and valuable, like a jewel found in
a deep dark cave. She would spin these tales about princesses
and castles and adventures. Sometimes she'd even wake me
up in the middle of the night to watch shooting stars or pull
me out of school because the day was perfect for a picnic. My
mother was a dreamer of the highest order, which was awesome when I was a little girl and still believed in unicorns
and fairy godmothers, but when I got older, it scared me."

"Why?"

"Because she would go after one dream this week,
another next week, and forget about paying the light bill or
dropping off the check to the landlord. I was eight years old
and writing checks at the kitchen counter, because she had
forgotten again. I had to be the responsible one, the one who
got the mail, sent out the bills. I vowed when I grew up that
I would never be like that." She sighed. "So I worked a job
I hated, got into a relationship as boring as paste, and put
all my free money into investments and savings."

He couldn't imagine this tempting, fiery woman ever settling for a dry, dependable day-to-day existence. The Lizzie
he had met, the Lizzie who had challenged him and teased
him, was far from dull. But he could see the responsible side
of her, the organized one with all the notebooks and redun-
dancies, probably making sure not a single stitch was dropped.
"But then you ditched it all for the chance to be a writer.
That's taking a chance on a dream. A big chance."

Lizzie gave him a half smile. "I guess there was more of
my mother in me than I thought. Then I met you. Another
dreamer. And wham, I was scared all over again."

"Me? I'm not a dreamer."

"Yes, you are. You look at this place"—she waved her
hand, taking in the stable, the horses, the green undulating

land—"and you see a future. You don't see work, you don't see bills. You see what it can be in a year, five years. Ten, even." She gestured toward Dakota, today finally standing in the paddock with the other mares, a little to the side, but out in the sun like any other horse. "You see a horse who has been hurt and thrown away, and see the spirit still inside her."

"Some things," Hunter said quietly, thinking of Dakota, of the woman beside him, "are worth saving, no matter the work involved."

"Even you?" she said.

The words hit him hard. He released her hands and stepped away. There was the crux of everything. The wall he had stood behind for so long. A wall built out of blame and regret and guilt. "Maybe. But I've been lost a long time, Lizzie. And I'm still trying to get myself back to where I was."

"You're further along than you think. I watched you work this ranch, and bring Dakota back to normal, and I see a man who is in exactly the right place."

He scoffed. "I don't know how much of a dreamer I am anymore. I think you nailed it earlier when you called me a porcupine. I have been one, a hibernating porcupine at that, all fierce and mean to anyone who gets too close. I've been using this ranch, my work here, as a way to stay insulated from the world. It was a lot easier than accepting what happened to Jenna and what part I played in losing her."

"You can't blame yourself, Hunter," Lizzie said. "It was an accident."

"I do. I have. It seemed the only thing I could do right after she died was take all the blame on me." He took off his hat and ran a hand through his hair. The merciless Georgia sun beat down on them, an angry fire that was soon soothed by a gentle breeze whispering across the Silver

Spur. "I thought I was doing the right thing by continuing on with the Silver Spur, keeping my head down and focused on the job, and instead, I was just . . . avoiding."

"I understand that, Hunter." She placed a hand on his arm, her eyes kind and sympathetic. "I've done the same thing with the issues I didn't want to face. If I just kept on punching a clock and putting money in the bank and, living from day to day, I could tell myself I was doing something different from the life I had in the past. But I hadn't really changed anything. Until I came to Chatham Ridge. To the Silver Spur." A smile flickered on her face. "To you."

He wanted to let those words sink into his heart, to give him hope, but he couldn't, not until he had told her everything he needed to say. He'd done a lot of thinking over the last couple days, the kind of thinking that set a man straight, and told him he was the biggest fool on earth, letting the girl he loved walk away. Now she was back, and he was going to do whatever it took to make sure she stayed. Including facing the wrongs he needed to right.

"The night that Jenna died almost destroyed me," he said, meeting her gaze, laying his own bare with the truth, "because everything was out of my control. The weather, the way she drove, the anger she had, the accident that happened because of all that. We fought because I thought if I kept her here, she would grow to love this place as much as I did. But what she loved was also out of my control." Hunter pointed at the corral, filled with the future of the Silver Spur, colts and fillies who were going to grow up and hopefully take this ranch back to the top. "I can hop on the back of a horse and control the direction he goes, how fast he runs, when he stops to take a drink of water. But I can't control the things that happen to the people I love or to how they feel about me. I can't control Amberlee's asthma, or her stubbornness in getting to ride again, and I can't control you leaving because I broke your heart."

Tears welled in her eyes, and he wished he could go back in time and erase that fight they'd had on the porch, the way he'd lashed out at her for something that was not her doing.

"I left, not just because I thought you didn't love me, but because I was scared," Lizzie said. "I had the very thing I always wanted, right here, and I was terrified that I was going to lose it all."

The two of them, scared and vulnerable, and instead of telling each other how they felt, they backed up, put distance between them. No more. Hunter pulled her into his arms, and inhaled the sweet soft fragrance of her hair. "You weren't going to lose anything, Lizzie. I was the one who was terrified of losing you if I asked you to stay."

She lifted her face to his. "Why would you think that?"

"Because I thought you were happier in your life up in New Jersey." There, he'd said it. Now was the chance for her to tell him he was right. That he'd imagined that happiness in her eyes when she was here. That she was only here to say good-bye.

"Oh, Hunter," she said, his name a whisper in her breath, "how could I possibly be happier there than I am right here? With the horses, the flowers and . . . you?"

He lifted her chin until her dark green eyes met his. "I want you to know that I would sell the ranch tomorrow if you wanted to live somewhere else. I lost everything once before because I was too stubborn to compromise."

"I don't see that as being too stubborn, Hunter." She curved into his chest and put her head on his shoulder. "You love this place, you love these horses, and you'll do anything to save them all and protect them all. That to me, speaks of a man who can love a woman and love her well."

He grinned. "Know anybody looking for a man like that?"

"I don't know." She put a finger on her chin and feigned deep thought. "Depends on what comes in the deal."

"Only one stubborn cowboy who can tie a cherry stem with his tongue, but was too much of a fool to untangle his tongue fast enough to tell the woman in his arms"—he looked down at her, thinking he could stare into those eyes for the rest of his life—"that he loves her."

"You"—her eyes widened, surprise flickering in the green depths—"what?"

"I love you, Lizzie." He cupped her face with his hands, ran his thumb along her bottom lip. "I have loved you since you showed up on my doorstep, soaking wet and as mad as a bee trapped in a paper bag. You have challenged me to be a better man, a stronger man, and one who stops being afraid to step outside this land and go after what he wants."

"Though you probably wouldn't have gotten too far in that truck," she said with a devilish glint in her eyes.

"Tomorrow morning, I'm buying the fastest pickup I can find. I don't want there to be any doubt in your mind that I'll go through heaven and hell to get to you if you leave again."

"I'm not going anywhere."

Her words settled like a balm across his heart. He drew her tighter to his chest. "I'm glad."

"I love you, too, Hunter. And I don't want you to leave this place, because I want to stay right here, with you, every single day." She rose to her toes and pressed a kiss to his lips. "I have loved you since I saw you with Dakota. The gentle way you tried to reach her, and how patient and kind you were with her."

He cocked a grin at her. "And here I thought it was my cherry stem skills that won you over."

"Well those skills are better put to use . . . elsewhere." She grinned, then curved into his chest again. The two of them turned toward the back of the ranch, where the horses raced each other around the pasture and the Georgia asters peeked a purple smile above the hill.

"When I marry you, darlin'," Hunter said, and felt Lizzie shift a little in surprise at his words, but he had learned some wise advice from Carlos today, advice he planned on taking, "I want to do it on top of that hill, so that we can look down and see everything we have—"

"And look out and see everything yet to come." Then she turned in his arms and kissed him, and in that touch, Lizzie finally knew what it felt like to truly come home.

Chapter 18

Noralee shepherded the book club women along like a gaggle of geese. She had on her best hat today, and a dress that she hadn't worn more than a handful of times, but she was already about to sweat clear through, given how worried she'd been about being there on time. "Lord Almighty, you girls are going to make me late for the wedding."

"Noralee, we are fifteen minutes early," Katie Ann said. "And besides, nobody's going to get married without the bridesmaids in place."

"I don't know about that," Rachel said. "I would have married J.W. in a cardboard box, with nobody but a couple rats for witnesses. I think Elizabeth and Hunter feel the same. I've never seen two people more googly-eyed about each other."

"I have," Noralee said. "You and J.W."

Rachel smiled, the kind of shy smile that said Noralee was right. "Well, he is a pretty awesome guy."

The others brought up the rear, each of them in pastel

dresses and low wedges perfect for walking up the hill to stand beside Elizabeth and her maid of honor, Sophie. On the groom's side, several of the men who worked for Hunter stood with J.W., looking dapper in jeans, white button-down shirts, and cowboy hats.

It was a small wedding, but it was also a small town, so just a handful of friends and family were in attendance. They sat in small white chairs that faced the field of Georgia asters, and several of the purple blooms were woven into the altar Hunter had built. There was a slight breeze, just enough to cool what would otherwise be a hot day. It was, as everyone would say that day and later on, a perfect day for a wedding.

The music swelled, and from either side of the bottom of the hill came the sound of horses. Dakota riding up the left, Loaded Gun on the right, each wearing a saddle all decked out for a wedding, their hooves drumming a low thunder against the earth. Elizabeth had taken riding lessons from Amberlee, and held herself tall and steady in the saddle. Hunter was as at ease on a horse as he was anywhere else, and kept pace beside his bride as they climbed to the top of the hill, then dismounted.

The minister said his words, Hunter and Elizabeth said theirs, then there was a kiss, and the ceremony was over. Hunter gave each of the horses a pat on the rump, and they charged back down the other side of the hill and into the field of asters. Elizabeth leaned into Hunter's chest, and they watched the horses chase each other among the flowers while the guests teared up. It was a perfect day, indeed.

After the wedding, Noralee took Hunter by the elbow. He was beaming from ear to ear, as happy as a pig in fresh mud. He could barely tear his gaze away from Elizabeth. "I'll have him back in just a second," she said to Elizabeth.

"Good. Because I hate spending even five seconds away from him." She smiled, and he echoed the gesture, the two of them about as goofy as two fifteen-year-olds.

"Oh, for goodness sake, you two will have a honeymoon." Noralee tugged on Hunter's arm, and they walked a slow path past the chairs. At the bottom of the hill, the caterer was finishing up the last touches for the simple reception Hunter and Elizabeth had planned. A little dinner, a little dancing on a portable dance floor, and a toast under the stars after the sun set. Noralee could smell the scent of the smoked pork they'd been roasting all afternoon.

"Thank you for coming today, Noralee," Hunter said, pressing a kiss to her cheek. "Wouldn't be the same without you and the book club girls."

"Rachel wanted to make sure you didn't make a break for it." Noralee grinned. "I told her you were so head-over-heels for Elizabeth, chances were better that the two of you would run off and elope."

"Can't say the thought didn't cross my mind." He grinned. "But today was perfect. Exactly what we both wanted."

"It was. And I'm glad to see you so happy. You deserve it." After all this poor man had been through. It was good to see him start over. Noralee had talked to Johnny Ray just the other day, too, and though he was still heartbroken over the loss of his daughter, she'd seen his excitement when he talked about the foal Dakota would give birth to in a few months. A foal that would mean a new beginning for all of them. Healing had come to Chatham Ridge, and it was a nice thing to see.

"Thanks, Noralee." Hunter pressed another kiss to her cheek. "Now, I hate to rush you, but I better get back to my bride—"

"Wait. I have a wedding present for you." Noralee reached

into her purse and pulled out a book. "You had to know I'd give you a book. I can't seem to think of any gift more perfect for all occasions than a book."

He unwrapped the package, then took the leather-bound hardcover out and held it up to the sun. He gave her a quizzical look. "It's blank."

"Yup. It's a journal. I figured going forward, the best thing the two of you can do is write your own story." She covered his hands with her own and looked up at Hunter. Noralee had a few regrets, one of them that she'd never had children. If she'd ever had a son, she would have wanted one just like Hunter McCoy. He was a good man, good to his workers, good to his family, and surely he'd be good to his wife and future kids. Elizabeth was a lucky woman. "The only requirement for the story is that it have a happy ending."

Elizabeth wandered down to them. She had on a simple cotton white dress with flat shoes. Her hair was tied back in a ribbon, fastened to a pair of those purple asters. "What are you cooking up with my husband?" she said with a smile. "Because I've been missing him something fierce."

Hunter drew his bride close and showed her the book. "Noralee says we have to make sure it has a happy ending."

Elizabeth curved into her new husband's arms and pressed a kiss to his lips. She looked beautiful and happy, and most of all, at home. Noralee couldn't think of a better pair than the two of them. She was so glad she'd made that call that rainy night and sent Elizabeth to the ranch to stay.

"I think we can do that," Elizabeth said.

"I think we already have," he whispered, then kissed her.

Neither of them noticed Noralee walking away, heading down to join the book club girls at the reception. The sun hung low in the sky, ready to kiss the horizon. Another beautiful day drawing to a close on the Silver Spur, and to

Noralee Butler, the entire scene was just as good as any she'd ever read in a book.

No, she thought, looking up at Hunter and Elizabeth, laughing together at something only they had shared, this was even better. And so much sweeter to see.

TURN THE PAGE FOR A PREVIEW OF THE FIRST BOOK
IN SHIRLEY JUMP'S SWEETHEART SISTERS SERIES

The Sweetheart Bargain

AVAILABLE NOW FROM BERKLEY SENSATION

Chapter 1

Olivia Linscott made the most insane decision of her life in less time than it took to microwave a burrito. Before she could think twice, or worse, hesitate, she'd packed what remained of her belongings into her car, loaded up on gas and 5-Hour Energy drinks, then ditched her life in Massachusetts and headed south.

All because a lawyer had shown up on her doorstep with a mysterious will, a crinkled photograph, and a butterfly necklace. Olivia's heritage, reduced to a nine-by-twelve manila envelope.

Now, forty-eight hours later, she was in sunshine instead of snow, catching the scent of ocean instead of exhaust. Outside the Toyota's window, the Florida coastline curved like a lazy snake, an undulating ribbon of blue-green punctuated by soaring seagulls and cresting whitecaps. It was a million miles away—and a good burst of salty, fresh air—from the choked, congested streets of Boston, where cars

played Frogger with each other and dodged potholes the size
of small elephants. Down here, Olivia could breathe, really
breathe, in more ways than one.

She pressed the speed-dial button on her cell and waited
for the call to connect. When her mother answered with her
familiar chirpy hello, a wave of homesickness crashed over
Olivia, and for a second she had the urge to turn around, to
head back to everything familiar.

"Olivia! I've been waiting for you to call," her mother
said. "How far are you now?"

"Only another mile or so to go." Olivia nestled the cell
against her ear. "I've been ready to crawl out of my skin for
the last five miles, just dying to get there already. Maybe I
should pull a Boston and put the pedal to the metal the rest
of the way."

"Olivia Jean, if you do, I'll fly down there and take away
your car keys," her mother said, with the same tone she'd
used when Olivia had been little and trying to raid the
cookie jar before dinner. "Even if you are over thirty."

Olivia laughed. "Okay, okay. I'll keep it to twenty miles
over the speed limit, like any respectable Massachusetts
driver." On her left, a half-dozen bright, happy shops lined
a wide boardwalk, across the street from the beach. A white-
and-pink awning fronted the Rescue Bay Ice Cream Stand,
a quaint little place with umbrella-covered tables and a giant
plastic cow sporting a bright pink bow. An elderly couple
enjoying swirled cones—one chocolate, one vanilla—raised
a hand in greeting as Olivia drove past. She returned an
awkward wave, just as a man walking his dog raised his
hand in greeting and a shopkeeper sweeping the walk did
the same. The instant welcoming atmosphere gave Olivia
pause. It wasn't that Bostonians were frigid, exactly, but
rather less overt in being neighborly.

There was something . . . warm about this town, something Olivia had liked the second she arrived. "Ma, you should see this place. It's like another planet."

"Well, we're still stuck on planet Arctic here. It's too darn cold to even look out the window, never mind go anywhere." Anna Linscott was no doubt bundled up by the fireplace in her Back Bay townhome. Olivia could see her now, sitting in the threadbare rose-patterned armchair Anna had owned since the day she got married, the blue-and-green afghan Nana Linscott had crocheted draped across her lap. "There was a ring around the moon last night. A storm is coming. I'm thinking three inches, maybe four."

"It's January and you're in New England. There's always a snowstorm coming."

Anna laughed. "True. But if I see a ladybug—"

"And she lands on your hand, spring is on its way." Olivia grinned at her mother's superstitious weather predicting. Half the time, Anna was more accurate than the guys at Channel 7, so maybe there was something to her folklore. Olivia glanced out the window again, drawing in another deep breath of balmy air. "This is bliss. Palm trees and beaches and—"

"Alligators and geckos."

"They won't bother you if you don't bother them." Olivia fingered the picture taped to her dash. A perfect Florida bungalow, painted in sherbet colors of pale yellow and soft salmon, trimmed in white, nestled in the middle of a neat yard, flanked by rows of blooming annuals and fruit-laden citrus trees. "Mom, do you think I'm doing the right thing?"

"I think you have to do this." Anna sighed, a mixture of support and worry. "Then maybe you'll finally have the answers you need, and deserve."

Olivia's finger danced across the picture again. Would

she? All her life, Olivia had felt like a lock without the right key, a puzzle missing a piece. Now, maybe here, she'd find what she was searching for.

Herself.

And if not, she'd at least get one hell of a tan.

"Darn," her mother said. "Your dad's beeping in. I sent him to the grocery store. By himself."

Olivia laughed. "Say no more. I'll hold." She glanced again at the photo on the dash, then up at the GPS. *Distance remaining: 0.9 miles.* Butterflies danced in her stomach.

When the lawyer had rung her doorbell last week, Olivia insisted he must have had the wrong address, the wrong Olivia Linscott, and the wrong will in his hands. Did she have any relatives in Florida, he'd asked, and she'd said no. Everyone in her little family lived in Boston, and always had. They'd practically come over on the Mayflower, as Aunt Bessie said. No one moved away, except crazy cousin George, who went to Alaska to marry an Inuit woman he'd met at a Trekkie convention. Olivia had seen the pictures of their *Enterprise*-themed wedding. Quite inventive, considering they'd held it outdoors. In February.

Then the lawyer had asked if she knew the identity of her biological mother, and Olivia's world flipped upside down. Her mother. The woman who had given birth, then walked out of Brigham and Women's Hospital, leaving her newborn daughter behind.

Her birth mother.

A woman she'd never met.

A woman who'd never contacted her, never done so much as send a Christmas card.

A woman who had left her property in Florida, a porcelain necklace, and not much else. There'd been no letter, no explanations. No idea of who Bridget Tuttle had been.

Or why she'd abandoned her baby.

All her life, Olivia had wanted to know why. She'd toyed with searching for her biological mother on the Internet, then drawn back at the last minute, afraid the answers might not be ones she wanted to hear. And now, that door to a personal connection, a face-to-face, was closed. Forever.

She swallowed hard and pressed a finger to the photo again. Her only link to Bridget Tuttle remained in this piece of property and the town of Rescue Bay. Someone here had to have known her mother and would be able to fill in the blanks that now gaped like black holes.

Maybe this desperate need to know stemmed from all the changes over the last year. Maybe it was finally having a tangible reminder of someone who had been, up till now, a mythical figure. A ghost, really.

Olivia had prodded the lawyer for more information, but he'd said he was merely the messenger, a Boston attorney hired by the Florida probate, and knew less than she did. He handed her the deed, along with the picture of the house and an envelope with the necklace, then wished her good luck.

She'd stood there for a long time, staring at that picture, before making the most impulsive decision of her life. Just . . . *go*.

Within days, Olivia had quit her job, loaded her car, packed up Miss Sadie, and headed south. And now here she was, hitting the reboot button on her life after a disastrous end to her marriage and too many years working a retail job that had been as fulfilling as cotton candy for breakfast.

In Rescue Bay, she wouldn't know anyone. She wouldn't turn a corner and expect to see the man who had promised to love her forever—which turned out to be one year and three months. She wouldn't face well-meaning friends determined to drag her to a bar, as if a few drinks and sex with a stranger solved anything. She wouldn't look around her half-empty Back Bay town house and think of dreams that had died a slow, reluctant death.

In Rescue Bay, she could start over. The sight of the sun and beach made her feel renewed, refreshed, reenergized. Maybe later today, after she'd settled in, she'd grab her suit and head for the beach. It was margarita weather, and Olivia wanted to soak up the warmth. To . . . thaw.

Yes, that was it. Thaw her bones, warm her heart again.

"I'm back," Anna said, her voice bright with laughter. "I love that man, but I swear, some days I could clobber him."

"Don't tell me. He was stuck in the bread aisle."

"He didn't even make it that far this time. He got side-tracked in produce. Apparently putting *apples* on the list had him flustered about Galas versus Fujis. And don't even get me started on the *bag of salad mix.*"

Olivia bit back a chuckle. "Dad means well." She reached out to the passenger side and ran a hand down the whisper-soft white fur of Miss Sadie, her bichon frise and fellow adventurer—who had slept in her doggie car seat from Baltimore to Rescue Bay, Florida. *Lazy little puppy*, Olivia thought, smiling at the snoozing dog.

"Since your father retired," Anna said, "he's trying to help out more. He says it's his way of learning how to survive without me, should I suddenly be abducted by aliens."

"Mars would have a force to reckon with if that happened, Ma." Blood relation or not, Olivia had always been close to her mother. She'd treasured the story of how Anna, an OB nurse, had seen the abandoned baby girl in the hospital and moved heaven and earth—and her cautious husband, Dan—to adopt Olivia and bring her home. Anna had nursed her adopted daughter through colic and chicken pox, puberty woes and acne battles, lost puppies and first dates.

"Me? I'm sweet. Mild-mannered. And don't you dare laugh, missy. You were the one who outcried every baby in that nursery."

That homesickness wave rose again in Olivia, but she pushed it back. Mom and Dad were coming down to Florida in March, and Olivia had already made plans for a return visit for July fourth. "Loud and insistent, right from the beginning, right?" Olivia said.

"I prefer to call it . . . determined. You're a strong person, kiddo, and you always have been. Your father and I thank God every day for bringing you into our lives."

"I'm grateful to have both of you, too." Still, a ribbon of guilt flickered in Olivia's chest. With parents like hers, why did she still want more? Why did she want a connection with the one woman who had never wanted her?

Palm trees spread their wide leaves over Olivia's car as she turned off the coastal road and headed toward the center of Rescue Bay. The GPS came on again, still sounding about as excited as an MBTA conductor calling "Ashland" for the thousandth time, and announced the last quarter mile to her destination. "I'm almost to the house," Olivia said.

"Oh, good. Tell me everything you see, the second you see it. Goodness, I'm excited and I'm not even there."

The GPS announced one last left turn, then a second later said, "You have arrived at your destination."

Olivia scanned the street for the pretty little bungalow in the pictures. This was it, the moment she'd been waiting for. She craned forward, looking left, right, north, south. "I can't find it. Maybe I got the address wrong—"

Then she saw the house. Or rather, what was left of it.

Not one part of the building before her matched the picture the lawyer had given her. Maybe the structure had once been that happy, cheery landscaped home, but if so, that had been a long, long, *long* time ago.

Holy. Crap.

Her elation deflated with a whoosh. The perfect little bungalow turned out to be a run-down building on a dead-end street, with an overgrown, sprawling backyard and a decaying wraparound front porch. A swing hung from the front, creaking back and forth in the slight breeze. Time and sunshine had faded the sunny yellow paint to pale butter, darkened the bright white trim to dingy gray, and worn down the salmon shutters to anemic pink. One shutter hung askew, another was missing altogether, and the window boxes that had once held blooming annuals now held nothing but dirt and desiccated stalks.

She checked the address. Twice. Right place, wrong decade in the photo.

This was her inheritance? It looked like one more rejection, only from the grave. The woman who had abandoned her in the hospital twenty-nine years ago had abandoned this place, too.

"So . . . what do you think?" Anna asked. "Is it as pretty as the picture?"

Olivia scanned the lot, searching for something, anything, to redeem this . . . legacy. Anchoring the yard was the Rescue Bay Dog Rescue, or so the sign said. The low-slung white building sprouted chain-link kennels on either side like tentacles. Chunks of grayed wood siding displayed worn, naked wooden faces underneath peeling white paint. The eastern corner of the kennels had rotted away, leaving a gaping hole to the inside. The roof sagged in the middle in a deep concave bow. One strong gust of wind, and what was left of this place—of Olivia's inheritance and her future plans—would crumble. She bit back a laugh before it became a sob.

"Olivia? Are you still there? Did you find the house?"

"Uh . . . yeah. It's . . . a whole lot more than I expected." She forced brightness to her voice. "Turns out there's an animal shelter on the property, too. It's . . . it's closed down now."

"Animal shelter? Why, that's right up your alley. Sounds like the perfect place for you."

"Yup. Exactly what I imagined."

Why was she surprised? Her biological mother had left her crying in a bassinet, alone, unwanted. Now Bridget Tuttle had saddled her daughter with a disaster that looked just as abandoned as Olivia had felt all these years. The letdown hung heavy on her shoulders, ached in her gut. She fought the urge to cry.

She drew in a deep breath, straightened her spine. She refused to let this set her back. She was here for a new start, and by God, she was going to get one, even if it meant calling in the entire crew from *This Old House* to help her.

"I better let you go now, Ma, so I can get moved in and settled before dark."

"Okay. Take care of yourself."

"I will. You do the same." She gripped the phone, her last connection to the life she'd impulsively left behind, and wished she could send a hug through the cell. "I love you, Ma."

"I love you, too, honey." A hitch sounded in Anna's voice. "Call soon, okay?"

"I will." Olivia tucked the phone into her purse, then parked in the cracked driveway. Weeds sprang up here and there, determined green stalks asserting themselves in the broken concrete. She unbuckled the dog from her doggie car seat, then put up a palm in command. "Stay here, Miss Sadie, while I check things out. Okay?"

Miss Sadie barked, bounced a couple of times, then settled in the passenger seat. Olivia climbed out of the Toyota and took a moment to stretch her legs, her back. Maybe if she got a little closer, she'd see that the house wasn't as bad as she thought.

Nope. It was worse. Like opening a candy bar and finding brussels sprouts underneath the wrapper.

"Damn." Olivia shook her head and had started to turn back toward the car when her gaze landed on a long, golden body beside the shelter.

Beneath the tattered remains of a red-and-white awning lay an emaciated golden retriever. Hurt? Dead? Sleeping? Olivia bent down, put out a hand, and kept her voice high, friendly. Nonthreatening. "Hey, puppy," she said to the too-thin, too-quiet dog. "Come here."

The dog didn't move. Didn't twitch so much as a floppy ear or raise its dark snout. Olivia inched forward. The golden retriever remained still. Olivia's gut churned, and she held her breath, waiting for any sign, any movement, anything.

Olivia took another step, then another, moving slow, cautious. All the while saying a silent prayer that the dog was alive.

And then, a slight flick of a tail, and Olivia's heart leapt. "Okay, puppy. Okay. That's good." She smiled and put out her hand again. A strong breeze whistled through and the building's roof swayed, creaked, then let out an ominous crackle. "Come on out from there, okay? Before you get hurt."

The dog didn't budge.

"Are you hungry? Hmm?" Olivia looked back at her

sedan, loaded to the gills with boxes and clothes. Miss Sadie's tiny white butterball body popped up and down, her excited yips carrying through the lowered window and into the yard. When Miss Sadie was working in a therapy environment, she was calm, even-tempered, obedient. When she wasn't, the nearly four-year-old dog was all puppy. Now wasn't a time for puppy energy.

Olivia turned back to the golden retriever and as she did, her gaze roamed the depressing scene before her: over the missing and cracked siding, the ivy weaving its way into the casements, the still, silent air conditioner covered with Spanish moss. The lawyer had lied. This wasn't a gift—this was a catastrophe. A catastrophe Olivia had almost no budget to repair.

Had she made an incredible mistake? Thrown away her life in Boston, on a whim?

But what kind of life had she had, really? One where everywhere she went, everyone she saw, reminded her of her biggest mistake. Where living in a town house meant for two, then inhabited by one, festered like an open wound. She fingered her left hand, empty for the past two years— two years filled with changes and new directions—and knew she'd made the right choice.

She wasn't going back. She would make this work. What choice did she have? Olivia was tired of being a failure. Failing at her marriage. Failing at her previous job. Failing at taking risks. She had changed careers, finally pursuing her degree in physical therapy, and the day had come to put all this education in practice. She had a new job, a new start. This time, she was going to plow forward and not let anything get in her way. Even this . . . mess. She couldn't do anything about the house right this second, but she could start with the dog.

"Come on, honey." She patted her thigh. "Let's get you out of there." Olivia kept up an endless soft stream of soothing words as she moved an inch at a time, slow, easy. She kept her hand splayed and her tone low, cheery. "You hungry, puppy? Thirsty?"

The dog's gaze darted from her to the dense, overgrown shrubbery on the right, then back again. Olivia closed the gap to five feet. The dog tensed, the fur on its back rising in a Mohawk of caution. The dark chocolate eyes grew rounder, filling with fear. "It's okay, sweetie," Olivia said. "It's okay. I want to help."

Wary eyes flickered, and distrust gave way to hope. An ear twitched. The tail raised, lowered, then swished slow against the ground.

"Let's get you something to eat. Would you like that? I bet you would."

The dog shifted, rising on its haunches, then dropping again to its belly with a high-pitched whimper. Dark crimson blood, dried, crusted over, smeared against the animal's side. All that beautiful golden hair matted in painful bunches. The dog had moved so fast, Olivia couldn't tell if the injury was new or old, or the extent of the damage. Whatever had happened, this poor thing needed a human, even if she didn't know it.

Olivia had to get this dog to a vet, but if she got too much closer, the wounded animal might panic and run. Or worse, bite her. The dog could be feral, scared. Either of which could make it react with its teeth.

In the car, Olivia had dog treats. Maybe if she got a couple of those, the dog would let Olivia get close and evaluate its injuries. She pivoted back to the Toyota and unlatched the rear passenger door, careful not to let Miss Sadie out. Just as Olivia snaked a hand into the bag that held the treats,

Sadie bounded over the seats, pounced on the bag, and knocked it to the floor. Olivia opened the door a few inches more, scrambling for the spilled dog biscuits.

A flash of white zipped past. Oh damn. "Miss Sadie!"

Too late. The bichon darted into the yard, barking hellos. The golden started, hips raised, ready to run. Damn, damn, damn. "Sadie! Quiet! Stay!"

The bichon heard the command in Olivia's voice and stopped running. She turned back, noted the displeasure in her mistress's face, and dropped to her haunches. Too late.

A glimpse of yellow fur, disappearing under the picket fence dividing her property from the house next door. A flick of a tail—

The dog was gone.

Olivia called the bichon back to the driveway and ordered her to sit. "Stay. I'll go look for him."

Miss Sadie sat, her pixie face filled with disappointment at missing the great adventure.

"I know you want to help, but you need to stay. *Stay.*" Olivia grabbed a handful of treats out of the car and headed for the hole in the wooden fence.

Hole was a generous description. Two boards were missing, a third broken in half. Olivia bent down and stepped one leg through—straight into a thick, green shrub. She pulled her other leg through and shoved past the jumble of green leaves and spiky branches that tangled in her hair, grabbed at her clothes, scratched at her face and arms. Finally, she emerged on the other side, a little worse for wear.

She straightened—and almost collided with a six-foot-tall wall of a man.

"What the hell are you doing?" he said.

Her mouth opened, closed. Not a single word came out. Her gaze roamed over him, and she had to remind herself to breathe. Damn. Hot, handsome, sexy. She swallowed hard and tried not to stare.

Too much.

Blue jeans hugged his thighs, and a black T-shirt sporting a Harley-Davidson logo outlined a defined, hard chest, muscled biceps. The man had short-cropped, deep brown hair, a chiseled jaw shadowed with rough stubble. Dark sunglasses hid his eyes, despite the setting sun behind him. On one side of his face, a jagged scar peeked out from under the sunglasses, which only added to the air of mystery. He looked—

Dangerous.

Not in the hack-you-into-tiny-pieces-and-bury-you-in-a-landfill kind of way, but in a mysterious, sensual way that said tangling with him would be unforgettable. That he was the kind of guy who could kiss her and leave her . . . reeling. Breathless. The kind her friends called a Mindless Man because one night with him would make a girl lose her mind—in a very, very good way.

Olivia brushed off the worst of the shrub debris from her hair and face. Chided herself for worrying about her appearance. Her priority was the golden, not some stranger with sex appeal and an attitude. "I'm looking for the dog."

"What dog?"

"The golden retriever that ran into your yard." Olivia peered around the man. She didn't see the dog anywhere. Then she spied the end of a pale yellow tail sticking out underneath the man's porch.

"Is it running away from home? Or from you?"

"Yes—no. I . . . I don't know." Damn, why did this man fluster her? "It ran over here because it's scared. I think the dog is hurt and needs to see a vet."

He leaned down, and she caught the scent of soap and sweat. A man's scent, tempting, dark. His sunglasses reflected back her own face, and nothing more. She couldn't see his eyes, but she could feel his assessing gaze. "Let me guess," he said, his voice low, teasing. "You hit the dog with your car and now you've had a sudden attack of guilt."

"Of course not!"

"Uh-huh." A slight grin played on his lips. "So you're just another Debby Do-Gooder, out to save the world?"

"I'm trying to save a dog, not the whole world. That's all." She thought of the house. Her complicated, disastrous new start. "I've got enough on my plate."

"You and me both, lady. You and me both." He let out a long breath and turned away.

In the distance, someone started a lawn mower. The low drone of the engine overpowered the chirping of the birds and sent the pungent smell of gasoline into the air. Crickets chirped in the deep grass, hidden under the carpet of green. A soft breeze tickled a path down the yard.

"Well, if you find what you're looking for," he said, "let me know."

"I already did." She bent down and splayed her palm to show the treats to the furry body under the porch. "Here, baby. Want some cookies?" The tail swished, but the dog didn't come forward.

"Sorry, lady, but I'm full. Though if you have chocolate chip, I'll reconsider."

"I'm happy to share, if you like liver-flavored biscuits."

"They make those?" He grimaced. "That sounds inhumane."

"That's because they're for the dog, silly." Olivia gestured toward the porch. "See him? Right there?"

The man turned. Scanned the space. "I don't see anything."

"What are you, blind?" She marched a few steps forward,

and pointed again. "Right there. Now if you'll just help me—"

The tail disappeared. An instant later, the dog darted out of the yard and into a thick copse of firs and palmetto palms across the street. Olivia sighed. "Great. Now he's gone. Thanks a lot."

"You're blaming me?" He arched a brow, and the earlier friendliness on his face had been replaced by hard lines. "I'm not the one trespassing. And possibly stealing someone's dog."

He had a point. She hated that, but he did. "Okay, maybe I was trespassing. But it was for a good cause."

He smirked. "That's what all criminals say."

"I am not a criminal. I'm a good person with good intentions." Her chin jutted up. "Unlike you. You . . ."

"Ogre?" he supplied.

Unbidden, her gaze trailed past the lean definition of his face, along those broad shoulders, down his strong arms. A dark heat brewed inside her, a heat she hadn't felt in a long, long time. What would it be like to have one night of hot, crazy sex with a man like him? He had this . . . edge to him, that whispered *dangerous heartbreaker*, yet at the same time, he carried an air of animal confidence that said a night with him would be amazing. Unforgettable. Curl-your-toes-and-smack-yo-momma amazing.

Clearly, she had gone way too long without sex.

She cleared her throat. Tried not to picture him in bed. Or naked. Or both. "I . . . I wouldn't call you an ogre."

"Oh, really?" He arched a brow, and something like a smile flickered on his face. A delicious quiver slid through her veins. "And what would you call me?"

"I don't know, but it sure as hell wouldn't be Mr. Rogers."

He laughed. "On that, I would agree."

The moment of détente extended between them. An olive branch, thin, but a start. She put out her hand. "We got off on the wrong foot. I'm Olivia Linscott. Your new neighbor."

He ignored her handshake. "Well, Olivia Linscott, do me a favor from here on out. Stay on your side of the fence. Us ogres don't like to be bothered." Then he turned on his heel and headed inside.

If this guy was indicative of the typical Rescue Bay resident, then she was tempted to get back in the car and drive home to Boston. At least there the crusty New England attitude came with the zip code.

Instead, Olivia headed out to the sidewalk. She cupped her hand to block the sun in her eyes and searched the dark wooded thicket across the street for any sign of the dog. Nothing.

"It's okay, puppy. I'll wait. I'm here for . . ." She glanced again at the decaying buildings she had inherited, now complicated by an injured dog off somewhere licking his wounds and a run-in with a surly neighbor. She had a mountain to climb ahead of her, but the sense of purpose surged in her chest. She could do this. She *would* do this. "A long while."

She dropped a treat from her hand onto the ground. There would be time to work with the dog, to earn his trust. Time to change the dog's life.

Olivia headed back to her property. She paused in front of the dilapidated renovation project that had become her inheritance and her home and called Miss Sadie to her side. Olivia had spent the year since her divorce trying to regroup, refocus, figure out who she was and what she wanted. Here in Rescue Bay, she had a chance to do all of that, while also finding her roots and discovering the truth about Bridget Tuttle. It was an opportunity, she told herself. The one she'd wanted for so long.

Miss Sadie propped her paws on Olivia's knee. She bent down and gave the bichon an ear scratching. "We've got our work cut out for us, don't we, Miss Sadie?" Then she glanced again at the house, and the reality of the disaster in front of her washed over Olivia. The place needed a new porch, a new roof, new siding—and that was just the *outside*.

"I don't even know where to start. Or heck, how to hammer a nail." What had she gotten herself into? Her resolve wavered and she glanced at the dog, trying to convince herself more than Miss Sadie. "We can do it. Right?"

The dog barked, and the bravado that had held Olivia together for fourteen hundred miles crumpled. Burning tears rushed to the surface and spilled down her cheeks. She dropped to the ground and gathered the only friend she had in Rescue Bay into her arms.